BRAD NORRIS

Division

The Chronicles of the Fallen State of America

The land will be scorched and the
people will be fuel for the fire

- Isaiah 9:19

Foreword

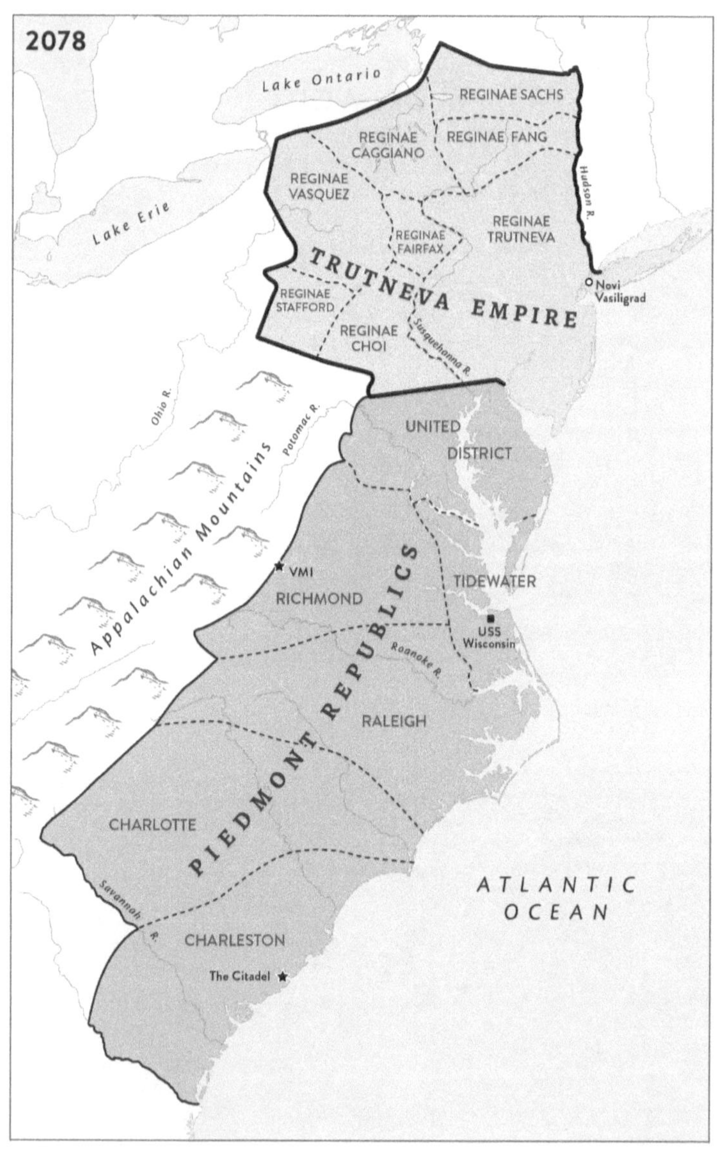

2078
Lake Ontario
Lake Erie
REGINAE SACHS
REGINAE CAGGIANO
REGINAE FANG
REGINAE VASQUEZ
REGINAE FAIRFAX
REGINAE TRUTNEVA
Hudson R.
REGINAE STAFFORD
REGINAE CHOI
TRUTNEVA EMPIRE
Susquehanna R.
Novi Vasiligrad
Ohio R.
Potomac R.
Appalachian Mountains
UNITED DISTRICT
VMI
RICHMOND
TIDEWATER
USS Wisconsin
PIEDMONT REPUBLICS
Roanoke R.
RALEIGH
CHARLOTTE
ATLANTIC OCEAN
Savannah R.
CHARLESTON
The Citadel

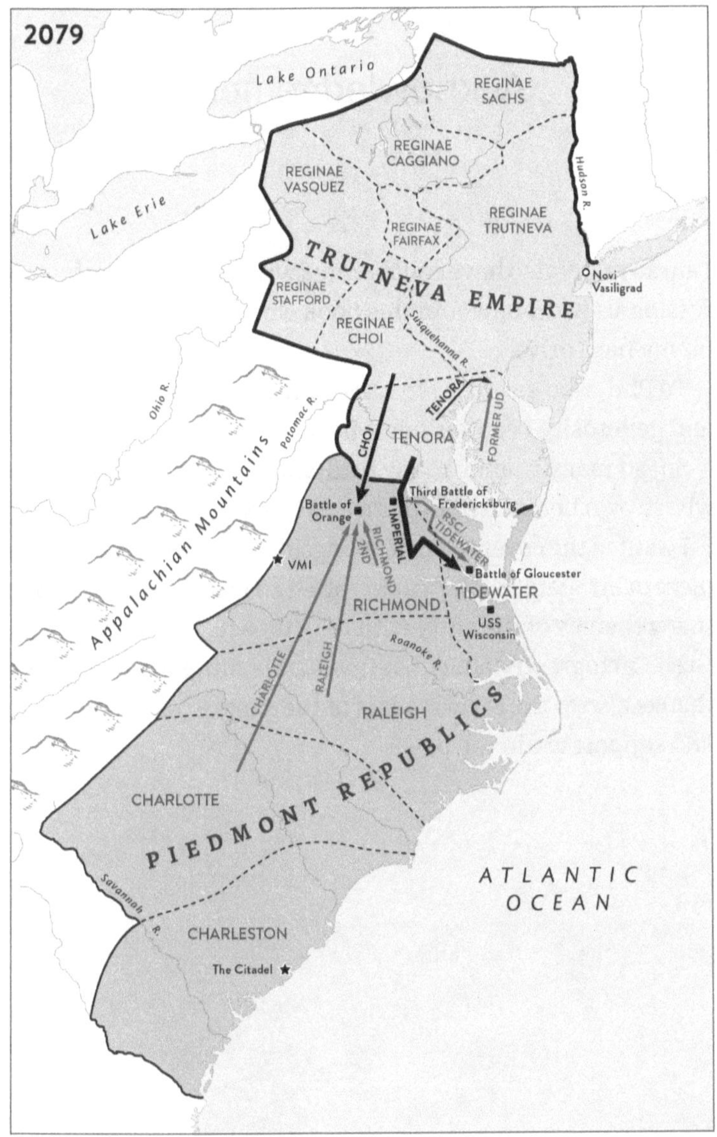

2079
Lake Ontario
Lake Erie
REGINAE SACHS
REGINAE CAGGIANO
REGINAE VASQUEZ
REGINAE FAIRFAX
REGINAE TRUTNEVA
Hudson R.
Novi Vasiligrad
REGINAE STAFFORD
REGINAE CHOI
TRUTNEVA EMPIRE
Susquehanna R.
Ohio R.
Potomac R.
Appalachian Mountains
CHOI
TENORA
TENORA
FORMER UD
Battle of Orange
VMI
Third Battle of Fredericksburg
IMPERIAL
RICHMOND 2ND
RSCI TIDEWATER
Battle of Gloucester
TIDEWATER
RICHMOND
USS Wisconsin
Roanoke R.
RALEIGH
CHARLOTTE
RALEIGH
PIEDMONT REPUBLICS
CHARLOTTE
Savannah R.
ATLANTIC OCEAN
CHARLESTON
The Citadel

Acknowledgement

I am so grateful to have collaborated with many wonderful professionals without whom this book would be just a document on my hard drive.

To Phil, who gave me the title. To my family whose patience and generosity I couldn't do without.

So, so many thanks to my brilliant editor, Margaret Diehl, whose own books are absolute treasures.

I wanted the cover to stand alongside the story as an original piece of art. Rafal Kucharczuk crafted an image that articulates many themes of the story with real impact. The maps by Erin Greb Cartography added an invaluable dimension. Deepest thanks also to the early readers of the story – your kind words and support are in the pages.

1

– Philippa – November 2078

Please be there when I come home.

Captain Philippa Calenos sat astride her stallion, Icarys, and looked through the binoculars. The ridgeline afforded her a panoramic view of the valley, the town, and the small farms below. Smoke curled out of several of the chimneys—a reassuring sign. The morning mist still hung heavily on the hills beyond. She rolled her neck to relieve the stiffness after the night on the bedroll in an abandoned farmhouse.

"Got the list?" she called to Lieutenant Meghan Scarbrough.

"Right here, Captain," Scarbrough replied.

"How many are we looking for?"

"Eighty-five names," she drawled.

"Let's get to it."

They rode in silence next to the crumbling byway. A faded sign welcomed them to the town with the European name—another lost connection. Getting closer, they saw signs of movement. People would be gathering in the market. That was always the best place to start.

Buildings on the outskirts had been stripped. Wood set aside for reuse or fuel. Copper, brass and any steel had been taken by Reclamation Units, leaving only foundations now surrounded by the remnants of rows of soybeans, corn, or sometimes marijuana. It had been a decent harvest despite the drought that had plagued much of the South. Even in late October, the temperature had been in the high seventies. Now, November brought the change.

Brick facades lined the main street, the paint faded and peeling. Stop lights and signs long gone. Like everywhere else they'd been, Philippa was struck with the feeling of retreat into the uncertain future. A small pack of dogs padded around a vacant lot. Getting closer, Philippa could see a dozen or so women setting up in their stalls. It was still warm enough to gather outside. Hearing the hoof beats, some looked up, immediately recognizing the insignia of the RSC, the Richmond Security Command.

"Peace to you, sister!" one of them called.

"Peace to all sisters," Philippa replied. "How goes it?"

She swung her leg across and dismounted. Lieutenant Scarbrough followed her lead.

The woman squinted. With a doubtful cackle, "We move forward. Not much else we can."

Philippa studied her face, ashen brown from the years outdoors. Her wiry gray hair was pulled back and tied off. When she spoke, Philippa could see some of her molars were gone.

On the table were laid skeins of wool dyed in black, yellow, orange and brown. On other tables were blocks of butter, eggs, jars of fruits and vegetables, herb cheeses in wax-covered crocks, glycerol, tallow candles, jewelry made from recycled

US coins, spare parts. Chickens in cages clucked nervously. The women moved with purpose, exchanging jokes. Some smoked the unfiltered Dominion brand cigarettes.

"The radiocast said there was war in the North," the woman said.

"There's always war in the North," Philippa replied. "The Trutneva sisters make sure of that. Anyone from the Council available?"

The woman pointed. "Paisley Wilson or Katlyn Falstaff should be there 'bout now. Others live outside town. Brick building, white columns two blocks that way. Can't miss it."

"Obliged." Philippa tipped her cavalry hat. "Tell folks that we'll be back. Lieutenant Scarbrough is a medic. If anyone needs help, that's why we're here. "

"A'ight."

Leaves swirled across the street as they led their horses. Some of the buildings sagged under the weight of neglect, but hadn't been torn down as if set aside, quietly waiting for an influx of new residents that would never come. One wide building with a brownstone exterior had become a machine and repair shop. The owner in her coveralls studied an object on the workbench, then looked up at the sound of the horses. Next to the wide building was the satellite office for the Piedmont Mutual Credit Association. Closed. Most remote branches couldn't be staffed more than one day a week.

They reached the courthouse and tied off the horses. Walking up the granite steps, Philippa took her hat off. The large old door groaned when she opened it. Inside, the hallway was lit with irregular fluorescent bulbs that hummed in the stillness. The dingy floor tile had come up in several places. Scarbrough stopped to study a portrait of the town council taken in 2002 that still hung on the wall. She wiped the dust away, revealing a man's face. His name had faded out. The councilman was a handsome late thirties, maybe early forties. Philippa was never certain in trying to estimate the age of one of those men born before The Forgetting. The man's confident smile and slightly graying hair assured the viewer that he could be a trusted partner in their bright success.

"It never fails," Scarbrough whispered. "Looking at them."

Philippa peered at the picture. "Yeah, what the hell happened?"

"Yeah."

Just ahead was a sign for the mayor's office. Getting closer, they heard the sounds of children behind the door. Philippa gave a knock and gently opened it.

Inside were over a dozen children—all girls—playing, reading or drawing. The toddlers and infants were on one side looked after by a couple of teenagers. The sunlight pushed its way through the grimy windows. The children were playing at a pretend wedding with two of the girls surrounded by the wedding party ready to throw confetti. They scattered and hid upon seeing the uniforms. Their whispered questions to each other gave them away though.

"Hello?" Philippa called.

At the far end of the room was an older woman, late forties, with fair hair cut at the shoulder, standing next to a desk with her back to the door. She wore a pair of faded jeans and a worn silk blouse under a pale green wool sweater. She looked around at the two visitors and waved them to a sitting area nearby. The two teenage girls—both more angles than curves—stopped what they were doing and studied the RSC soldiers.

"Morning, ma'am," Philippa offered.

"Captain, Lieutenant. Welcome. I'm Paisley Wilson. Sit." To the girl, "Phoebe, please run and get these women some mint tea. Thanks.

"We've been expecting you. It's been about four months since the last survey. What news?"

Philippa settled into the musty sofa. "Overall, the news is good, although the summer hurricanes were some of the worst we've seen. The harvests have been strong – thank the longer growing seasons. Births are steady. Ratio remains somewhere around three and a half to one. Trade with the northern Reginae has brought needed parts, drugs, diesel engines. The Trutneva sisters control the transport. Relations with them are always tenuous at best."

"Mmmm," the mayor nodded. The tea arrived.

Philippa extended her hand. "Thank you.

"The Piedmont Republics reaffirmed the Shared Aid treaty at the Convocation in August. Technical, military, relief cooperation guarantees. God help us if we ever have to invoke it. How are things here?"

Wilson stirred honey into her tea. "Same. We probably have enough bio to go the winter. Might be mild, they say. The solar grid's doing alright. Clear days we get close to what we need. At night we run the generators for electricity but shut down at midnight, except the clinic. After that it gets pretty dark."

The wedding had resumed. "From two women, you are now one wyve. Caretakers of each other and all humanity. You may kiss." The girls giggled.

Confetti flew in the air. The girls rained paper over the visitors. Philippa and Scarbrough clapped for the new couple.

Wilson flicked her wrist. "Very sweet, girls. Now shoo!

"Where were we? Yes. Power is stable. Our water tests good.

Don't even ask me about sanitation. Always digging up old pipes. We have stocks of food. Plenty of deer. Some of us trap critters to supplement. Ever eaten groundhog?"

"I've had worse." Philippa grimaced and shook her head. "Skunk."

"Ewww."

"It's worse now thinking about it. At the time, I didn't know what it was."

Scarbrough asked, "Any births?"

Wilson nodded. "Two, both girls."

Scarbrough wrote down the names. "There were eighty-five last count. Any deaths?"

"No, but we haven't heard from Martha and Wayne. The Cargills. They're out on their farm south of town."

"Would you show us on the map?" Philippa asked. "We'll ride out there."

"I'd appreciate that."

Philippa stood up. "Anything you need?"

"The usual," Wilson said wearily. "Sterile dressings and needles. Antibiotics. Ammo—30 ought 6. Machine oil. Insulated copper wire. Central Production has our requisition."

"Well, we're riding back to Richmond tomorrow. Lieutenant Scarbrough will treat what she can, and we'll leave the supplies."

Wilson smiled. "Thank you. Are you staying here tonight?"

"Yes, ma'am, that was the plan."

"Very good. I'll arrange for accommodations." Wilson raised her arms. "As you can see, we've got plenty of space!"

* * *

While Lieutenant Scarbrough treated the townspeople, Philippa went with the mayor and inspected some of the power infrastructure. Geese huddled in a nearby field, picking at leftover seed. Cold wind came strong out of the north. When she was younger, Philippa imagined that the winds carried what had been forgotten, that they had swept through furiously gathering lifetimes of memories exhaled in dying breaths. She and the mayor walked among the rows of solar panels, Philippa occasionally kneeling down to check a connection. The one-megawatt system had been installed ten years ago, and with care, should keep producing for the next twenty. Philippa had worked on dozens of similar installations across the Richmond Territory and outside in cooperation with the other Republics.

"I was ten when the United States finally gave up," Paisley began. "'There was still Internet then. 'Bout a year later cat six Hurricane Karl—funny how they were all named after guys once we knew the score—sank New Orleans. Near half a million dead. No National Guard, no FEMA. Just human misery. We watched it happen."

Philippa had heard hundreds of these stories—of the slow-motion train wreck—and figured that she was just a new audience for the mayor. The regional survey had dragged out longer than she'd expected, and she was ready to go home for some rest in her own bed. Maybe Astrid would still be there. Springtime was always the better rotation, but she hadn't pulled that assignment. The short days and low, pale light held a quiet despair she found hard to shake. Especially when camped in a shell of a building from those times. Stories like the mayor's only gave substance to that feeling. *The cold end of things. We, the dispossessed.* She nodded and gave a sympathetic look.

Paisley continued, "Seeing that drove home that nobody was going to look after us anymore. We had awoken in a wilderness to a terrible reckoning, which we are still paying for. I've been mayor for twenty years and I've spent every day fighting to hold it together."

Though she felt a surge of impatience, Philippa had to admit that women like Wilson were the reason that they held onto what remained of civilization. Tough, organized and compassionate women who'd dug in as crisis followed crisis. They'd made hard decisions and had to live with the results. Still, every one of these speeches ended with some version of It's Your Turn Now.

"You women coming along, you'll see the sacrifices in time. You'll need to be ready. You can't stop what's coming."

"Yes, ma'am," Philippa replied as she moved along the row.

* * *

Scarbrough had seen to about twenty women while Philippa inspected the power. Sprains, infections, a laceration that needed stitches. She checked blood pressure, felt for lumps, listened to chests and examined feet for ulcers. Given the need, she was prepared to perform one of two dozen minor surgical procedures. Word had spread quickly throughout the town, and the people had lined up. By early afternoon, she'd treated everyone who'd come. She waited in the vestibule of the town hall where she'd set up the makeshift clinic, watching the children play in the hallway.

"He's sick," a woman's voice said behind her.

Scarbrough started. She hadn't heard or seen anyone approach. She turned around and saw a woman, maybe twenty-five, wearing an old print sundress under a moth-eaten sweater. In her arms she held a small child, wrapped in a wool blanket.

Scarbrough waved. "Come in, come in."

She took the child and gently laid him on the table, unwrapping him carefully. Without the blanket, the child huddled in on himself. The skin was warm. The boy's eyes were closed, and a thick layer of mucus had formed a crust. His breathing shallow and raspy.

Scarbrough felt his pulse. "How long has he been like this?"

The woman clenched her hands. "Four days. He don't sing. Barely eats. I've been trying to get him to drink."

Scarbrough rummaged in her medical bag. "That's good. How old is he?"

"Three next month."

Scarbrough removed an otoscope, looked in the left ear then the right. "Ear infection with conjunctivitis. Very common with this age. I'm going to give him an injection that should speed his recovery. He'll be fine in a couple of days, but he does have a fever, so keep pushing the fluids. Now, let's get you cleaned up, little man."

She took a piece of clean gauze and moistened it with distilled water. Tenderly, she softened the yellow-green goop and wiped it away. The boy sniffled and suddenly his eyes popped open. Although Scarbrough had seen eyes like these hundreds of times, they never failed to send a shiver through her. The boy's eyes had no pupil and only a deep blue ring outlining where the iris should have been. The sclera was a milky-blue that dimly glowed like the ghost fireflies in her native North Carolina. Blind—the same as every male child for the last fifty years.

"That's better, yes," she cooed. "What's his name?"

"Sawyer."

"That's real nice, real pretty. Hold him close now. I'm gonna give him his shot."

* * *

Later, Scarbrough and Philippa rode south to the spot on the map where the Cargills lived. The wind continued blowing hard and cold from the north. Both women pulled the hoods up on their gray RSC parkas. Leaves tumbled and swirled, mixed every now and then with an old, shredded plastic bag, the store name illegible and forgotten. Trees grew out of an old cineplex whose roof had collapsed. Philippa and Meghan rode in silence through the landscape of modern ruins.

The long driveway led up a hill and ended at a farmhouse Philippa guessed couldn't have been less than 150 years old. A traditional two-story frame building that had once stood proudly atop the hill. Now it was held together with whatever materials had been available. Four different colored shingles on the roof. Two by fours tacked up for a handrail across the rotting steps. All the windows on the second floor had been boarded up to save heat. Pumpkins rotted in the nearby garden. Crows squawked on the nearby fence post. The laundry on the line billowed and shook like broken mourners.

The two soldiers tied off their horses to a post on the porch and climbed the steps. Philippa rapped hard on the door with her gloved hand. No answer. They waited a moment and

Philippa knocked again, harder. Still nothing. Trying the knob, Philippa discovered the door was unlocked. Slowly, she opened the door.

"Hello?! Mr. and Mrs. Cargill? We're from the RSC. Mayor Wilson sent us! Anybody here!"

They stepped inside. Philippa pulled off her hood and caught a glimpse of her face in the hall mirror. Her black hair flew every which way, and she spent a moment brushing it down with her fingers, looking in disgust at the aggressive gray streak that had invaded. *Not even thirty,* she mused.

"Hello! RSC!" she called again.

Sounds drifted from the back of the house. Cautiously, they followed them down the hallway. The door was cracked open an inch. Gently, Philippa knocked on it and pushed it open.

Inside, a tiny old woman wrapped in a blanket sat next to a bed. Her shoulders heaved in time with her quiet, breathless sobs. On the bed lay Mr. Cargill, his dead white eyes—normal, not filled with unknowable radiance—staring at the ceiling. His emaciated frame was stiff under the covers. Mrs. Cargill held his hand. The room was cold, and the smell of death had begun to gather in the still air. The love that Wayne Cargill had felt for his wife, his memories, and regrets all converted to methane, hydrogen sulphide and ammonia. The alchemy of death.

Philippa shuddered. Scarbrough knelt down and wrapped her arms around the shaking woman, trying to offer some small measure of comfort.

"Oh, dear thing. I'm so sorry. So sorry."

Mrs. Cargill didn't move. She continued sobbing into Scarbrough's shoulder. Philippa imagined icy waves of grief, of loss, washing out of the old woman and feeding into that dark, gelid ocean that always threatened to pull her, Philippa, down and away. Scarbrough held her more closely. Philippa gently took the dead husband's hand away and closed his eyes.

"I'll look in the kitchen for some tea."

Philippa found the kitchen and was relieved to find the woodstove still held some glowing embers. She rekindled the fire and found the teapot and the black Lowcountry tea from South Carolina. While the water heated, she went back to the bedroom.

Meghan was still holding Mrs. Cargill. Philippa looked around the room. The wallpaper peeled in many places. On top of the dresser stood a photo from their wedding day, dated 2021. Fifty-seven years. She tried to imagine the wedding night as she looked at the corpse. Then tightened her lips, both disturbed and annoyed at herself for wondering. *Get moving, Philippa!* As much as she felt sympathy for the old woman, practical matters intruded.

In a whisper to Scarbrough, she said, "We need to...you know. Take him outside."

Scarbrough furrowed her brow. "We have time. We have time for Martha."

Philippa shook her head. "I'll check on the tea."

Moving back to the kitchen, she found the water boiling. She poured a cup and carried it back to the bedroom. Scarbrough took it and cupped it in Martha's hands. She stood up.

"Martha, we need to lay Wayne to rest. Can you show us where?"

"No, no! Not yet!"

Meghan hugged her again. "It's unsafe. You'll get sick. We're going to take you to town."

"I don't care. I want to die! There's nothing left!" She shook her head and broke down again.

"It'll be dark in a couple hours. I'm going to look outside," Philippa said.

She left the house and found a shovel in the tool shed. She walked to the highest point on the property and looked out. A beautiful view. The afternoon sun added golden highlights to the smoky lavender mountains. A handful of purple leaves drifted through the long, coarse grass, brush and saplings of the backyard. It had been a few years since the Cargills tended to their property beyond collecting windfall. She started digging. After a few minutes, Scarbrough joined her with another shovel. The two worked in tandem, chiseling away at the hard earth. Dusk was approaching.

They returned to the house. Philippa lit a lantern.

"Martha, dear. It's time," Scarbrough said.

The tiny lady stood up. Her hands were gnarled with arthritis. *Beautiful, even now*, Philippa marveled.

Martha clasped her hands to her chin. "May I have some of his hair?"

Scarbrough reached over to her. "Of course."

Meghan retrieved her scissors from her bag and carefully cut the soft white wisps that fell across his forehead. Afterwards, she and Philippa wrapped the body in a sheet and, each carrying an end, took the body up the hill. Martha followed, still wrapped in her blanket.

Depositing the body in the grave, Scarbrough recited:

"Dear heavenly Mother. Welcome your son, Wayne, to your breast. Give him rest from his labors.

I am the life, the sacred source of life saith the eternal Mother;

whomever that believeth in me, though they were dead, yet

shall they live;
    and whosoever liveth and believeth in me shall never die.
    For none of us liveth to themself,
    and no one dieth to themself.
    For if we live, we live unto the Mother.
    and if we die, we die unto the Mother.
    Whether we live, therefore, or die, we are the Mother's.
    Blessed are the dead who die in the Mother's grace;
    even so saith the Spirit,.

The words said, the two soldiers filled the grave. And in the November gloaming, the only sound was the cold north wind paying its respects and collecting what it was owed.

2

– Philippa – November 2078

Philippa paused outside the door of her (their?) apartment, the key poised in front of the lock. The ride back with Scarbrough had been uneventful. In all, she had been gone three months. Three months with no word from Astrid. Philippa had posted letters from a few of the towns where they had stayed. She closed each of the letters with: *Please be there when I come home.* Of course, it would have been impossible for Astrid to write back, having no idea where to send replies. Tomorrow, she'd go down to the post office where she'd probably find the uncollected letters.

She turned the key and the bolt slid. The door creaked open and Philippa was greeted by cold still air and silence.

"Astrid! It's me!"

She turned on the lights and hung up her parka. She shivered a little and thought about putting it back on until she could get the radiators going.

Philippa tried again. "Astrid, I'm home!"

She could be at the store. The thought gave her hope until

she was reminded of how cold it was in the apartment. Astrid despised the cold. Philippa would open the windows during winter Astrid kept it so warm. Astrid dreamed of cycling through the south of France. Always in motion.

She turned the valve on the old radiator. It thumped and wheezed while it warmed up. The bedroom was empty, the bed made. Everything perfectly organized, but no Astrid.

The note was in the kitchen. Astrid's elegant, ivory Smythson stationery from seventy years ago. A relic from before The Forgetting. Philippa stared at it for a while before picking it up. She knew what it said already—they'd said the same words so many times. Resign her commission from the RSC, move south where they would raise sheep and Astrid would paint. *Maybe one of them would win the Lottery to have a baby.* A crazy idea, Philippa thought. Even if she could, what sane woman would bring a baby into this world?

They'd lived there three years. Their aerie on the eighth floor. The elevator hadn't run for ages. Other women and families lived on the first and second floors, but only Philippa and Astrid were fool enough to make their home at the top. The fin de siècle apartment was stunning: parquet floors, eighteen-foot ceilings, Biedermeier furniture, fireplaces in every room, built-in bookshelves bending under the loads of books. Von Neumann nestled up against Goethe. Monographs of artists ranging from Renaissance to early 21st century, a section devoted to mysticism. Another containing extensive studies of nuclear events and the aftermaths. The collected transcripts of the Nuremburg Trial. Thinkers of the early 21st century, literature, architecture. A massive National Geographic atlas in a sleeve. Leatherbound collections, many in foreign languages. Endless worlds to explore together. The atelier had a southern exposure with which Astrid fell in love. It offered a sprawling view of the James River. Her studio! she proclaimed. The place had remained untouched for maybe thirty years. Whoever had lived there had left everything behind.

Now it appeared Astrid had done the same. Her paintings hung on the walls: small canvases with detailed portraits of boys and young men, as if they might be the only archaeological record in some distant future. When she'd get a commission, she would paint a second portrait to keep. Philippa remembered her crushing old cobalt glass to a powder to make the smalt for the eyes. Other pieces hung interspersed. A portrait of Philippa in shades of pink, Astrid's favorite color.

She sighed. The entire ride back, she had tried to steel herself to this outcome. To be alone, again. Always the orphan. The survey tour had exhausted her. Long days and cold nights. Now it felt like her last reserve of strength was slipping away. All the air was leaving her body, replaced with a bottomless void where she couldn't breathe. She gasped and the tears fell from her eyes onto the envelope.

She allowed herself only a short cry. *I'm a soldier, an officer, not a child.* She wanted to forget everything for a while. Astrid, the Cargills, the Piedmont Republics, the Trutnevas, the daily struggle. So much of the world had already been forgotten.

Philippa dragged herself down the hall to the bathroom and filled the claw-and-ball tub with steaming water. She arranged burning votives around the room. The light softened and diffused in the steam. She found the pack of Dominion Cannabis and lit one before slipping into the welcoming bath. She closed her eyes and let the heat and smoke sink in. Soon she was filled with warmth and her thoughts drifted in all directions. They lost substance and meaning, becoming disconnected, dissolving into a whispered static. *If I'm thinking this, how can I see myself thinking this. Weird.* Her thoughts hovered and melted in the pale glow. When they alighted again on her departed lover, Philippa's heart filled with grief. *How can such delicate shoulders carry the weight of this unrelenting world?*

* * *

Rain pattered against the windows, murmuring in its ancient language. Philippa stirred and looked at the clock. 4:11 AM. She closed her eyes again and tried to find her lost thread of sleep. The empty half of the bed where Astrid should have been sparked a painful reminder and summoned images of her. Sleep would never return now. She stared into the darkness of her room, replaying memories. Maybe what Astrid wanted wasn't so crazy. *Maybe I can't see things for what they are.*

Restless now, she rolled out of bed. A stomach pang reminded her she hadn't eaten since noon yesterday. Probably nothing here, she mused. She padded to the kitchen and put the kettle on for tea. Astrid's envelope still rested on the counter, unopened. She snatched it up and tore out the letter.

Dearest, dearest P –

I heard there was a ship bound for Europe leaving from Baltimore. Such a hope! I knew there was no way that I could convince you to go. You'd tell me I was being foolish and I probably am. There is so much more. You just have to open your eyes to it. You are an honorable, decent woman and I love you. I will always love you, P. Think of me only on sunny days, a bright ray of light that takes the chill away.

Au revoir,
Astrid

North? A ship to Europe? Those things no longer existed and even if they did, how would Astrid survive?

The kettle whistled. Philippa dropped the letter and steeped the tea. She strode into their living room and curled up under a blanket on the aged leather sofa. Across the room was Astrid's joy—the ProForm Tour de France stationary bike. Philippa's mind wandered back to when they first found the apartment. Tucked away in a closet was the bike. It was probably seventy-five years old. An antique – the gears rusted and the screen smeared with dust.

Astrid cried, "Mine!"

Philippa knotted her face. "You can have it, but I predict we'll be taking it for scrap."

Astrid rested her hand on Philippa's arm. "You'll see."

Astrid mounted the bike, pressing down on the pedal with all the power in her slim body.

Screeechh. The bike groaned. Philippa winced, certain that damage had occurred. Astrid powered the other leg round with the same tortured noise. She hopped off, shrugged her shoulders and smiled. "It's gonna need some work."

Astrid was right, Philippa reflected. She found oil and lovingly brought it back to life. The gears ran smoothly. Then, one day, magic.

Astrid had been pedaling for twenty minutes when the small screen lit up. Only a few other times had Philippa seen video images—one more casualty of The Forgetting. They both huddled around the display. Astrid pushed one of the buttons. The screen changed. Suddenly they were flying through the streets of a charming town. *France?* Astrid pedaled harder and they sped up. She slowed and so did the video.

Astrid was transported. Everything on the screen was perfection, a long-ago wonderland. Vittel, Vesoul, Foix, *Paris!* Miles and miles she rode, pushing herself towards some expectant singularity where it was only her and the bike streaking past endless fields of lavender. Away from the world's fever dream.

Philippa hadn't seen it then—the tiny spark in the machine that set off a chain reaction within Astrid. Astrid was always four feet away, but all the while going further and further into that distant sunset.

Philippa shuddered, returning from her reverie. Baltimore was part of the United District, one of the Republics. Maybe she could confirm the story about the ship; she'd had virtually no contact with command during the survey tour. An event that significant couldn't have gone unreported. Rumors were part of the daily fabric these days—part entertainment, part hope. Women held their breath and slipped under the warm, liquid surface of belief. Some sought connection in the myriad cults that had spawned out of the Forgetting—new deities for a world staggering under the hostile climate: Illustral, Goddess of What Was Lost; Othere, warrior goddess of the battlefields; her unfaithful consort, the unnamed Scorched God of Drought; The Shipwrecked Goddess raging at the coastlines. Others craved myths of faraway places where maybe things hadn't changed, where the temperature hadn't climbed. Alaska, Iceland, the northern island of Japan. Places where maybe there were still men.

A wasted hope. *Thou hast delivered us into the hand of our iniquities.* In 2023, the last normal male children were born.

They had been replaced by the eldritch, blue-eyed changelings. *Homo sapiens* became *homo mysterium. Homo fatuus.* A cruel joke. Philippa couldn't stand the sight of them.

Her stomach growled. Philippa dressed in RSC fatigues and strode up Main Street to the Old City Hall building. The commissary would be open. The lightest sprinkle of rain fell, but Philippa didn't pull up her hood. A couple of RSC trucks rumbled past, leaving the smell of burned cooking oil behind.

From her earliest days at VMI, she knew she belonged in the RSC. A sisterhood like no other. The exhaustion, the pain, the abject abuse of the drill sergeants only drove her harder to demonstrate her worth. The RSC held for her a nobility in its ideals of service and self-sacrifice. The promise of meaning in the chaos of the fractured world. Security from the mocking north wind and the beckoning dark water that were never far from Philippa's thoughts.

She returned the salute of the guard posted at the entrance and marched straight ahead to the dining hall. There were few other personnel at that hour. The custodian, Edward Vaughan, was pushing a mop across the hall, balancing it on the stump of his right arm. Nearly eighty, his sunken face, crowned by mangy gray hair, poked out of the tattered tweed overcoat he wore regardless of the weather. He'd folded the sleeve and stitched it so it wouldn't hang loose. His incoherent mumbling drifted into a song Philippa didn't recognize. Vaughan endlessly repeated a few of the lyrics '...and with fear and trembling stand'. An escapee from the Trutnev labor camps, he kept to himself, never making eye contact. He'd washed up, literally, on a dam just south of the Mason Dixon Wall. He had been one of the exhums, the term the Trutnevas used for their labor inputs, although he was known to have once been high up in Vasiliy Trutnev's government. Pity mixed with distaste. *Can barely do the job. Why even keep him around?*

Philippa exchanged nods with a sergeant. She queued up and served herself a plate of scrambled eggs and grits and poured a cup of Lowcountry tea. She sat down in a remote corner and tore into the food. A furious hunger overcame her, and she hunched over the plate, shoveling the food in. She didn't notice the figure approaching.

"Keep your seat, Captain."

Philippa looked up, panicked. Not all the food had made it into her mouth. She grabbed at her napkin while standing up to salute.

"Ma'am!" she cried, but it came out sounding like "Mm-mmm."

"At ease."

Philippa choked down the mouthful. General Poole returned the salute and pulled up a chair. As every other time Philippa had seen her, the General wore her steel-gray hair pulled back, revealing the thick scar that furrowed from her left eye to her jaw. Whatever had done it had also severed the optic nerves. The eye always looked straight ahead, never moving. The sight of it always unnerved Philippa slightly. Philippa suspected the eye saw things on a spectrum not revealed to anyone else. Nobody knew how she had been injured.

Poole shifted in the chair. "How was the tour, Captain?"

Philippa replied, "Overall, satisfactory. We covered the arc out up to old route 33, followed the mountains and back 60. Soybean, tobacco and marijuana prices have been good. Folks have enough stockpiled for the winter. Could wind up being mild. Usual issues surrounding labor allocation—never enough. Population, in that sector at least, is stable. A few tool and die shops have started up for farm equipment. Engines. Scrap foundries. I officiated two weddings and one funeral."

Poole raised her good eye. "Funeral?"

"Sorry, ma'am, not really the right word. An old man. Lieutenant Scarbrough and I buried him. He left a wife behind. The mayor took her in."

The General nodded. The gold stars gleamed on her shoulder.

Philippa lifted her cup. "What's the news?"

The General stared at Philippa, the dead eye appraising her. Philippa dropped her eyes, afraid that the General was seeing *too much.*

Poole exhaled. "We have concerns."

Philippa sipped her tea. "The Trutnevas?"

The General nodded. "The Sisters are hemmed in on the east. They won't cross the Hudson—the non-aggression treaty with New England. New England supplies many of the Empire's armaments and a war now with them would be costly. The Trutnevas have grown powerful over the years by establishing those client states, but some of them have grown strong. Could turn rabid. It would only take one or two of the Reginae to turn against them and the sisters would be put to the sword, Dirae Corps or no.

"On the western border of their lands, the Newmarked of Pittsburgh held out against Gael Stafford's army. An army of religious fanatics convinced the mutation was God's will. They dug in up in the mountains and bled Stafford white. Ran the Viet Cong playbook. Stafford tried her gambit and lost. Not a lot of meat left on that bone for the Trutnevas, but I think they'd rather hold Stafford close to keep Venoma Choi in check.

"To the north, there's nothing until Montreal. Too far with an exposed flank to New England. Trutnevas are too smart for that."

Philippa tried to hide the alarm in her voice. "That leaves..."

Poole nodded. "Right. The United District."

Philippa tore at her cuticle. Astrid headed straight into the Trutneva mandibles.

The General continued, "An invasion of the U.D. would trigger the Mutual Defense Treaty. The Trutnevas know this. They'll try to divide and conquer. Come at us one by one. If the U.D. falls, we're next. Our embassy reports that for months now, the Trutnevas have been conducting a silk glove insurrection. Look at this."

The General pulled out a 100 libra banknote. "Look it carefully."

Philippa studied the bill. She held it to the light, rubbed it. Everything appeared right. Libra notes bore an engraving of a symbol of each of the Piedmont Republics on one side. This one displayed the Lincoln Memorial on the reverse.

The General took the bill back. "It's counterfeit, but an exceptional job. Ultraviolet light puts the lie to it. These started circulating last month. Some merchants in the U.D. now will only accept the Imperial ruble."

Philippa gasped. "They're trying to destabilize the government."

"Correct. The Trutnevas have seeded the population with hired sympathizers, wagering they will get a share of the spoils. They hold demonstrations against the government demanding trade deals with the Empire."

A chill crept through Philippa. She glanced over at Vaughan. "Everyone knows what *they* trade in. What about Pallas

Evermore, the Premier?"

The General shook her head. "Her health is failing. She's not the leader she used to be. She's attended to by Antenora Sware. Treasonous bitch, that one. Never leaves her side. I guarantee she's Imperial Intelligence Service. Put my life on it. She opens the door—the Trutnevas walk in. All under the guise of a 'Peace Treaty.'"

"What are estimates of the Trutnevas' troop strength?"

"Maybe eleven regular divisions—fifteen thousand each and two divisions of the Dirae. Each of the Reginae could field an additional five to eight. Choi more."

Philippa took a deep breath. "General, that's close to three-quarters of a million! Combined, the Republics couldn't draw three hundred thousand. Are they mobilizing?"

"No, not that we can tell. But they don't need to—that would show their intentions. No, they will pursue this course until it's no longer profitable.

"The Senate has ordered me to ride to the U.D. and assess the situation. You're assigned to my security detail. Pick two of your best for the mission. We leave tomorrow at dawn."

Philippa saluted. "Yes, ma'am."

The General stood up. "Carry on."

Philippa stammered. "Ma'am? Any news of a ship sailing from Baltimore?"

The General never looked back. "Of course not."

Philippa pushed the tray away, her appetite stolen. For years there had been an uneasy detente with the Trutnevas. Before the time of The Forgetting, Vasiliy Trutnev, with uncanny prescience, had sold all of his paper assets at their peak and bought control of railroads, Pennsylvania shale gas, radio, and munitions. While the United States collapsed, he offered food when people were starving and forged a mercenary army to hold onto his nascent empire. Men could be bought cheaply. He groomed the twins, Myrmica and Solenopea, to be as ruthless as he was, and they didn't disappoint. Some whispered they killed him in the bath, like Marat. They built upon his empire using the economics of control. They controlled the energy, the labor, the military and most critically, the reproductive ability of the Reginae.

The General said to pick two. Lieutenant Scarbrough was the natural first choice. Philippa hated to take her from her well-deserved leave. She couldn't think of the second name. She didn't expect there would be fighting—this was strictly reconnaissance—but having a markswoman was a smart piece of insurance just in case. Maybe also, while she was in the U.D, she'd find some clue to where Astrid had gone.

She stuck her tray in the window for the dishwasher and climbed the stairs to the RSC local command desk. Sergeant Chavez sat at the desk. Philippa looked through the window at the building across North 10th Street. The windows were still dark in the early morning, but someone had hung a strand of blue Christmas lights around a window on the fifth floor. Their muted, lonely glow summoned a wave of sadness. *Oh Astrid, it always rained on Christmas.* She turned back to the Sergeant.

"I need a shooter. A no-shit femme fatale."

The Sergeant reviewed some papers, comparing them with others. She looked up. "I got a name. Corporal Merika 'Sodapop' Johnson. One hundred ten percent lethal. Probably out on the range now. They say she lives there."

Philippa raised an eye. "Sodapop?"

"I'll let her tell it."

"Let's go see."

The two women marched back down the stairs and out of the building. The range was located where the old Library of Virginia building stood, much of which had burned a decade ago. Blunt concrete walls surrounded it. The Sergeant led Philippa through the gate and across the courtyard. In the distance, Philippa could hear *Crack!* pause *Crack!*.

A row of targets stood at the far end. Distance marks were painted on the grass in white. At one of the thousand-meter marks, a woman in fatigues lay splayed on her stomach, her eye pressed to the scope. The rifle—one Philippa had never seen before—was supported by a bipod towards the end of the barrel. The woman never moved, even when Philippa knew she must have heard their approach. She seamlessly ejected the spent cartridge and bolted a new round. *Crack!* Again *Crack!* Completely one with the weapon. The holes in the target formed a tight circle around the mark.

"Corporal!" Chavez bellowed.

With one fluid motion, Johnson rose up and shouldered the rifle, her right arm in a polished salute.

"Ma'am, yes, ma'am!"

"At ease."

The arm went down, but Johnson remained rigidly erect, staring straight ahead. Lanky and broad-shouldered, she appeared taller than she was. And she wasn't only standing still—as any decent soldier would—she was statue-still, not a quiver or a twitch.

"Corporal, this is Captain Calenos. She has orders for a mission. Highest priority. She's looking for muscle, but no flash. Respectable, like. Can you do that?"

Eyes still forward. "Ma'am, yes, ma'am."

Philippa asked, "What kind of rifle is that?"

"Accuracy International L115A1, ma'am."

"Where did you get it?

"It belonged to my father, ma'am."

"What do you call her?"

Johnson's eyes narrowed, the whisper of a smile. "I call her *Vengeance.*"

Philippa studied her. She was hard, no doubt about it. Her stony face revealed nothing, her dark half-moon-shaped eyes a mystery. In contrast, her hair was like chocolate spun sugar.

"Corporal, we will be assigned to General Poole's detail. We will leave at 0500 tomorrow morning. We will observe the proceedings and provide security to the General. We will be among friendlies but on guard for trouble. Are you as sharp with a pistol?"

"Yes, ma'am."

"Good." Philippa locked eyes with the soldier. "Why do they call you Sodapop?"

The elusive smile flickered across her face again. Her eyes showed nothing. "It came from a time my squad was on a patrol down Danville way."

"Go on."

"We found this case of soda, old Mountain Dew, I think. I'd never had one. There were twelve cans and twelve of us. I drank my can. Like bang! It was sure good. I wanted another. I told e'vryone of them I'd fight them for their can. Give 'em 100 libra if I lost."

"How many cans did you win?"

"Nine, ma'am. The other two got wise."

"You'll do just fine, Corporal. See you in the morning."

3

– Evermore – November 2078

A pigeon alighted outside her window, puffed up for insulation against the gusting rain. Its blood-red eye stared straight at her. Pallas Evermore turned away. *Pigeons carry disease,* she shuddered. *Tuberculosis...can feel it already spreading in my lungs! Something must be done!* She clenched her fists. *Antenora will fix this.* The thought quieted her mind. She exhaled deeply, not realizing until then that she had been holding her breath.

She sifted through stacks of papers. *It must be here!* Piles of documents covered her desk, tipping and mixing with other piles. Some drifted down to the floor where they melted with other piles. Drafts of legislation, maps, budgets, requisitions, the whole of the workings of the United District layered the desk, the edges blurred. Past and present knitted together.

Protests on the mall, protests in the streets. *When did this begin?*

Alarm swelled. *The letter had just been here! The ultimatum from the Trutnevas.*

Pallas grimaced and rubbed her gnarled hands. The wet and the cold amplified her arthritis. She rummaged around the desk, pushing other papers onto the floor. Soon to be lost like raindrops in a puddle. Pallas spun around. A second pigeon had joined on the window ledge. She flung open the window. "Go!" she cried into the wind, which responded by blowing more of the papers across the room. Pallas's throat tightened and her face flushed. She banged her fist, immediately regretting it. Her hand throbbed.

"Antenora, please!"

The massive oak door opened. Antenora—always dressed in black—tiptoed in, gracefully as a wasp descending on a leaf. She was tall and her body almost skeletal. The skin was pulled tight across her mouth in a rictus. Her teeth jutted in different directions out of her pale gums. She closed the window, took Pallas's hand and led her to an upholstered chair in the sitting area. "Sit. You'll catch your death."

Pallas sat, her furrowed brows giving way to a child-like look of relief.

Antenora knelt beside the chair. "Now, what troubles you?" She smelled of tea and ink and something else, something like the whisper of an old, dead thing. Pallas breathed more shallowly. She was too sensitive lately.

The Premier's office had been in the Capitol Building since the White House burned in 2026—the same year the US government defaulted on its debt. Riots had scarred much of the city in the early days of the Forgetting.

Pallas's eyes were moist. "The-the letter. From the Trutneva sisters. I need it. I need to draft a reply. It must be handled very delicately. What they propose is utterly untenable. They offer protection from that blood-thirsty bitch, Choi. She's demanded all the land south of the border until Frederick. The Trutnevas have stated they would intervene on our behalf, but there's a cost, a high one. There always is. The Trutnevas would garrison three divisions—two here and one in Baltimore. We would pay for their maintenance and submit to the Protsent."

Pallas closed her eyes. "It's unspeakable."

Antenora stroked her hand. "These are troubled times. No one wants war, but we of the United District will never give in. Do your hands hurt? Do you want some white birch tea?"

Pallas shook her head, staring into the middle distance. The different options blurred when she tried extending them to their logical end. A strategy of appeasement of the Trutnevas was impossible. The U.D. could defend against Choi, she was certain of that. The U.D. had always been on the front line, always prepared for this day. There would be casualties. But would fighting Choi enrage the sisters and lead to an invasion by combined Trutneva/Choi forces? There must be some way to thread the needle. At least buy more time.

Pallas turned to Antenora. "We must affirm the Treaty."

Antenora nodded slowly, her eyes wide. "Yes, that *might* be prudent."

Pallas's face radiated with the idea. "We will deliver a letter signed by the heads of the other Republics affirming the Treaty and their willingness to stand by the United District. In the meantime, Colonel Kincaid will move the Second Army to Frederick."

Antenora lowered her voice. "We must ask ourselves: what has the Treaty done for us? The other Republics look to us to protect them. They hide behind our defenses, never offering anything more than token sacrifice. They are the lesser part. The Trutnevas know this. *You* know this. They will not come. Involvement from the other Republics will only inflame the sisters at a time when we need them to help maintain peace."

Peace, Pallas mused. For thirty years, the United District had maintained peace in the region, paying a tremendous price. Who was left to remember the twenties and thirties when the United States flailed, like a drowning man, to hold itself together? The fighting, the hunger, *the rapes as men demanded they would not go quietly?* A hollow pang crept through her insides. When she sifted her mind for thoughts of a happy yesterday, they vanished, leaving her with only bad memories. Failures, small betrayals, arrogance, shame. They crowded together, multiplied and rose up, unbidden. Her face burned. Lost was the voice that put her thoughts to right, lost the faith that the spell would pass. Drowned by the cawing, squawking maelstrom. She clenched her hand repeatedly and concentrated on something else (anything else!) to stop the damning images from replaying. Peace. Peace was what she needed.

She rubbed her hands. "No, they will answer. They have to. Prepare a letter."

She strode back to the window. Her eyes, dull moments before, shone with a fierce determination as she dictated.

"Cherished Sisters –

We face each day knowing the struggle. Our peace—hard-fought—has persisted because of our resolve to maintain the dignity of all sisters and to never yield to the temptation of power. I celebrate this victory every day. We have never sailed into the storm but have deftly ridden the waves of conflict and always greeted the sun again.

The Trutnevas to the North have conspired with Venoma Choi to play a gambit that would draw all of us into war. The United District stands as the bulwark of the Piedmont Republics against their aggression. For thirty years, our strength has shielded all the Republics."

Antenora captured her words in her beautiful flowing script.

"*To you, Richmond, Charlotte, Tidewater, Raleigh, and Charleston, I ask that you affirm the Mutual Defense Treaty. I must stress that we are not invoking the Treaty—that would play into their game. But these are perilous times, and we must be prepared.*

You must respond. State clearly that the Treaty is as unbreakable as the day it was signed. Show them we will never submit, that we will sacrifice for what we have built.

May the Mother keep us,

Pallas Evermore"

Antenora nodded and wrote. Pallas peered through the window. Echoes of chanting protestors trailed on the wind. *When did this begin?*

Thwump!

Startled, Pallas gripped her chest. An object had smacked against the window. *Violence? It can't be.* She looked at the ledge. A pigeon lay lifeless, its head twisted unnaturally.

"Antenora, it flew into the window! How terribly sad." Her voice quavered.

Antenora set down her pad.

Pallas lifted the window. "Oh, never mind about the bird. Proof the letter, encrypt it, then send it through secure transmission. Now go."

The heavy door closed behind her. Pallas rummaged in her desk, then the closet. The cold, damp wind swirled the papers around the floor. Finding what she wanted, she returned to the window. Tenderly, she lifted the bird to her cheek. Finally, she wrapped it in plastic and tucked it in her pocket.

* * *

Antenora retreated to her desk outside of the Premier's office. Always the same scene, always the same dialogue, Antenora thought. It must always be her idea. Walk her through the fog of her own decaying thoughts. Her lip curled and she stilled, waiting until her face was blank again.

Patience. The plan will succeed. Soon I will be one of the Reginae and rule over the U.D. This is not a setback. She studied herself in the mirror next to it. A crown, yes, a crown of platinum or white gold with diamonds. Strong, yet graceful. I will commission a crown from the finest Imperial artists. Antenora Sware will take her rightful place. Regina Sware.

A knock on the open door. "Ma'am?"

Antenora snapped around, brushed her hands on her hips.

The young clerk was new. Antenora had been introduced but had forgotten her name. Her skin was clear, and her chestnut hair fell in luxuriant waves on her shoulders. Antenora glanced at her cleavage, imagined the girl's nipple hardening to her touch.

Antenora smiled. "Yes?"

The girl paused, then stepped to the desk. "There's a communique from the RSC. General Poole has requested a meeting with the Premier. She will be here tomorrow."

Antenora almost scowled but caught herself. "Odd that this is the first we're hearing about it. When will she arrive?"

"The message said around 0800." The clerk took a tentative step back towards the door.

Antenora clasped her hands. "When they arrive, let them know the Premier will see them." Antenora pointed a chair, "Sit."

The girl cautiously lowered herself, her cushiony hips warming the chair. Antenora glided around to her side of the desk, nostrils flaring slightly. *She's been burning scented candles. Rose. Mint. How wasteful. How delicious.*

"Were there any other details?"

"No, ma'am. Just that she would be travelling with her security detail."

"Very good."

Antenora laid her hand on top of the girl's. Her finger traced the butter-soft café au lait skin. "I know a quiet restaurant, quite exclusive, but they always reserve a table for me. They manage somehow to stock the most delicious vintage reds. Smuggled from the North."

The girl looked at the floor. "I have to get home to my wyve. She's pregnant."

Antenora pushed a strand of hair behind the girl's ear, fingers trailing down her neck. "Oohh, how lovely. When is she due? You must tell me when the blessed day comes."

The girl stood up, tipping the chair over. She dashed to set it upright.

"Sorry, very sorry, ma'am."

Antenora pasted her smile back. "Don't give it a thought," she cooed. "You run along now."

The girl fled. Antenora balled her fist. *How dare she deny her queen?* She would keep working on the girl. *Perhaps her wyve will die in childbirth. So many do. Soon, everyone will want to be close to me.* The appearance of General Poole was distinctly unwelcome. Poole was the smart bet for the next head of Richmond. A brilliant strategist and shrewd diplomat. Antenora knew she would have to prepare Evermore for the meeting—give the failing Premier her lines.

There would be no letter to the Republics. For years Antenora had provided a deep channel of intelligence to the Trutnevas. Troop strength, crop yields, male births, energy production, command and control centers. She'd laid bare the throat of the U.D. and handed the Sisters the knife. They'd hammered out the plan. First, Choi provides a diversion by crossing the border. Not an all-out invasion. District forces mobilize and move to defend. Then, sign the treaty and let the imperial troops roll in. Far more than three divisions stood ready. The Trutnevas would control the cities before U.D. military command could take action. Regina Sware is crowned, and Choi gets a small piece of the territory as payment for her part.

A perfect plan.

4

– Philippa – November 2078

At 0500, Sodapop Johnson was waiting for them outside the motor pool. Durham Arms 9MM strapped to her hip. *Vengeance* had been traded in for the RSC issue M-21 with a forward grip. The rifle slung over her shoulder. Her half-moon eyes revealed nothing.

Phillipa and Scarbrough approached. Johnson offered a tight salute, which Philippa returned. Scarbrough exchanged nods with the Corporal. They plunged their hands back into their pockets. A cold front had dropped the temperature twenty degrees from the day before. Rain had fallen most of the day before. Scientists had pronounced that the two degree rise in temperature from the time of the Forgetting had made volatile weather more the norm, but for Philippa, it was the only weather she knew.

Philippa hadn't told Scarbrough any details or, more specifically, any of her fears. For years the six Piedmont Republics watched the seasons pass, living in a cloud of uncurrence—a state of shared denial that events were heading in a certain direction that no one was willing to acknowledge. The Empire in the North loomed more threatening by the day. The Trutnevas would never allow the Republics to rival them. War was inevitable, but no one spoke of it. The Trutnevas controlled vast reserves of Marcellus shale gas. The gas supply was one more means of control They supplied the energy to the Reginae and shut it off at any hint of rebellion. No heat, no lights, no power for their factories where the victims of The Protsent toiled.

In little more than a year you who feel secure will tremble.

General Poole arrived just as the truck was brought around, a JLTV without the gun mount. Built in Charleston in the former Mercedes Benz factory, it ran on biodiesel, like every other vehicle in the Piedmont Republics. Petroleum was scarce and used only for specific purposes. In the early years of the Republics, planners prioritized canola and other oilseed crops to provide fuel. Shipments of oil from Mexico and the Permian Basin had ceased. Even before the oceans became too treacherous, the massive oil tankers stopped arriving from the Middle East—nobody wanted the worthless currencies. Philippa got behind the wheel, the General next to her.

No one spoke as Philippa pulled the JLTV out onto the highway. Interstate 95 remained the primary north-south roadway. They rolled along the highway, veering around holes and buckles. Philippa kept the speed down while freight trucks barreled past.

Prince William Forest marked the boundary of the UD. To the east was Quantico, which housed one of their four armies. More UD vehicles filled the road as the morning opened.

They passed Crystal City, the Pentagon, and rolled into Washington DC across the 14th Street bridge. The street lamps bore ten-foot banners with the UD crest, hanging lifeless in the still morning.

"Drive around, Captain," the General ordered. "We're early."

Philippa headed straight up 14th Street, towards the Mall.

Ahead, a large orange detour sign loomed. Concrete barricades closed the street. A dozen or so UD soldiers stood behind them.

"Captain, pull over," General Poole ordered.

"Ma'am."

They turned on Independence, just before the barricades and pulled up to the curb. They strode the short distance to the guards, General Poole leading.

"What's going on here, soldier?" she barked. "Why the blockade?"

Two soldiers approached. Both enlisted, by their stripes. Neither offered a salute or other acknowledgment of the General. Both Latina, hair pulled up under their caps, wearing the gray-green U.D. fatigues and parkas. The one on the left, a sergeant, held up her hand.

Philippa pulled ahead of the General and spoke sharply. "Sergeant, Corporal, the world has turned on its head when an allied general doesn't command respect in the District. I suggest you take a careful look and adjust your attitude."

The two snapped to attention. The sergeant spoke, "Ma'am, yes, ma'am. Apologies."

The General returned the salute. "At ease. You're among friends. Now, situation briefing."

Sergeant Borquez (Philippa read the name patch) pointed towards the Mall. "Street's shut down. Protestors are rolling in. Whole Mall is cordoned off."

"How long has this been going on?"

"Two, maybe three months."

Philippa peered off to where the sergeant had pointed, east, near the National Gallery of Art building. Papered across the buildings were posters of starving children with WHY EVERMORE? superimposed on the image. A tent city in faded blues, yellows, reds and greens sprouted in the distance like a shattered rainbow. A crowd of several hundred ragged women and some men had assembled around fires burning in oil drums. Signs slung over shoulders read 'Evermore must go,' 'United Against Corruption,' and 'United Disgrace.'

In the mud where once grass had grown, a crudely constructed podium had been erected, a hollow parody of a courtroom. A weathered UD banner hung behind the judge's bench, on it, in red paint:

Evermore = Traitor

Everywhere Philippa looked, litter covered the ground.

Borquez pointed at the crowd. "Every day, they hold a 'trial.' Should start any minute. Been doing it for weeks."

General Poole stared out with her good eye. "This is a disgrace. Clear them out."

"Can't. Orders."

"Orders?"

"Orders to leave them alone. Don't engage. Close off the streets and keep a distance."

"Orders from whom?"

"Secretary of State Sware."

Poole scowled. "We're going to take a closer look. Stay here." To the RSC, "Leave your weapons here. "

Johnson shook her head, barely noticeable.

Philippa cleared her throat. "Ma'am, I respectfully state I

disagree with that plan."

"In my gut I do too, but we can't give them any reason to start something."

"Yes, ma'am."

They deposited their firearms in the JLTV and secured the vehicle. Crossing the grounds, Philippa made a quick assessment of the security situation. UD troops, some on horseback, maintained a loose cordon around the Mall like the one with Sergeant Borquez. Maybe a hundred total. On the Mall, she estimated two thousand protestors. Several trucks rolled into the camp from 7th St. She shook her head. The UD hadn't had this kind of unrest in years. What could be behind it all? She knew the answer. *Trutneva insurgency.*

From the back of one of the trucks, costumed characters emerged. Twelve solemn figures wearing agonized, oversized masks made from papier-mâché lined up and stepped in funereal unison. Gaunt-faced masks, terrified masks, diseased, sore-riddled masks. The crowd divided, knowing their path, their ritual. Their clothes were tattered, offering no comfort from the cold. People from the tents hurried over. More wood was added to the bonfire. *The show is about to begin.*

General Poole led the four RSC soldiers. To their right, the old Smithsonian castle. The banner advertised the exhibit *Plants near Extinction.*

The figures wended through the crowd and up the stairs to the stage. From the second truck, three new figures climbed out. Two of the women wore vintage business suits, one a blue pinstripe, the other charcoal gray. The last woman to leave the truck wore black judicial robes and powdered white wig to match her chalky makeup. A gruesome smear of claret lip color accentuated her mouth.

The crowd whooped and hooted. *All cheer the carnival trial.* Current surged through the ranks. Towering over their heads ranged one of the biggest men Philippa had ever seen. Six feet six, maybe 280, mangy gray beard, red-ringed eyes. Like a caged animal, he paced in circles around the perimeter with his sign, hollering, "Hear it! Truth! Traitors!"

Out of the crowd, a woman carrying a scarecrow dressed in a UD flag and blindfold heaved it onto the stage. The two women in suits propped it in a chair on the middle, hanging a sign that read 'Pallas Evermore' around its neck.

The RSC stopped thirty feet away. Philippa scanned the mob. Chanting, frozen breath vaporous and hate-filled. The fire blazed higher. Their eyes reflecting it, expectant. They swarmed around the stage. In their fury, Philippa saw the face of something ancient and unappeased, now stirring. Something blood-soaked. She looked at Corporal Johnson. The soldier stood with her feet apart and shoulders squared, eyes roving between the General and the crowd. Normally expressionless, they glittered with anticipation.

"Traitors," the crowd roared.

Gray Beard raised his fists high, snarling.

The judge produced an old megaphone. "My people! Justice is a gift that can only be given by the citizens. Justice lives in your hearts. Justice feeds your souls. You, the long-suffering, know its price. You who are cold know its price."

She pointed to the twelve 'jurors' shivering on the stand.

"You who are oppressed know its price. You who are hungry know its price. Today, we measure Pallas Evermore to determine if she should pay. What does she owe to the citizens she claims to govern? We will hear her defense in her own words. We will also hear the account of her greed, her corruption, her incompetence, her base disregard for the citizens of the United District. What say you?"

The crowd roared its rapturous approval. A beer bottle flew at the straw figure on the stage.

Philippa studied the UD soldiers, casual almost bored against their vehicles. *This happens every day?*

Protesters stoked the bonfire, the flames rising like their collective rage. Sparks exploded and swirled in the frigid air. The bearded man paced and howled, eyes glazed and bloodshot. "Hear it! Now it comes, now they see!"

The judge barked through the megaphone, "We will hear from the prosecution!"

The woman in the gray suit strode over, taking the megaphone, addressing the scarecrow. "Premier Evermore. You stand accused by the citizens of the United District. How do you plead?"

"Guilty!" the crowd roared.

A mocking grin crossed the prosecutor's face. "Your Honor, the defendant has chosen not to enter a plea."

"Continue."

"Premier Evermore, is it true that only a quarter of the United District has electricity?"

What happened to the power?

"Is it true that starvation threatens nearly half of your people?"

"True!" the crowd erupted.

Lies! Philippa turned to General Poole; whose jaw clenched.

The prosecutor strode to the chair with the straw doll, jabbed at it. "Is it not also true that you have profited immensely from property stolen from the citizens? That you have diverted trucks and train cars and sent them south to the criminal governments of Richmond and Tidewater?"

The scarecrow slumped sideways in the chair.

The prosecutor threw up her hands. "Your Honor, the defendant refuses to answer the court's questions. The prosecution has no choice but to rest."

A sneer crossed the hideous face of the judge. She cried out, "The court will now hear the defense."

The blue-suited woman snatched the megaphone from the prosecutor. "Citizens! Pallas Evermore has no defense for the crimes committed against the United District, but our court must be impartial. We must look at the prosecution's allegations and see for ourselves." Turning to the scarecrow. "Do you deny the charges against you? Do you deny that you have turned sister against sister and child against parent?"

Across the crowd, Gray Beard bellowed, "Now they see! Now the blood!" Eyes bulging, swinging the sign over his head.

Danger infused the air. Philippa pulled close to the General. *When does the deer smell the wolf? When does it realize the distance is too short to run?*

"Ma'am, we should go. This isn't safe."

Poole drove her fist into the palm of her other hand. "Hold your position."

Johnson fixed her eyes on Gray Beard. Scarbrough took a step back.

Before handing the judge the megaphone, the woman in the blue suit called forth, "Your Honor, the defense rests,"

The judge rose from her chair. "Citizens! Justice must be paid. You give it with clean hearts, with the righteousness that your will is pure."

"The blood is the will!" Gray beard smashed his sign on the ground until only a two-by-four remained in his enormous hands.

To the scarecrow, the judge rendered the verdict. "You have rejected peace!

"You have denied your people.

"You have stolen their future."

To the crowd, "How do we find the defendant?"

With one voice, "GUILTY!"

What is the sentence!"

"Burn her!"

The judge and lawyers dodged the trash and bottles that rained on the 'court.' The crowd surged, climbing over each other. Two of the protestors reached the scarecrow and hoisted it on their shoulders.

"Burn her!"

The crowd centered around the scarecrow. The two carriers paraded it towards the bonfire. Angry hands tore the blindfold off and waved it at a UD patrol.

Philippa scanned the perimeter. *Why are the UD soldiers doing nothing?*

"Enough!" the General bellowed. She strode towards the mob.

The crowd stalled. The scarecrow swayed. Gray Beard snapped around to see who dared to interrupt the proceedings. He shrieked, "There they are! Vultures feeding on our misery. Smash them."

His eyes narrowed, he raised his smashed sign pole and charged. Others fell in behind.

General Poole stopped.

Waving her arm, "Sergeant Borquez, NOW!" Philippa hollered.

Gray Beard raced across the Mall, an ancient Viking destroyer. Borquez would never get to them before the giant hammered the General into the hard ground. Hammered all of them.

Scarbrough and Philippa grabbed the General and pulled her back towards the perimeter.

Sergeant Borquez and a small squad charged towards the RSC, weapons drawn.

Gray Beard closed the gap in a handful of strides. Ten more steps and he would be in striking distance.

Philippa turned towards the giant. "Take the General," she ordered Scarbrough. "Johnson, you too. I'll hold him off." *This how it comes. Her hand close and the spotless beyond. Astrid forgive me.*

Johnson didn't respond. She stood braced for the giant's attack.

Gray Beard homed in on the General. Philippa dropped her shoulder and crashed into the raging giant. She caught him squarely in the legs and bounced off the hurtling force. Gray Beard stumbled but caught himself. He swung the board, hitting her in the shoulder, knocking her to the ground. Pain sheared her arm. Regaining his momentum, he charged again towards the General.

Like a shadow, Johnson slipped between the giant and his prey. Gray Beard roared and swung the club at her head. Johnson dropped to her knee; the club hissed through the air above her. Gray Beard lurched, the force of the swing pulling him left. Johnson feinted with her right fist and jabbed with her left. The punch connected with his jaw, lifting him barely off the ground. His head snapped back, and his eyes rolled up. His body slammed against the ground, the club dropping on his face.

CRACK CRACK – shots fired. Borquez aimed her pistol in the air. Her squad behind her, rifles leveled at the crowd. More UD followed, hustling the RSC off the scene as the protestors hurled bottles and insults.

Back at the JLTV, the General had regained her composure. Waving her arm out at the scene, "Remember this. The United District we knew is a mirage and the fierce sun is fading quickly. Thank you all. Such courage. Especially you, *Sergeant* Johnson."

Johnson saluted. "Ma'am." But her eyes betrayed nothing.

5

– Evermore – November 2078

General Poole paced back and forth in the antechamber to the Premier's office. The molding was interspersed with plaster Ionic columns. The faded gray carpet had a path worn through it connecting the Premier's door to the entrance. The furniture was a mismatched collection of once-expensive furniture with a vaguely Chippendale theme. The cushioned seats were shiny with wear, the wood finish chipped and scratched. With so much left over from before the collapse, new furniture was a luxury. Evermore would never spend tax libra on such trivialities. Johnson worked crosswords from a small book she'd brought. They'd been stuck there for two hours. From time to time, Antenora Sware would drop in with an 'I'm so sorry, but the Premier's schedule is quite full. I'm sure it won't be much longer,' but everyone saw through her petty game.

Around noon, Sware escorted Poole into the Premier's office. The entire room was spotlessly clean and organized. Pallas Evermore stood waiting on the faded, threadbare Oriental rug and wrapped her arms around the General.

Evermore pulled back, grasping the General's shoulders. "Well, well, my old friend, Karyn. Look at you. Just to lay eyes on you again heals my soul. The one person I seek in these difficult times. Karyn will help set things to right."

"My dear Pallas, how are you?"

"Slower than I'd like to be. So much needs to be done. I would be lost without Antenora. Did you receive the letter?"

"Hmmm, no, what letter?"

Evermore furrowed her brow and looked askance. "I think it went out last week." Sware led Pallas to the upholstered sofa in need of mending, sitting next to her. Poole took a chair to the side.

"Do you know what I think about, Karyn?"

"No, tell me."

"The men. Their half of the species condemned. Why didn't they tear it all apart? Burn it all to the ground. Yes, many tried, but why did some fight to hold civilization together with the remaining time they had? Fought and died while so many others tore at the marrow. I think about that with wonder. How proud they were, the adult men of our childhoods. I thought my father hung the moon. And then.... Should we be grateful?" Her eyes lit up. "Do you remember the Convention of 2050? You were just a junior delegate from Roanoke, and I introduced you to the people who were really trying to make things better for everyone. We helped forge the Mutual Assistance Treaty. We locked the doors and set guards to make certain no one left until we reached a consensus. That fellow from Baltimore, what was his name?"

Poole cocked her head without reply.

She leaned in. "You remember! Fat! Fat red face he kept pushing at people. 'No deal, no deal,' he kept saying. You know who I mean."

Poole shrugged.

Evermore stared at the General, smile trembling then turning to a scowl. "No, that wasn't. That wasn't you. You weren't there. Never mind. I'm sorry." She wrung her hands.

"That happens to everyone, Madame," Sware murmured. To the General, "What was it that you wanted to meet about?"

The General eyed Sware, fearing that anything she said would be fed to the Trutnevas. "Madame Premier, I've come to hear your assessment of the situation. We've received reports of blackouts lasting for days. Engineers from Richmond and Tidewater have been attempting to divert what they can off our grids to shore up the situation."

"Blackouts? I wasn't aware of any shortages. The wind farms along the Delaware coast provide what we need." She peered wide-eyed at Sware.

Sware lifted her chin, her voice unctuous. "Terrorists, Madame Premier. Terrorists have been attempting to cripple our power supply. But we've stopped them at every instance. We have it completely under control."

"Terrorists?" The Premier glanced from Poole to Sware. Distant cawing. Swarms of oily grackles and starlings merging into a billowing figure clad in judgment. The hot breath suffocating. She clenched her hand. *Peace. Grant me peace.*

Poole eyed the Premier narrowly. "The situation is far from under control. Counterfeit libra are legion in the U.D. We've traced arms shipments from the North. This is an insurgency."

Evermore shrank in her seat, blotches of color staining her soft old cheeks.

Sware leapt to her feet. "Your intelligence is wrong, General. No such problems exist here in the District. What kind of an ally comes here to spread patent lies! You and the other Republics have never measured up. It's always been *our* burden." The light glinted off her teeth. Like a hyena, the General thought.

Poole spoke calmly, but with force. "Madame Premier, there is revolution right outside your window. Your Secretary of State, Antenora Sware, permits this, perhaps even *encourages* this."

Sware took the Premier's hand. "An exaggeration. Such disrespect she shows you! Yes, there are protests, but these are the freedoms that we defend. The citizens are free to express their dissatisfaction even when we may not approve or even like what they say." Rounding on the General, "I suppose you would treat your citizens differently?"

General Poole dodged the question. "We're not talking about Richmond. This was no exhibition of civil disobedience; this was Trutneva poison infecting the U.D.!"

Evermore pressed her fist to her lips and peered up at Sware. "Is this true? Trutnevas? Here?"

Sware smiled and stroked Evermore's hand. Tears formed in her eyes. "If I haven't served you to the utmost of my abilities. If you have even the slightest doubt of my fidelity, I should resign immediately."

Pallas trembled. "NO! No, Antenora, you misunderstand."

Sware shot the General a look. *She does what I say.*

The Premier stood up and walked to the window. The crowds on the Mall chanting. *When did this begin? Is that my name?*

Sware gripped Poole's shoulder. "The Premier has many matters to attend to at the moment. The interview is concluded."

Poole twisted her hand and tossed it off. *Damned hyena.* Sware winced.

"Madam Premier...Pallas, please! We must work together. We can find a peaceful solution."

The Premier turned, eyes clear. She sighed, "Peace, yes, peace. Our hopes of maintaining peace are dwindling, Karyn. Venoma Choi is threatening in the west. There have already been small incursions past the Mason Dixon Wall, near Hagerstown. She's testing our resolve. The Trutnevas have offered to broker a truce. But what they really demand is an occupation. We can't fight them both."

"How much time have they given you?"

"A week." *Was it really a week?*

Poole put an arm around her and pulled her close. "We will solve this, Pallas. I will remain here, and we will formulate a strategy."

Antenora interrupted, voice pitched high. "I'm sure that won't be necessary, General, although we are deeply grateful for your offer."

Poole stared at her, the dead eye passing judgment. "I'm staying. Let me inform my staff."

Sware bowed her neck. "Of course."

Sware and Poole strode towards the door.

"Karyn! Wait!"

The General turned.

"Do you remember when we were both junior delegates at the Convention of 2050? Remember 'No deal. No deal!'"

Poole nodded. "I do. It was the best time of my life. Thank you for reminding me." A lonely tear ran down her right cheek. She wiped it away.

Pallas beamed.

Phillipa, Scarbrough, and Johnson all snapped to attention when the General reappeared. Sware dashed over to an attendant and whispered.

Poole began, "The situation is worse than I feared. I am going to remain here. We have to draw out the poison if we have any chance of stopping this." Grabbing a sheet of paper from the desk, she began hurriedly writing. "Give this to the Council. Their eyes only."

Sware stepped in, her jutting teeth in a distorted smile. "Write all you want. If you choose to stay, I will have you arrested for espionage. It's your choice."

Poole spat. "You don't dare."

Johnson and Philippa drew closer to the General, hands slowly moving to their hips.

Sware laughed, a screechy, stuttering sound. "Go. Now. When we meet again, maybe you'll have a better idea of who you're dealing with."

Armed guards burst through the door.

"Just in time. Escort these women to their vehicle and make sure they cross the border. Safe travels, ladies. A real pleasure."

* * *

Later, one of the attendants built a fire in the Premier's office. The wood smoke smell captured the essence of warmth and safety. The Premier sat in one of the upholstered chairs next to it, gazing at the flames—that pure blue at the base so exquisite!

Antenora brought the tea and set it on the table next to the Evermore. "Here you are. There are shortbread cookies."

"Mmmmm. Thank you. Where is General Poole? Where is Karyn? Isn't she here?"

"No, dear one, she couldn't stay after all. Pressing business in Richmond. Very regrettable. But we will carry on."

Evermore clenched her fist and stared back at the fire. *There was something else.* Shadows from the fire stretched their arms towards her. The faceless judge in *his* obsidian robes that mercilessly held her. *Please not again!* She closed her eyes.

Sware slid the treaty documents over. "Madam Premier, we need to speak about the Peace Treaty with the Trutnevas. The Republics have not replied to your letter. We need to review their offer. It's the only means to secure a lasting peace."

Pallas sighed. *A peace lasting for centuries. Wrapped in plastic.*

6

– Summer 2020

Ninety-three degrees outside and flashing red screens every-where across the trading desk. Fifth straight day. Through the glass wall, Josh watched the trading room. Watched the world going to hell. His wife home from the hospital since yesterday, calling on the cell phone again. *Better than the margin calls.*

Josh answered, "Hey, babe."

Her voice fragile, barely holding it together. "I'm watching the news. SARS, Zika? They said it might be a new Zika virus."

Josh huddled over his desk, cupping his ear against the panicked din. "Charlotte, no one knows. We have to figure this out." Two months in the house in Greenwich, their dream home. The eight million dollar note they signed. The furniture they'd found in Paris hadn't even arrived.

Charlotte's voice cracked. "I knew something was wrong. I just knew it! He never kicked."

Josh twisted his back to the desk, pictured her face, her blond curls, her anguish. *I should be with her.* He sighed. "NIH, Hopkins, Mayo. Everyone's working to understand this. The

World Health Organization is having a press conference this afternoon."

"They're everywhere. These babies. Spain, China, Australia. What does it mean?"

Josh could hear the child in the background, the strange melodic cooing. "I wish I knew. The news is killing the market. Much worse than '08." *You can't tell her how bad.*

Charlotte started crying. "He's so perfect."

"I know. He's ours. He's gonna be great. Just hang in there."

"He doesn't cry, he just kind of...sings."

Josh sighed. "That's beautiful. You're beautiful. Let me jump. I'm so sorry. I've got Goldman lighting up the phone. Got to try to keep them at bay. Have me by the balls, the cocksuckers. I love you."

"I love you too...so much."

Therefore a curse consumes the earth; its people must bear their guilt.

Josh Arajanian. Master of the Universe. 2011 Caltech, computer engineering and mathematics. 2013 Warton MBA. CFA. Two years with a high frequency shop and then his own artificial intelligence hedge fund, Quicksilver Capital. Four billion hard under management and 39:1 leverage, syndicated through Goldman Sachs, mostly derivatives. Five years averaging seventeen percent returns. Two and 20 bought the Greenwich house and the flat in London. Now all of it wavered like a mirage.

Josh ran his hand through his gelled curls. "This is Josh."

"Josh, guy, it's Sam. We're downside nine percent today. Can you post more collateral?" His voice resigned, inflectionless.

Josh gritted his teeth. "You know the answer. We're both at

the same party."

A long silence. Sam cleared his throat. "I hate this part Josh; I want you to know that. You've been a real good story. Money in the bank, but there's nothing in the equity account."

"Just give me till Monday. They'll come up with a plan over the weekend. Things will come back."

Sam's voice flat, "This is not my call."

"Fuck, Sam, you can't do this. I built this. You can't come in and take it away!"

"Hey, I don't like being the guy. You're one of thirty calls I gotta make. Risk is all over us. It's fucking DefCon One. The Feds are going to shut down the market. Who knows when *or if* they are going to reopen it? Their liquidity flood wasn't enough. Japan's already gone dark. I'm giving notice in accordance with our deal. We're taking the collateral against liquidated damages. You're on your own. We're all on our own. Maybe I'll see you on the other side of this. God help us."

Josh hung up.

Over. Gone. Five years gone in five days. Was their son really a gift? Or was it a curse?

Rachel, the head trader—phone in each hand—called over, "Josh, Josh! What the fuck's going on? The account is frozen. I'm locked out. The partners are freaking out. Answer me!"

Clarity. Utter clarity as when a fever breaks and the illusions are revealed. Josh looked at his hands.

"Go home," he mumbled.

"What?" Rachel yelled. Others joined in.

"Go home. GO HOME! There's nothing left. We're shut down. Goldman pulled the plug."

Curses, expletives. One trader smashed his phone on the desk. A line from a Ben Folds Five song—not heard since college—interrupted his thoughts.

'*...Seems that all men want to get into a car and go anywhere*'

Josh jumped on the desk. His throat tightened. "Working with you all these past five years has been a tremendous privilege. You're the smartest, toughest bunch to have on my side. We all did great work. But there's nothing more we can do here."

Rachel, tough, always the hammer in search of the nail—that's why he'd brought her in—collapsed in her chair, face in her hands.

His voice cracked. "I don't know where this is heading, but it's pretty bad. Now, go home and be with someone you love. Tell them that you're sorry, for...whatever. Tell them they are what matters."

He strode to his office, locked the door and turned off the light. He looked out of the midtown tower. A cathedral stood across the street, its Gothic architecture a staggering achievement of humanity. *Nothing is permanent.* In the street, life carried on. Sleepwalkers soon to wake up in the nightmare.

A quick calculation. *After fifteen seconds, the human body in free fall will reach terminal velocity. From this height, only about ninety-three percent...*

He thought of Charlotte pregnant, his hand caressing her nine-month belly. "We're having a son," she told him on New Year's Eve. He remembered the tears in his eyes, his gratitude. But now...a simulacrum in place of a child. Was it gift or a curse? Josh imagined some dark emissary, a skeletal man in shabby clothes—the Pied Piper, betrayed by the greed of men. Opening the windows of the houses, taking the sleeping babies and replacing them with blue-eyed dolls. Taking all the babies, keeping them till a distant Day of Atonement when mankind again understood that God was to be feared.

7

– Brick – December 2078

Brick stared out the window at the street nine stories below, scratching her armpit. Cars and trucks lined the street. Servants hoisted trunks onto carts. Freezing rain fell, the hiss of it muting the sounds that drifted up. She coughed a deep-chested, phlegmy cough and lit a Dominion cigarette. The smoke and nicotine immediately settled things down. She exhaled and turned around, studying the slender blonde still asleep. Smells of sex and resignation. She'd instructed the girl not to say anything, no words. Nothing to break the illusion, however thin. And for a few hours, she had been able to imagine herself among the lucky who had wyves or someone who loved them. She'd paid the escort service for the night, but now that was over. Time for work. The Trutnevas always got what they were owed.

"Get up!" she shouted.

The girl stirred, rose up on an elbow. Long legs, smoky eyes and pouting lips. *Worth the price.*

"Now! Out!"

Groggy movement. Too slow for Brick's taste. She threw a shoe, barely missing the girl's head. *Bang!* It bounced against the headboard.

"I said, get the fuck out!"

Gathering her clothes and coat, the girl raced out of the apartment.

Fifty years ago, the building had been the Federal Reserve Bank of New York. Vasiliy Trutnev—father of Myrmica and Solenopea—had claimed it as a prize after his forces had routed the remains of the New York National Guard. After his victory, he renamed the city Novi Vasiligrad. Somewhere deep below was a vault with racks of gold bullion. Six thousand tons of it. Brick couldn't have cared less. The stuff wasn't worth much these days. Deadweight.

Brick stretched and lumbered to the bathroom, reminding herself not to slouch. Naked, she inventoried her deficiencies. Different sized breasts, shapeless ass and the trail of wiry hair leading down from her navel. She scratched her labia rings. Six feet one. Thick—she'd always been thick. Thick lips, thick-bodied and thick-witted, so they all told her. Her greasy straight dark hair covered the scar from when she'd been kicked in the side of the head. Her six-year-old brain had swelled. It took almost a day to get to a doctor. That swift, skull-breaking instant had defined her. She picked at a scab on her elbow.

Happy birthday, Myrmica and Solenopea. You made it to forty.

Later that day, the sisters were hosting the collection of greedy, treacherous sycophants known as The Reginae. The seven queens of the Trutneva empire. Each of these cunning women knew that they ruled *because* of the Trutnevas, but each one hated the twins and wouldn't hesitate to try to overthrow the sisters if they thought they had the odds on their side. Brick made sure that didn't happen. She knew the color of their lies.

Brick showered but didn't bother cleaning her hair. She combed the greasy brown strands flat to her head. She dressed in the uniform of the Trutneva House Guard—deep green, almost black jacket, white shirt, narrow, eggplant-colored tie with the Trutneva crest—the golden two-headed eagle. On her lapel she pinned the emblem of the House Guard, signifying her position as a commander in that elite company.

Looking around the luxurious apartment, she acknowledged she had a first-class setup. Good food and plenty of it. Heat. Sex. The respect (be honest, fear) of the other officers. The Trutnevas had the winning hand and she'd play out their game.

Skipping the elevators, Brick tromped down four flights of stairs, past guard teams, to her office. Marijke was waiting for her as usual. Camo fatigues, ultramarine beret with the Trutneva crest, chipped Tiffany blue fingernail polish. M&P 380 Valkyrie holstered on her hip. All the same colors. She lowered her eyes as Brick entered. She started to hand Brick a sheet of paper then just as quickly recoiled as if burned. "Situation briefing, Commander."

Brick growled, "Read it."

Marijke stammered, "All of the members of the Reginae have arrived. Queen Choi insists upon a meeting with the Sisters."

"What does she want?"

"Reproductive requests."

"That won't happen today. Next."

"There are complaints about the security measures. The container searches. The dogs."

Brick cocked her head. "Too bad. That comes straight from the sisters. They all know by now what the rules are."

Trutneva security was looking through every case, trunk and bag the Reginae had brought. Everyone in the retinues were searched for weapons and explosives. The dogs were almost for show, Brick thought. Only an idiot would try to hide powder or C4 with its telltale odor of motor oil. Pure Semtex would be the choice. If it was smuggled in, Brick would find it though. *She* would smell the lie. That was her gift. Her gift from the mule.

"Any men?"

"Several."

Good, she thought. The tired old husks, whiffs of urine, greedily hanging on to the past, always presented a ridiculous sideshow she enjoyed watching. There were lots of things about the lost world, as she understood it, that she envied; men were not among them.

Brick lit a cigarette, squinting, "How are preparations?"

"No issues reported."

"Review the schedule."

Marijke cleared her throat. "Twelve o'clock luncheon. Two to four-thirty meeting of all the Queens. Six o'clock reception. Seven o'clock dinner. Festivities afterwards."

"Has the food been checked? Any new staff?"

"All tests clear. No new staff."

"I want to see for myself." Trust was the scarcest commodity in the Trutneva empire.

Brick stormed to the vast kitchens, Marijke in her wake. The servants were swarming about, tasting sauces, chopping vegetables. Heat and steam permeated the air. The gleaming stainless steel amplified the sounds. Smells of all varieties: vanilla, garlic, roasting meat, anxiety, soaps. Brick inhaled them all, categorizing them mentally. Lifting each aroma to seek what might be hiding underneath. So far, nothing. No poisonous hints. No hidden treachery.

She paced around the room, leaning in to question the servants. The head chef was first. An ample middle-aged woman who clearly enjoyed her work.

Brick leaned in. "Don't stop what you're doing. Tell me what you are making."

The chef carried on. "Lamb chops. The Sisters' favorite."

"You know everything that goes on here. Have you seen any new faces? Any new delivery people?"

The chef looked up. "No, Commander. Not to my knowledge."

Everything the chef said was true. Golden-copper sparks surrounded her words, gleaming like the patina on the saucepans. Brick grunted to herself and moved on. One by one, she questioned the servants, watching each time for the gray ash, the tell, but each time it was bright, like metal on a grinder.

Brick cornered one of the newest servants, a plain-looking, petite redhead, mixing batter. The newest servants always got the lowliest jobs. Seeing Brick approach, she dropped her spoon. The clatter echoed through the kitchen.

Brick stared down at her. "Where did they find you?"

The terrified girl shrank into the floor. Brick smelled black treacle fear and waited.

"Burlington. Queen Sachs' soldiers raided our farm. I was sent here as part of the Protsent."

Brick lifted the girl's chin and gave her a predatory smile. "Too weak to do any real work, eh? Not pretty enough for the bed either, I wager."

The girl said nothing.

Brick dropped the girl's chin. "What are you making?"

"The cake, Commander." Her eyes returned to the floor. Brick caught the bitter aroma of burnt sugar.

Brick studied her. "Tell me, do you stock the shelves?"

"Yes, Commander."

The words looked right, but a thought nagged her. *She doesn't know what she knows.*

"What else? *Tell me.*"

The servant's eyes lit up. "Wait! The girl who delivered the candles told me to be careful. I thought that was strange. Very strange."

Copper sparks swirling around the words. *The candles.*

Brick growled, "Bring them to me."

Work had stopped in the kitchen.

The servant scurried off and returned with a box of eighty candles. Each one was the same ultramarine color as Marijke's beret.

Brick studied one of them, held it up to the light, sniffed it. She snapped off the end with the wick. Nothing. Picking up a knife, she scraped the wax at the base. Nothing. She tossed it aside. *It's here!* She reached in and sampled ten more at random. On the tenth one, two passes of the knife revealed the fuse. She sampled another one—same deadly result.

Clever, Brick thought. The explosives had been placed deep in the candle to allow enough time to get them all lit. Enough time to wheel the cake out. But not too deep to risk never igniting. If it had worked, no one in the room would have survived the blast.

Brick turned to Marijke. "Go now and find eighty candles that match these exactly. We need bait for the rat trap. And post guards at all these doors. No one leaves this room until I give the all- clear."

Marijke saluted, "By your command." Then she glared at the servant, who stood shaking.

"How about this one? Should I take her to The Quiet Room?"

A look of unalloyed terror crossed the poor girl's face.

Brick narrowed her eyes and smothered the momentary surge of pity drawn from the unfortunate servant's panic. Pictured her strapped in the chair, waiting, the bland face streaked with tears. Helpless in front of what was coming.

Brick sighed. "No, not her. We'll have our prize soon." To the servant, she barked, "Now get back to work!"

The girl's eyes rolled back, and she collapsed on the floor.

8

– Brick – December 2078

Assassins, I knew it! But who?

She tromped up the stairs, rolling the names of the individual Reginae around in her head, scratching for clues. Brick wasn't cleared to hear the intelligence reports from around the Empire and beyond. She was a specialist, personal detail to the Sisters. She heard scraps of information and coarsely patched together the stories. Greed and treason. Venoma Choi, brilliant and violent. Gael Stafford, licking her wounds but loyal...for now. Brick fought for a year in her mercenary army against the fanatical Newmarked. Latrobe, Greensburg. Of Fairfax, Caggiano, Sachs, Fang and Vasquez, she knew less.

Myrmica Trutneva lived on the top three floors of the Reserve Building. Solenopea had travelled from Philadelphia and stayed in the guest quarters. Brick slowed while climbing the last flight. She held the rail, panting, before opening the door. *Gotta quit smoking.*

The attendant looked up from her work and the guard struck a defensive pose until they recognized her. Both Dirae

Corp—both hated her.

The attendant offered a lame salute and looked down at her papers. "Commander, what do you need?"

Brick replied with a salute. "I need to speak with the Sisters."

The attendant didn't look up. "We have orders that they don't want to be disturbed. What's this about?" Words like volcanic ash falling and blowing.

"You're lying and you know it," Brick growled. *Ignorant bitch.*

The attendant flicked her head at the guard. "Go. Tell the General the commander wishes an audience."

"Yes, ma'am." *Click clock click* of the boots in the hall.

Brick flexed her hand, clenching and releasing. She could still hear the long-ago-never-forgotten taunts: *You're a freak. Stupid as a brick.* She inched closer to the desk. *I know her kind. Thinks herself too important for someone like me. Fuck her.* A calmer voice intruded, but just as quickly overridden. *Just step back. No, fuck her.*

CRACK!

Brick smacked the attendant's head against the desk. She pinned it with her elbow while the other hand twisted the attendant's arm behind her back.

"Aaahhhhh," the attendant grunted, her left arm flailing for her sidearm on her right hip.

Brick leaned in and whispered. "You should know better by now. Do that again, I'll see you're in Cayuga buried alive in salt, working fifteen hours a day with the old men. Never see the sun again." She released her with a shove.

The attendant rubbed her wrist, eyes narrowed. Wisely, she kept her mouth shut.

The attendant returned. "They're in the Her Grace's private

office. Second door on the left."

"I know the way."

Brick tromped the marble floors, eyes fixed forward. The walls were punctuated with large paintings, ancient and modern. The kind people wrote books about. Books Brick hadn't ever read. The Sisters had many of them, entire rooms of shelves. She doubted they read them either. The double doors opened on the meeting room.

Inside, the sisters sat at the end of an enormous conference table. Gray light diffused through arched windows set high in the two-story room. At one side of the room stood an eight-foot-tall white box with glass panels. Inside the box hung two slaughtered sheep—entrails exposed—nailed to a St. Andrew's cross. The whole sacrificial assembly submerged in formaldehyde.

Myrmica and Solenopea. The twins. Statuesque warrior-goddesses summoned by blood sacrifice out of some mythical Siberian killing field. Othere's handmaidens. Their blazing infernal hair fell in rich waves down their shoulders. Myrmica's left eye sparkled ice blue while her right was limpid amber. Solenopea's eyes were reversed—right eye hazel, left radiant sapphire. Brick had lost count of all the fights she'd been in, had been shot at a dozen of times in combat. She always kept her head together when threatened, but there was something unnerving about the Sisters. Something unnatural.

Swarming around the sisters was their small army of advisors, military officers, house servants, and strategists. Brick recognized Del Fuego, the ranking general of the Dirae and Glott, Supreme General of the United Imperial Army. Glott parodied the image of a fit, rigid military commander. She seethed like a jellyfish, billowing each movement. Her dull gray uniform adorned with medals. Narrow-set eyes with a burned-in, paranoid squint. Rumored to have violent sexual proclivities.

Glott was speaking, "...over ten thousand operatives active in the District. Two weeks, maybe less. Sware is in regular..."

Brick stopped.

Myrmica looked up. "Speak. What..." Her voice cool, almost musical.

Solenopea completed, "...have you come to tell us."

Brick nodded to each. "Your Grace, your Grace. We have discovered an assassination plot."

Conversation in the room froze.

Brick cleared her throat. "The candles, for the cake. A portion of them were Semtex, shaped and dyed to look like the others. We've quarantined the staff for interrogation. I've instructed one of my soldiers to find candles that are the exact replica. With your permission, I propose we continue as if nothing happened."

Solenopea stood up. "And whoever leaves before the cake..."

"...is the traitor," Myrmica added. She licked her lips.

Brick nodded. "Yes, your Graces."

General Del Fuego smacked her palm on the table. "Well done, Commander."

Brick mumbled. "Thank you, ma'am."

Glott interrupted. "Still, that could have been a decoy."

Brick turned. "I agree. I've ordered a sweep of the dogs through the halls and doubled the guards at all exits." She turned to the twins. "What about the daughters? Of the queens."

Solenopea answered. "Allow them to attend. A change like that at the last minute would signal our discovery." A ray of sun caught her left eye, the blue foundation of fire.

Myrmica added, "We don't want to cause any suspicion. If the daughters aren't there, the traitor will suspect that they've been found out. General Glott, what would have been the damage if the explosives had gone off?" Her hand lay on her sister's arm, smoothing the bare, gold-tinted skin.

The General shifted, an amoeba drawing in, reaching out. She wheezed, "Total destruction. Blast radius of fifty, sixty feet. No one would survive. Whoever plotted this had murderous ambition." The words looked right, but Brick stepped towards the General. Closer was better.

General Glott waved her fist. "We will find these traitors and show the world what happens to anyone who dares cross the Trutnevas." Brick sniffed. Her breath—a sharp tang of acetone—coated the General's words. Nothing alarming, no ash. Still, *there's always someone inside.*

Brick scowled. Schemers and liars, all of them. Nothing to strike at. Nothing to wrap her hands around. She turned to leave but stopped short. "General Glott, if I may. A word."

The General tilted her head. "Yes?"

"Tell your doctor to check for diabetes."

The General's head recoiled into her neck.

Brick saluted. "By your leave, your Graces."

9

– Brick – December 2078

Soft light glittering from the dozens of candelabra reflected off the crystal chandeliers. Hundreds of tiny white lights adorned the giant potted Ficus trees spaced throughout the ballroom. The twenty-piece band played up-tempo songs, the bleach blonde front girl wearing a sheer black dress slit up the thigh. The seven Reginae and their entourages had staked out their territories in the room, creating small encampments with suspicious glares for outsiders.

Brick surveyed the room. Anastasia Geftman, head of the Novi Vasiligrad Central Bank, huddled next to a far column speaking with Xi Fang who held the territory just north of the Trutnevas. *Lining up financing to buy off the Trutneva army once the Sisters are gone?* Fang's luxurious, glossy black hair piled high on her head. Her eyes, ringed in silver shadow, met Brick's, missing nothing. Her daughter—a younger replica—sipped a drink nearby.

Julia Fairfax and Katherine Caggiano sharing a table. *Planning to seize the gas fields in their backyard? The source of*

Trutneva power.

The daughters reunited with the Queens—the Sisters demanded that each of the Reginae send one of their daughters to live in Novi Vasiligrad. The girls were lavishly pampered and looked after by the Sisters, hiding the reality that they were hostages, kept to ensure obedience. They competed quietly and nastily, each bent on seducing and betraying each other. Much was promised; little actually happened, save for the odd servant inexplicably bruised (and they knew better than to complain). Brick would like to release the lot of the girls, in their wispy gowns and shiny jewels, into the dirty back streets of the decaying city.

Servants carrying sweet gin cocktails and Dominion Cannabis circulated wearing tight-fitting corsets and patent heels. *I'd kill for a cigarette.* Not now. Work to do. Wealthy old men, deathly gripping their waning power, surrounded themselves with younger women. *Typical.* The Sisters had made certain to supply the party with compliant escorts on the payroll of Imperial Intelligence. *Compliant but not without hate.* She had heard that in the old days, women feared men because they were stronger and more aggressive. She believed it but doubted it had ever been that simple. Women had power now; they must have had it then too. The power of sex, lies, intelligence, cunning.

The two-story ballroom overflowed with pre-collapse decadence. Tapestries in ultramarine. A fountain of sparkling wine, hundreds of Calla lilies cultivated in Harlem hothouses. Tables laden with delicacies not found anywhere else in the Empire in such abundance: lobster from New England, salmon mousse, turtle soup, crowns of lamb chops. Another table loaded with gifts from the Reginae and others. Brick glanced at the kitchen door. The cake lay baited within.

Myrmica and Solenopea worked the room, a full head taller than most of the women. Covered in diamonds. Whispering with Gael Stafford, laughing with Bianca Vasquez, always a glass in their hands, but never a taking a sip. Never compromised. Never far from one another, either. Even across the room, their gazes met regularly, and thoughts were exchanged: that was obvious, though the mechanism wasn't clear. She had seen them once, through a window, in bed together, a blue-eyed boy between them. He was doing what it was males did, but the sisters were kissing each other. They reminded her of hibernating snakes.

Here, Brick drew little attention. Far more interesting and important people for the guests to study.

Camphor-scented Arturo Giacometti, head of the Imperial Rail System, sat nearby, next to a teenage boy. The boy's blind, enigmatic blue eyes drifted in his head. *One of the fragmen. No point trying to talk to them, but at least they don't lie.* The label captured the essence of these creatures. Broken men, merely a remnant of what they once were. Healthy in body, able to learn a few things; who knew what they thought or felt? Who knew their purpose? Well, humans always found a purpose for one another. Giacometti and the teenage boy both wore tuxedos with matching silver bow ties. Brick studied Giacometti, watched him lovingly cut the boy's food and hand him the fork. Their two faces bore similar features. *Must be his son, not his lover. Fatherhood is one more thing that will soon be forgotten. My father worked himself to death and still couldn't protect his family, feed them. He was decent. Mother hated him. Called him weak, a failure. She never missed an opportunity to remind me that to be ugly was to be alone and that I should get used to it. The fragmen ushered in this world, put women in charge. Now they are our pets. Our burden.*

Brick gazed out at the gathering. *Which one, which one?* With this much noise, focusing on one conversation proved nearly impossible. So many lies permeated the room, it hardly mattered. Her work would come later in The Quiet Room amid the pleas for mercy.

Fifteen minutes until the cake.

Moving around, Brick sifted through the aromas. A secret richness for her alone. The heady lilies, a hint of lavender from the linens, the latest Chanel creation—subtle edge of cedar—wafting from Regina Sachs, juniper undercurrents from the drinks. Then, honeysuckle, sweet and patient.

Honeysuckle.

I think I love you.

Brick's heart dropped. She looked around desperately, eyes wide, sucking in air to quiet the throb in her chest. *It's not possible. She can't be here.*

She wiped her hands on the hem of her jacket. *Stay focused. Find the assassin.*

She allowed herself a moment to reclaim the delicate honeysuckle and traced the source. A near table with a drunken attendant to one of the Reginae. The girl threw her a lopsided look and broke into laughter. Brick clenched her jaw and glared at the ignorant fool.

I think I love you. Brick shook her head. *God, I was so fucking stupid then.*

9:00 o'clock

Bang!

The double doors to the ballroom burst open. Acrobats clad in gold and ultramarine leotards leapt and handsprung towards the fountain. Flaming batons twirled through the air. Trailing behind, the pastry chef pushed the cart on which the three-tiered cake burned with treachery. The candles curved alongside the edge in pairs, snaking up along the outside. The band broke into a languid version of "Happy Birthday."

Myrmica and Solenopea exchanged those speaking glances and beamed at the crowd.

The guests closed around the cake. Brick counted the Reginae: Sachs, Caggiano, Fairfax, Choi, Stafford, Vasquez. *Where the fuck was Fang?*

"Happy Birthday to you"

Brick pushed through the crowd, staring at faces. No Fang. She stormed to the door.

No one in the hallway.

"Happy Birthday, dear Myrmica and Solenopea
Happy Birthday to you"

She had doubled the guards at the exits and given strict orders that no one was to leave. If Fang didn't hear the explosions, would she guess they'd been found out or would she think the candles had failed? Smart bet was to run. Increase the distance. Buy time.

Brick thundered down the stairs, smashing through the ground floor door. Ahead, she heard, "Stop, no one is allowed to leave."

Fang's voice precise and commanding, "Do you know who I am? I'll have you court martialed. Let us pass."

"Arrest them!" Brick hollered. She turned the corner, chambering a round in the M&P 380.The granite hallway with the black wrought ironwork opened up into a cavernous vestibule. An enormous bronze mechanical clock hung on the wall, its hands frozen at 5:13.

The first guard fumbled for her sidearm. Fang wheeled around, her high-necked scarlet jacket conveniently stretchy, and leveled her with a roundhouse kick. The guard slumped over.

Fang's daughter, in an emerald dress petaled like a flower for ease of movement, flew at the other guard, hammering her with a kick to the chest. The guard bounced against the wall, falling to her knees. Still conscious, she was struggling to stand when Xi Fang snapped her neck.

Brick leveled her pistol, jerking it between Fang and her daughter, gasping, "Stop, dammit."

Fang crouched, lithe as a cat. "She can't shoot us both." She lunged at Brick. Brick snapped the gun away from the daughter and fired. CRACK. Fang was too quick. She spun and brought her elbow down on Brick's gun arm. Brick barely held on.

The daughter flew at her as she had the guard. *I've seen this trick.* Brick caught her ankle and wrenched her off-balance. The girl tumbled to the floor.

Brick twisted and aimed at Fang. CRACK. Fang leapt and kicked off the wall, flying over Brick's head. CRACK CRACK. Always an instant too slow.

Fang landed behind her. Brick spun around and immediately dodged, losing her balance. Fang's roundhouse glanced off her shoulder. Brick tried to steady herself when another kick sent the gun clattering across the floor. A snapping sound and pain shot up Brick's arm. *Fuck, it's broken.*

Boots running in the distance. Fang's daughter pulled herself up on one knee, eyes narrowed in hate. Fang bobbed, fists raised, looking for an opening.

Stay focused. This one is deadly. Put her down.

Brick couldn't make a fist with her right hand. It hung down at her side. Turning sideways, she raised her left hand and threw a jab. Fang blocked and connected with a left to Brick's left eye. Brick staggered.

You got one chance left.

Fang weaved. The daughter wobbled to her feet and lunged for the gun. Brick lowered her head and charged, wrapping Fang around the waist with her good arm. Fang clawed and bit at her back and head. Brick spun around and threw Fang at her daughter. Both crashed to the floor. Brick grabbed the gun.

Four Trutneva guards, pistols drawn, charged the scene. In moments, the Fang women were restrained, hands cuffed behind their backs.

Brick bent forward, good hand on her knee. "'Bout fucking time."

"Are you okay, Commander?"

Brick gingerly probed her eye. "Yeah, had worse," she growled. "Everyone in the Fang entourage is under house arrest. Keep it quiet. None of them are to leave. Take these two to the holding area. Separate rooms." Pointing to the two dead guards, "Clean up this mess."

Fang's daughter wrestled against the arms that held her and yelled, "Your day will come. I'll look forward to killing you myself." Brilliant copper words.

Brick smirked and shook her head. "That day is coming for all of us." Still, the girl's threat echoed in her head, unsettling her, spoiling her triumph. Turning to the guards, she stuffed her hand in the breast pocket of the closest one. "Which one of you has a cigarette?"

10

– Brick/Quiet Room – December 2078

Brick slammed the door to the Quiet Room behind her. *Just kill them and be done with it.*

Day four of the interrogations of the Fang retinue.

Brick ran her hands through her hair and paced back and forth. She squeezed her eyes closed. *What time is it? 2 AM, 3?* Inside The Quiet Room, the Fang Chief of Security hung by her wrists, arms spread, balancing on her toes. Everyone waited.

Brick marched to the bathroom, peed, splashed water on her face and through her hair with her good arm. The matted clumps glistened in the garish light. She scrubbed her hand under burning water, wincing. Satisfied with the angry, red skin, she tucked in her shirt, lit a cigarette and strode back.

The Quiet Room—the lair of Irma Greist—the She Wolf.

For seven hours, Brick had listened to the answers the woman had given. The Chief of Security was a trained liar, but Brick had never known anyone to hold out against the She Wolf's 'attentions.' Brick watched the words, measured them, signaled when the ashen lies swirled. The She-Wolf often circled back, asking the same question with slight variation in her flat, inflectionless voice. Bureaucratic efficiency. Mid-fifties but excellent skin carrying the lingering citrus smell of her moisturizer. She wore her gray hair pinned up. An attendant recorded the sessions.

The Quiet Room existed as a mental space as much as a physical space. Pride, ego, illusions, all stripped bare. Inevitably, people taken there found themselves alone in the primal truth: *Everyone betrays.* Located in one of the basements of the Reserve Building, it represented a special dark star in the Trutneva constellation of terror. On the gray-green door hung a black and white silhouette of a woman with her finger pressed to her lips – somebody's sick joke. The room stank of sweat, fear, and ammonia.

The She Wolf picked up where they'd left off, coiled whip in her hand. "We need to talk about the candles."

The woman's head lolled on her chest. Unwashed gray-streaked blonde hair draping down. A hot spotlight shone down from above. Sweat beaded on the unfortunate woman's brow. Her only clothing, a print hospital gown tied loosely in the back. "I've told you everything I know. I don't know where they came from." Coppery-gold gleaming trailings.

The She Wolf held one up and approached. "Clever, really. Semtex is quite hard to come by."

She circled the prisoner. "Let's review the names of every-one you traveled with."

The woman panted the thirteen names. Her calf muscles trembled. The She Wolf compared the names with what she'd confessed earlier.

"Who did you speak with since you've arrived? Take your time. I'm going to help you out. I'm going to name people and you are going to reply. Anyone from Gael Stafford's delegation?"

The woman clenched and unclenched her hands to regain circulation. "No." Brick nodded to the attendant, their signal she was telling the truth.

In her slow monotone, The She-Wolf asked, "Anyone from Julia Fairfax's party?"

"No."

Golden, flashing words. Brick nodded again.

"Bianca Vasquez or anyone she traveled with?"

"No." Another nod.

"Farrow Sachs?"

"Yes."

"Tell me who you met with."

"I met with Colonial Oswald. She has an informant in Syracuse. We share intelligence regarding Regina Caggiano." Dry, gray words. The prisoner was lying. Brick, sitting at the table just outside of the spotlight, shook her head. The attendant clicked her pen—the code between her and the She Wolf.

The She Wolf lifted the prisoner's chin, smiling her worthless smile. "That's *very* interesting. You know just what to say, don't you?"

Brick scowled. *The fool thinks she's going to trade. Give the Trutnevas something and spare herself.* The amber glass ashtray overflowed with butts.

The She-Wolf droned, "Tell me more."

The woman shifted to attempt to relieve the strain. "They have been holding back on their percentage. Holding back on the Protsent. They falsify the reports. I have proof." Ash and cinders. Brick shook her head. *Click.*

The She Wolf traced the line of tears down the prisoner's face with a polished nail, never revealing she knew of the lie. She established a perverse parody of trust. "We have *so* much time, you and me. See, you give me something and I accept it as a measure of your willingness to help. What do you owe your mistress? I know that you didn't know anything about the plot. We all do. You were in the room. You would have been blown to shreds like everyone else. Your Queen was happy to sacrifice you."

The She Wolf pulled the string on the gown. It fell open and hung off the prisoner's shoulders. Brick let her eyes drift over the woman's figure. There was a mixture of pity, disgust and indifference in her gut that she was used to, that defined her working days. Only in these early moments. Only when the prisoner was still a person.

"Fuck Xi Fang," the prisoner spat.

"That's the spirit! The spirit of cooperation. I can tell we're going to be close friends. Now, this is important, so I will need your full attention."

Brick recognized the technique. She'd seen it many times. The She-Wolf would punish the prisoner for lying, make her excruciating situation worse. The She Wolf pulled the handle on a winch attached to the wall. The prisoner lifted higher with each crank. Toes trying to grip the floor, then pedaling in air. Manacles cutting into her wrists, she groaned.

"Now, why do you think Caggiano would..."

SSSSSSSS CRACK!

The She Wolf laid a stripe across the unfortunate's back. The woman cried out. Brick imagined the heavy blow followed by a searing burn. Immediately an angry weal raised where the braided leather had struck.

Three more strokes followed, the She Wolf snapping the whip for effect in between. She eased off the winch, lowering the prisoner. The woman's knees buckled, and her face collapsed in deep sobs. Snot ran from her nose.

The She Wolf would now give the prisoner time to reflect. She took a seat at the table and reviewed the notes from the interrogation. Agonized cries filled the room. Not a lie among them.

The She-Wolf was working her way through Fang's retinue. Meticulous, never rushing an interrogation. Xi Fang and her daughter would be the last, and certainly the worst.

Brick looked around the room at the cruel devices: an angled table where the limbs were stretched till they broke. The Fang bodyguard had spent fourteen hours on it, head below her feet, body taut as a bowstring while other prisoners were interrogated. A medieval pear-shaped device pried her jaw open unnaturally wide. The She Wolf periodically removed it for questions.

The chair with straps. The Fang driver, eyes wide with terror, shaking his head—*would snap it off if he could.* Straining at his bonds in desperation. Covered in vomit. The She Wolf wedging the funnel down his throat and forcing another gallon of water into his distended stomach.

The dentist's drill, pliers, electricity. Best to unfocus her eyes and feel a shiny, humming nothing.

Sometimes, another prisoner was brought in to witness the torments, a premonition of what they faced. "More conducive to an atmosphere of truth," the She Wolf had sneered. Certainly, that would happen with the Fangs. Daughter in front of the mother. Vice versa. "Shall I do it to her or to you?" How long before the mother said "Do it to her"? Brick shook her head. *How long is this going to go on?* But she knew the answer: as long as the Trutnevas want it to. *Yeah, well, I didn't sign up for this twisted shit.*

Brick took the break in the interrogation to let her mind drift.

Fishersville, 2052. Six years old. Parents working as farm help for food and shelter. The mule rearing up, smashing her head. A day before they found her, another day before they made it to the hospital. She remained unconscious for weeks. Waking up with a new, strange gift. A type of synesthesia, they said. Something about the smell and the sound working together. Words had color. Lies did too. She learned that she had to be close to the person for the connection to work.

VMI, 2069. Mopping floors, cleaning stables. Odor of horse shit always on her clothes. The library wood smell mixed with the old paper. Looking through books, concentrating until her head hurt. Words played tricks on her, never meaning what she thought they did. They tumbled around the pages, hiding their meaning. She had just an instant to catch them before they fled. Even when she slowed her eyes down and held each word, pinning it to the white paper, the letters flew away, leaving nothing but an empty circle with the black characters laughing at her from around the periphery. Brick slammed the book closed.

But *she* had noticed. *She* had cared.

Would you let me help you?

The long oak table in the library. Early morning, an hour before the cadet had drills. People would laugh if they knew, would humiliate the cadet. Honeysuckle and dyed wool. Dark hair cut regulation length. Never lying. Resigned to some barren future Brick couldn't understand.

Use the ruler. Good, now try again. Read it to me. Take all the time you need.

Brick shook her head. *Stupid!*

Charleston, 2073. During the day she sank pilings to maintain the seawall. Working with a grizzled man and two other women, they anchored offshore and hoisted the six-hundred-pound driver twenty feet in the air and let it fall, driving the creosote-soaked logs into the ocean floor. Twenty times an hour, eight hours a day. *Thump, thump, thump*—the tidal heartbeat of The Shipwrecked Goddess coming to reclaim her lands. In the Atlantic deep, the Goddess yearned to draw the city to her watery tomb. The temperature on the water easily broke a hundred. Nobody spoke, nobody had an ounce of energy for anything but pulling the ropes.

At night, she went home to Blanca, a shy Latina with sleepy eyes. Blanca fed her huevos rancheros, roasted poblano chilis stuffed with spicy meat. Rubbed her burning shoulders. Evenings together, drinking cheap tequila at the waterfront bar. Suspiciously eyeing the gang of black girls who seemed to speak their own language and whose fists were like concrete. They always took too much interest in Blanca. Did they want to fuck or fight? *One's almost as good as the other.*

At times she'd felt an urge to go further south, to the Island of Miami where it was rumored there were pirates who raided the cities along the Gulf coast. They profited from trading captives for sugar in Havana. There were always rumors. Instead, she left Blanca without saying goodbye and jumped a northbound Trutneva freight train and rode it as far as Baltimore. From there, she hitched and hiked northwest across the Allegheny Mountains to Altoona where Gael Stafford had just struck a pact with the Trutnevas to expand west. Stafford's bold and reckless plan was to capture

Pittsburgh, controlled by the Newmarked. She was paying dear for mercenaries.

That's where she'd met the Sisters. Where they'd taken an interest in her special gift. They opened up a new world to her of wealth and power. They trusted her—as far as they trusted anyone—gave her authority. Compared to her years of living rough, this was a world she'd hold onto as long as she could. Brick hadn't ever profited from her ability before. In so many ways, it limited her, prevented her from friendship, intimacy. Brick had seen thousands of lies. Lying was so easy for so many—just like breathing—an invocation meant to reshape reality.

SSSSSSS CRACK!

"AAAAAAHHHHHH!" the Fang officer cried.

"Now tell me again about the meeting with Colonel Oswald."

Brick started, looked up. The She Wolf lashed again across the prisoner's back. A trickle of blood formed at the edge of the wound. *Back to work. The Trutnevas always got what they were owed.*

11

- Winter 2020

Keep them in the hospital until we know more.

Javier held the bottle while the infant boy pulled on the nipple. The luminous eyes of the child stared at him. The deep blue ring where the iris should have been. Ten fingers, ten toes. A perfect mystery. He rocked the child, smiling at the four other babies who needed to be fed. *My boys now.*

Within two weeks of the first births, virus had been ruled out. Not pathogenic. Cellular. DNA testing confirmed a mutation of the Y chromosome. No cure. This discovery was about the same time his credit cards stopped working.

The baby closed his eyes. A smile spread across its face.

Javier sniffed and kissed the boy's forehead. "You are ripe, little man! Must have been good, eh?"

He set the bottle to the side. With a warm cloth, he cleaned the boy's bottom and changed the diaper. *How much longer will the supplies last?*

"There, better, right? I'm going to check on your brothers."

He rubbed the scar on his forehead and picked up another

baby.

Javier and a small group kept coming to work after the administrators told the staff that they wouldn't be paid past September. The cot in the examination room was Javier's new home. He was lucky to grab a few hours of sleep a night.

Maybe they'll foreclose on my house, maybe not. Maybe nobody goes to work at Bank of America anymore. They can have the car. What good is it if there's no gas.

Javier remembered some of the images from the summer when the economic collapse began: TV news reported on the dozens of suicides that ringed the perimeter of the global banks. Someone had written *It has found us* in blood on a window. The (less?) fortunate were shown carrying their personal belongings from their bankrupt employers.

Over eight days, four trillion dollars was wiped out. Governments closed the exchanges to slow the crisis. Within two weeks, all credit had dried up despite massive interventions from central banks. Payrolls weren't met, inventories couldn't be financed. Smaller banks failed. Soon the massive layoffs began, and power stopped flowing. In the new darkness, the stars were again revealed. Now, the federal government controlled everything (at least that's what they said), utilities, media, food distribution, communications. Vasiliy Trutnev, one of the country's wealthiest men, had been named the Secretary of Economic Resilience. Black markets, however, were where people went when the situation was serious.

The arrival of the strange baby boys shook the world's economies. But what was really lost was trust in the future. Was this the end of the species? If global population was going to collapse, better to take what you can now. Why lend if there weren't going to be people to repay? After discovering all the boys were blind, people asked how could they ever be anything but a liability?

Javier glanced at the boards on different windows. Late afternoon sun sparkled around the edges—a strange afterthought to the freak hailstorm earlier. Security had held back the first wave of looters. Javier shrugged, thinking about the irony of having to treat the wounded who had just tried to kill him.

Javier slid the bottle in the tiny pink mouth. "Here you go, nice and warm. Just how you like it."

In the second wave, the pharmacy had been looted. Opioids, insulin, ZPacks, Viagra. *Guess you gotta get it up for the end of the world.* Javier got clocked with a crowbar to his skull. Knocked out—concussion, but no fracture. Carried a .38 Ruger on his side from that day on. The situation had stabilized a little since the nationalization brought reservists. Now, the few of them who remained bartered their services. The dollar was barely worth the paper on which it was printed.

Monitor their condition. Run tests. Compare findings.

Some of the mothers refused to breast feed.

"No, no, I was told I was having a *normal* baby. They showed me on the screen. That's something from a freak show."

Javier pled with her. "Please, he really needs you as much as when you carried him. This is a critical time in your baby's life."

Some never returned. Javier and one of the remaining nurses looked after those babies. Better him than many other options for the boys.

What triggered the mutation? Nobody knew. GMOs? Microplastics? Bisphenol A deposits in human tissue? Earth surface temperatures two degrees higher? Some combination? Evolution had turned a page. Sealed a door. There was little anyone could do but face the new reality. Javier reflected on his med school biology class. *Mutations may produce more adaptive examples of the species.*

For in perfect faithfulness you have done wonderful things, things planned long ago.

They never cry.

12

– The Shipwrecked Goddess

The Cult of the Shipwrecked Goddess. Abandoned in a lifeboat as a child in 1917 after the ship, the *Laconia*, on which she was travelling, sank. Two weeks she drifted without food or water. Finally, half-mad from the sun, parched, her skin blistered, she could endure no more. She mumbled a prayer and slipped into the sea.

She sank, breathing in the brine, embracing her fate. Looking up, the sunlight above, once so painful, dazzled on the surface—brilliant and intoxicating. Rays glimmered and danced around her. Lower she sank, expecting her consciousness to drift away. The pressure rang in her ears. *She was still alive.*

Hours (days?) later she touched the bottom. Her new life, transcendent, was revealed. Here she waited and grew in the cold lightless depths. Her heart slowed to the tidal rhythm. Her skin, translucent and soluble, permeated the waters stretching for leagues. All of life once began here, all of the ancient secrets long forgotten. Rage filled her thoughts. Time and pressure ground away the little girl she had been, releasing her of sympathies, charity and any joyful memories of before. All that remained was a white-hot diamond of fury. The surface world was abomination. Salt the land and drown the heretics.

For her believers, she is the watery chaos that claims more land each year. The relentless pounding against the fragile sea-walls. The terrifying storms she wields rendered transoceanic travel impossible. Only once the continents submitted again and the oceans reunited would she rest.

* * *

The Saffir-Simpson Hurricane Wind Scale measures the intensity of sustained wind speed. Until 2029, the highest score was Category 5. Category 5 storms leveled trees, tore roofs off homes, knocked down buildings. The dying United States Federal Government could, at that point, only offer token assistance to the affected areas.

In that autumn, with Earth surface temperatures now two degrees warmer, hurricane danger evolved. Storms with winds greater than 180 mph raged through the Atlantic, sprawled over 300 miles. Swallowing even the largest ships. They devoured everything in their paths upon landfall. An inexorable force, unrelenting in its merciless destruction. To the people living in fear, trying to understand the loss of boys, the storms portended a verdict against humanity. In other times, these would have been labeled Category 6. In 2029, while civilization tore itself apart, these storms represented something more dire. These were the labor pains of the new deities. *For something that was yet to come.*

They became known as Leviathan.

13

– Sware – December 31, 2078

"Antenora! Antenora!"

"Yes, ma'am," Sware replied.

Antenora circled the room, stopping to tap on the window or replace a book on the shelf. Shrouded in black turtleneck and slacks. Papers carpeted the floor. On the mall, the New Year's Festival was taking shape. U.D. troops had cleared out the tent city. *No more need of them. They will get theirs.* Tonight would be fireworks and the ascent of a new Queen.

Evermore sipped her tea, shrinking into the upholstered sofa, her glassy eyes unblinking. "I think we must send a letter to Tidewater. To Elora King. And I need to prepare my New Year's Day address. We need to stir their hearts. We will expose the Trutneva offer for what it is."

Sware replied crisply, "She's dead."

Evermore recoiled, "Dead? Who?"

"Elora King."

The Premier's eyes widened in panic. "That's not possible! Where have I been? I've failed her too."

"She's dead. Quite sudden." The smallest smile played on her lips that had to work to cover her teeth.

"Then we must send condolences and ensure—"

Antenora slipped behind the sofa. Evermore's brittle gray hair pushed high with a sterling clip. Shae laid a hand on Evermore's shoulder, "No more letters, dear. Your work is finished."

"Antenora?"

"There is one *last* thing."

Antenora pulled the plastic bag (always so many of them around) over the Premier's head, twisting the opening tight around her neck. Evermore's hands flew to her throat, clawing at Sware. The Premier reared up on her heels; the tea spilled down her front. The cup smashed into the saucer.

Antenora gripped the bag tighter. "Shhhhh, dear. Shhhhh." She grimaced—for such a frail creature, the Premier was surprisingly strong in her desperate resistance. The plastic perfectly conformed to Evermore's face when she desperately sucked in the remaining oxygen. A death mask. Her breath fogged the inside, blurring her distress. Only her wide staring eyes, their light dimming. Sware looked away while cinching the little remaining slack. *Would she miss the old fool? So easy to manipulate. A doll. A living doll.*

Evermore's grip loosened. Soon, her arms fell limp to her sides.

Antenora slid the Premier back onto the sofa, removed the bag and stroked Evermore's face. She closed the panic-wide eyes. *At last! No, she wouldn't miss her.* "Pallas Evermore, long serving Premier of the United District. Ever faithful, ever vigilant. We will always remember your sacrifice. There will be a week of mourning. You will look lovely."

A small, hand-picked corps of officers had been preparing for the coup. Loyalists who understood that power was the only language people understood. The other U.D. leaders would either fall in line with her new government or suffer the consequences. She had prepared a list of ministers and officers to be arrested immediately and had taken steps to ensure they were separated from their soldiers. Trutneva troops were *en route* and would control key facilities by nightfall. At midnight she would proclaim her ascension. The new year will herald the reign of Queen Sware.

14

– Vaughan – Spring 2062

Are you going to die like a man?

Behind him, the dogs barked, fierce clipped bursts. They would tear him to shreds if they got to him before the guards could shoot. Vaughan stumbled forward through the downpour. His feet slipped, but he staggered forward. The bone-on-bone pain in his hip seared with each step. The darkness and rain limited his vision. He knew he had to run west, but was he? He could hear it. His head swam from exhaustion, hunger, and desperation. *I should have made it by now!* Not daring to look back, he plunged forward. The sole on his left boot flapped where it had peeled away. Vaughan panted, near-crawling up a small hill, feeling his small reserve of strength slipping away. He'd saved a portion of his meager rations over the last week and had eaten them right before his escape. Cresting the hill, he nearly wept.

There it is! The river.

He pushed on. *Just a bit more.*

Five days of hard rain had caused the Susquehanna River

to flood. The banks extended for hundreds of meters beyond where they should have stopped. Ahead was a clearing. Debris scattered through the shallows. Vaughan splashed towards it, squinting in the darkness, discerning a collection of items, both natural and man-made, that had washed up. Upriver, the trunk of a slender, dead tree extended out, the water coursing through the branches.

Vaughan gasped, wading further out towards the tree. *Yes, a young one, that one could work. Maybe not too heavy.* His starved brain had lost its ability to hold any other thoughts. The frigid water momentarily shocked him out of his exhaustion, numbed the pain. Strands of his long hair fell across his eyes. He wiped them aside. Pushing against the current, strong, even so far from the center of the river, he reached the tree.

The barking sounded closer. Two shots echoed, muffled by the crackle of the rain.

He'd stolen an extra length of rope from the camp storeroom and had worn it around his waist for a month, under his pants. His skeletal fingers tugged at the knot, slipping on the wet hemp. It refused to yield. *No!* Viscous panic oozed in. He thought about why he'd stolen the rope, regret welling up. *I should have hung myself.* Finally, the knot came free, and he looped the rough cord around the trunk, then around his chest, tying off the crude harness.

Are you going to die like a man? All the failed possibilities of his life had winnowed down to that one last question.

He heaved against the trunk, pushing towards the river. The tree shifted slightly. On the hillside he'd just crossed, lanterns flickered in the darkness. The dogs had almost reached the edge of the river. Vaughan panted. He pushed again, his feet sinking in the mud. The tree twisted and angled towards the current. Vaughan's left boot remained stuck. He slid his foot out in time for the tree to pull away and drift along in the edge of the river. A volley of shots erupted. Vaughan shifted as much of his body under the water as he could while trying to steer the tree further away from the shore. He picked up speed and peered ahead into the glistening darkness. *Safe from the dogs and the butchers.* He shuddered from the cold, congratulating himself for the pair of woolen socks he'd taken from the exhum who'd died earlier that day. After several miles, the rain stopped and the moon reflected on the surging current, casting a million glimmering fragments in pale gold. Vaughan huddled against the trunk, doing what he could to steer the vessel of his salvation.

Remember.

Vasiliy Trutnev had come to *him*. Sought his counsel during the early years of the crisis. A multi-billionaire before the collapse, Trutnev's power and influence had only grown in the year after. A state of emergency had been declared with no foreseeable end. Trutnev had proposed a vast nationalization scheme, the Resilience Effort, and Vaughan would be part of the leadership. Trutnev had taken control of Range Resources and Talisman Energy when their shares had lost 98 percent of their value. He used his position to bankrupt or consolidate all other Marcellus operators. The vast shale deposits were his, and he alone decided who would enjoy the light and heat they provided.

The state of emergency allowed sweeping changes without oversight. Trutnev exploited every opportunity. The judiciary presented an intractable obstacle to progress as they held on to an outdated set of laws. Trutnev quietly established a new legal system that operated on the principle of expediency. That which did not advance the Resilience Effort would be considered a criminal act. In two generations, who would know anything different in the growing isolation?

At first, the mutation had been spotty, random. Women who'd conceived at the same time gave birth to profoundly different baby boys. Coordinated government efforts were made to confront the health and financial crises. China and North Korea responded with mass sterilizations of women who'd borne one of the blind changelings. Like an invasive species, they overwhelmed the natural order within five years of the first appearances. As they grew, their helplessness only added to the challenges.

Vaughan clung to the tree trunk, enveloped in frigid numbness. *Hold on. Hold on. Hold on.* He couldn't stop his teeth from chattering. With his tongue, he probed the area inside of his mouth where the guard had knocked out three teeth with the butt of her rifle. *Dirae bitch!* Hours passed. The sun rose, illuminating the river and the shore. The brown water foamed in small rapids. Even where the river widened, he still moved swiftly along. Debris floated alongside him. Bloated animal carcasses bobbed, carried along by the torrent. A four-foot, plastic Santa spun past, its muddy, jolly face winking at him, holding him to the now-forgotten secret of wonder they'd once shared.

Remember.

Hope and Resilience. The slogan for Trutnev's grand scheme. Public service ads ran on TV in the years before broadcasting stopped. Trutnev relied on radio—a simpler technology—to tell the story he wanted heard. The country ripped itself apart at the seams. By 2030, the former United States had fallen.

Series of wars with forgettable names followed: The Wheat War, The Texas War of Separation, The Thirteen Month War, The Second Civil War (followed soon after by the Third and Fourth). Wars of faith and famine. Rapacious leaders, like Trutnev, seizing as much as they could.

All the while, nature steadily reclaimed its own. Farms in flood plans were abandoned. Towns devastated by tornadoes were nothing more than names or memories. Endless deserted roads scarred the country. The boundaries of the known world blurred, became unmapped.

The problems Vaughan faced were immense. He needed to improve the national food distribution system to help stabilize the country. He had to pick up the pieces of the financial ruin and forge them into a new economy. Manufacture jobs out of air. Industrial strategy for Trutnev was centered on the gas fields. Enormous reservoirs of energy could be harnessed if he could successfully keep the rigs operating. Building upon the available resource of the gas, Vaughan initiated a massive project to convert millions of vehicles to run on it. Military and government vehicles took precedence. Vaughan opened hundreds of factories to build the components.

But Trutnev, student of Beria, knew the solution: create an endless supply of political prisoners, starve and work them to death. An economic necessity, but more importantly, *a climatological necessity.* There were too many people and the food should go to the loyalists. Within years, fences topped with concertina wire surrounded the factories and the filthy, disease-riddled camps that housed the workers. Impossible production norms were demanded. Vasiliy always regarded men as the greater threat to his power. *Oh, how wrong he was, eh sweet daughters?* They had no place in the future. Women were rewarded for denouncing their husbands. Large institutional orphanages (Another slogan: Our Society is Family!) were created to maximize the labor from the population. *Where else would they put the children whose parents had been arrested and from where else would you draw your Dirae?* Later they transformed them into the fertility institutes.

We at the top had anything we wanted. My wife, home in Ithaca with her family. Is she still alive? Telling her nightly on the phone that I missed her. That I loved her. That the work that kept me away was important to the future. But for me, a different girl every night. Desperate to eat, to feed their children or to vainly attempt to influence the fate of their husband or relative who'd been arrested.

The tree trunk bobbed. Vaughan clung to it. A rock loomed ahead. Vaughan heaved against the tree but was too weak to steer it to the side. The branches crashed. The trunk twisted. Vaughan scraped against the rock, his back and hip erupting in pain, but distant, almost detached from his frozen body. He winced. *Worse when they interrogated me. I wasn't sure I would walk again.* The tree cleared the obstacle and again he drifted free. He blinked his eyes from the spray. The remains of houses appeared along the banks of the swollen river, chimneys towering over the drowned walls.

They always come at night. Treason. They pinned that on everyone. I demanded to see Trutnev. They showed me the report my wife had filed describing my crimes. Her signature at the bottom, but was it? They kept me awake for three days in that box, on my toes, arms manacled over my head. In the end, I couldn't spell my own name, but still I signed the confession. I consumed the lie. Mandatory twenty-five years. Men had been condemned; why shouldn't I suffer?

A fragment of an old hymn surfaced. *Picardy. I haven't thought of that in decades. We sang it at King's. What could have become of that?*

Vaughan shivered. His beard and hair matted to his head. Hunger gnawed at him as it had for eleven years. The first years of his sentence, forced to work on the Resilience Effort. Fourteen hours a day he dug canals to relieve storm surge. He hauled block for retaining walls. He watched as men around him died from exposure and dehydration or were hanged for not fulfilling their quota. He witnessed starving men steal bread from the sick and dying. It was there that Vaughan made the choice to survive at any cost.

After seven years, they transferred him to a timber camp in West Nanticoke where they made ties for the ever-expanding Trutnev railroads. They worked the inmates through winter when the temperatures fell below zero. He'd lost two toes from frostbite. They worked in the summers, with temperatures over a hundred. In the camps, everything narrowed down to a crude stub. Thinking devolved, became base—how to get more food, how to not freeze, how to not draw attention. Life in the camp didn't allow for a time frame beyond 24 hours.

He drifted by a decaying, miniature replica of the Statue of Liberty standing atop a crumbling brick railroad pier. The headless body still raised its arm in defiance. Passing Harrisburg, he slunk low to the waterline, hiding from people crossing the bridge. Rescue meant return to the camp. *I'll drown myself first.* The river narrowed passing the otherworldly nuclear power plant. Three Mile Island. The forbidding cooling towers loomed over the abandoned facility.

The sun rose higher and started its descent. His only warmth would soon fade. Exhaustion and the cold gripped him, tempting him to sleep. He closed his eyes only to snap his head up moments later. *Rest. Need rest. Once I'm past the wall, I'll steer to the shore.*

Ahead, the Mason Dixon Wall spanned to either side. The water flowed around the bottom of the gray monolithic slabs. *Thousands died building it. Bones in unmarked graves.* A guard tower stood nearby on the eastern shore. The trunk wagged in the current, speeding up. Vaughan sunk low again, trying to keep an eye on the tower. He heard the dim echoes of shouting over the rush of the water. Guards rushed about.

CRACK

CRACK

One of the shots hit the trunk, splintering a limb. The others hit the water. Vaughan shifted, sinking as low in the water as the harness allowed. *Not like this!*

The river carried him onward. Minutes later, he was out of range and the shooting ceased. Vaughan slid back up on the trunk. The waning sun drowned the scene in brilliant gold. He panted. *Safe in Maryland. I made it! It's over!* Tears streamed down his face. *Just push to shore.*

A distant hissing sound caught his attention. He turned a bend. The river widened out. The distant hiss crescendoed into a rushing, thunderous roar.

The dam!

Vaughan's mind reeled, thoughts slow to form, crowded out by his rising panic. *If I pass through the gates, I'll be crushed against the rocks below.* Ahead, the dam rose from the river. In the twilight, the lurid orange-red neon letters glowed: Conowingo Hydro Electric Plant. Searchlights weaved across the expanse. The openings of the flood gates were packed with debris: tree limbs, siding from houses, ruined cushions, plywood, shreds of blue plastic tarp. Vaughan thrust against the tree, furiously kicking with his remaining strength. The tree shifted, but instantly settled back on its course. Vaughan clenched his teeth and heaved again. The trunk spun, the back kicking out. Vaughan clawed to hang on; his pulse pounded in his ears. Even if he weren't starved and broken, the fatal trajectory couldn't have been altered. Inexorably, the tree sailed towards the gaping sluice.

He accelerated as the pull from the dam grew stronger. His numb hands clutched the trunk, bracing for impact. *So close and this.* A mirthless smile tugged at his lips. *God does enjoy his jokes.* The tree slammed against the wall. Vaughan lurched forward, held by the rope harness. The trunk swung around, now almost perpendicular to the dam. Water heaved and crashed around him. Vaughan sputtered and coughed, unable to avoid the turbulent waves. A searchlight crested across the opening next to him. The tree twisted, forcing him lower, barely over the waterline. The pressure from the water pinned his arm between the tree and the dam, crushing it. He fumbled with the other hand to untie the rope. *Where is it? WHERE IS IT?* He couldn't time his breathing with the water smacking against the concrete side. With each breath he inhaled more of the fetid water. Panting and choking, he flailed weakly, searching for the knot.

"Help me!" he called out, but his weak voice couldn't carry over the roar of the water.

The twilight faded to darkness. The searchlight drifted slowly across the opening, illuminating the detritus and the brown-gray foam. It hovered briefly over him. Vaughan raised his hand, fingers outstretched. The light began to move on, then jerked back to his position. High above he heard, "You!

Hold on!"

Vaughan's vision blurred. He mumbled. Merely keeping his head above water seemed impossible. He blew water out of his nose and gasped.

"Hold on!" From over the railing, a worker rappelled down the side of the dam, her body harness secured to a thick rope. She inserted a length of cut hose into his mouth. Vaughan could breathe again. Bracing herself against the dam wall, the worker placed one boot against the tree and pushed, freeing his arm. Slipping lower into the water, she tried to pull him from the trunk. Vaughan's rope held him. The worker studied the situation in the spotlight glare. She glanced around, seizing upon a bottle bobbing nearby.

"Close your eyes!" The worker smashed the bottle against the dam wall. Using the jagged neck, she sawed the rope until it snapped. Vaughan started to slip, unable to hold himself any longer. The woman grabbed him, wrapping his arms around her shoulders. Vaughan convulsed, muscles no longer responding to his will. She gave a thumbs up sign and slowly the two of them rose above the watery chaos.

Other workers took Vaughan from her as they topped the guardrail. One of them wrapped him in the tweed overcoat and carried him inside, propping him on a chair.

"Get him some tea!"

Someone wiped the hair from his eyes. "What is your name?"

Vaughan's lips moved, but only incoherent sounds emerged. He doubled over, coughing, collapsing in the small puddle of water he'd brought up.

15

– Astrid – January 1, 2079

Five-four-three-two-one—Happy New Year!

"Kiss me!" A redhead popped up in front of her—sweet smell of gin on her breath, eyes droopy. A festive miniature top hat in purple held to her head with an elastic band.

Astrid leaned back. "Hm, what?"

The girl flopped her arm on Astrid's shoulder and pressed her lips closer. "Kiss me, it's the new year!"

Astrid pushed past the girl. "No, no." *Didn't want to be alone, but I can't stand being here.* Everywhere she looked couples were tangled in passionate embraces, celebrating. *I just see her face again and again.*

A Mount Vernon neighborhood bar. The wood paneling and snug booths gave it a cozy feel. Glass beads had been strung from the ceiling. The light hitting them produced the feeling of being in a giant champagne flute. Confetti littered the floor.

Astrid tucked her chestnut hair behind her ear. *A ship! Of course, there was no ship. What were you thinking? They laughed at me at the Maritime Office. Tomorrow I'll go home. We can work it out. I just needed some space, Philippa's so suffocating sometimes. So fatalistic.*

She picked up her coat and hat, squeezed through the throng and out into the clear night. *Need some air.*

The cold midnight brought relief. She inhaled and watched the vapor of her breath. Her friend's apartment was a twenty-minute walk up Charles St. The monument stood straight ahead. *There's Washington's giant cock. Ready for action. Watching over the city, kind of a watch–cock.*

In the distance, towards the harbor Pop Pop Popop. *Fireworks?* Popopopopop popopopop. *Weird, that sounds more like gunfire.*

Last New Year's, we had a dinner party for just us two with the fine chartreuse Villeroy & Boch. Phil strung white lights. Candles everywhere. We danced on the parquet floors to old records in our pretend world. We dressed in elegant gowns we found tucked away in the apartment, but soon they were piles on the floor next to the bed. She pulled the flaps down over her ears. *I'll call her when I get to the flat. It's not too late. She tries so hard to protect everyone. She needs someone to look out for her.*

Astrid stuffed her hands in her pockets. *So cold. So different from when I met Philippa three years ago.* The memory cheered her, filled her with hope. *It's not too late.*

They'd met during a Richmond summer afternoon thunderstorm. The temperature had rapidly fallen ten degrees. The leaves on the poplar tree turned over in anticipation as the wind gathered strength. Astrid set the crate of pears down and watched through the bank of tall windows. The light before the storm was always so exquisite—pale gold, almost green. So alive. It held everything in timeless suspense before the looming darkness.

Lightning flashed, followed by the distant rumble. Fat drops spattered the road. Moments later, the downpour erupted, the wind driving it in swarming bursts. Rushing streams soon flowed along the curbside.

Astrid had been working at the food co-op for a few months, rotating between the orchard and the store. The store operated in one of the many abandoned brick warehouses. She'd taken it upon herself to paint a mural across the side wall. In one of the back rooms, she put together a small studio with a bed. Sketches covered the walls, often studies of life and death—a baby chick emerging from the egg, infant hands, the fresh carcass of a deer killed by a wild dog. She kept a white marble mortar and pestle where she ground some of her pigments. An edge of turpentine hovered over the earthy fragrance of the store. She didn't mind the work at the orchard—the men and women there a sort of family—but running the store allowed her more time to focus on her art.

The bell on the door rang. A woman dashed in out of the storm. Her sleeveless print sun dress clung to her long torso. Faded ianthina-gray with abstract shapes in pale gold. *Woven from the storm light.* The woman ran her hand through her short, dark hair, the dampness bringing out soft curls. Erect posture, not self-conscious of her height. From her time in the service, Astrid guessed the woman was an officer. The earnestness in the woman's face tried to hide a profound sadness in her eyes. *Where has she been? What secrets does she keep?*

Astrid's face flushed. Tingling heat spread through to her fingers.

The woman stood on the mat. "Do you mind? It's really coming down."

Astrid wiped her palms down the front of her t-shirt, meeting her eyes. "No, sure. Stay. It's been pretty quiet."

The vulnerability in the woman's smile. "Thanks. I was walking along the river and the storm came out of nowhere. I haven't been in this part of the city for a while." She looked around, focusing on the mural. "That's nice. I really like the colors."

"That's mine. I did it. It was just kind of a dull gray before... made me depressed."

The woman's eyes flashed. "Wow, I'm so impressed. You're really talented. I don't know anything about art. Nothing but gray walls for me. People who can do anything creative, painting, music are so rare and wonderful."

Astrid's expectant heart refused to quiet—a euphoric feeling her insides would melt mixed with fear the moment would pass and she would be gone forever. Graceful neck and tanned arms. The woman shifted her backpack. Astrid studied the hairline fold of the woman's axilla, the flex of her triceps, not realizing until that moment how famished she was to press that skin against her lips.

"I'm Astrid."

"Philippa."

Astrid met her gaze. "I was just about to close up. Do you like chiles rellenos? They make the best a block down the street. Maybe once it stops..."

And thus, we began. A convoy of trucks rumbled past, black with no insignia. At the old United Methodist Church, bells pealed. *Now, we'll make a new start.* Doors all around flew open. People rushed out to the streets. Lights snapped on in dozens of windows.

Ahead, a group of people had gathered. Coats half-open,

hands waving. No party hats, no bottles. Astrid's heart skipped a beat. *They aren't celebrating.*

Astrid approached. "What's going on? Did something happen?"

A tall man with a fine head of gray hair replied, "Antenora Sware is on the radio. She says there's been a coup by some of the District generals. Imperial troops have been brought in to protect the citizens and maintain order."

Another one chimed in, "Those trucks. I've been watching. Dozens of them."

"Fucking Trutnevas!" A woman swore.

The tall man offered, "Sware said this is a temporary situation and we should go about our routines."

Someone else spoke up, "That's just more bullshit. Look around, we've been invaded."

16

– Astrid – January 4, 2079

Astrid peered out the small window in the door. Her stomach gnawed at her. She hadn't eaten for hours. The small, high-ceilinged cell was windowless. The guard had taken her watch, Philippa's RSC-issued mechanical. The corridor outside was empty. *Have they forgotten about me?*

Two bunks extended out of the wall. A stainless-steel toilet snugged in the corner behind a small partition. Fluorescent lights hummed above, the only sound.

Three days had passed since her arrest. From the checkpoint, she had been marched to the train station and loaded into a freight car along with a hundred other unfortunates. Her only clue to her location was that they had traveled north.

At the far end of the hall, a door opened. Two guards led a girl with Asian features by the elbows. The guards wore dark gray uniforms with the Trutneva insignia on a shoulder patch. The girl's ankles were shackled and her wrists cuffed to a wide leather belt around her waist. The orange jumpsuit ballooned around her; three sizes too large.

They stopped in front of Astrid's cell. "Back away from the door!" one of the guards barked.

Astrid retreated to her bed.

The guard opened the door and shoved the girl inside. One held a baton ready while the other unlocked the cuffs. "Better not have any trouble," she growled. She fumbled for the key.

As soon as the second cuff was off, the girl lunged at the guard, grabbing her belt, reaching for her sidearm. Instantly, the second guard brought the baton down square across the girl's head. The girl spun, then collapsed on one knee, her bared teeth twisting into a confused frown. She swayed and finally sprawled flat on the floor, unconscious.

The first guard straightened up. "Bitch gonna get fucked up acting like that. She's in our world now." Turning to Astrid, "Meet your new playmate, sweetheart."

Astrid cowered in the corner.

Minutes later, the girl stirred, pulled herself up to sit.

Astrid leaned forward, "Are you okay?"

The girl rubbed the back of her head, blood trails on her fingers when she pulled her hand away. "I'll kill her. I'll kill all of them."

"What's your name?"

"Mind your own business." The girl stood up, bracing herself against the bunk. She studied the room. Small vent, no windows. "When do the guards change?"

Astrid stammered, "I... I don't know."

"Then what good are you?" The girl spat.

Astrid pulled herself up to the wall, wrapping her legs with her arms. "Sorry."

The girl paced, eyes never leaving the door.

Astrid curled up in her bed. Minutes stretched to hours.

Through the slot in the door, two bowls of yellow-gray stew slid in on a tray. The girl took one, tilting it to her lips. Astrid scooped up the other.

The girl ran her finger around the inside. "Is that it?"

Astrid held out her bowl. "Here, take some of mine. "

The girl grabbed the bowl and devoured the remains before Astrid could change her mind. She thrust it back to Astrid.

Staring at the door. "I will kill her. I will kill them all," she recited, her face set, the fierce words falling into Astrid's mind like glowing stones. Glancing back at Astrid, she muttered, "Oh yeah, thanks."

Astrid nodded. A shiver ran through her—the impression she was in the presence of something dark and elemental. A ruined divinity.

In time, the girl asked, "Are you from Baltimore, U.D?

Astrid shook her head, "No, Richmond. I live with my wyve."

The girl cocked her head. "You know where we are, don't you?"

"What do you mean? We're in jail."

"This is central labor induction. Funny, right? Chester. Part of the Imperial penal system. Abandon all hope ye who enter here. This is where they decide where to send you to work off your crimes. Say the wrong word—crime. Borrow from the wrong people—crime. Found in the wrong place—crime. Who you work with can be a crime. I know what I'm talking about."

Astrid stared at her, remembering what she'd heard, what she'd never wanted to think about. The girl smirked.

"You've probably never seen them, the walled factory towns, the agriculture work camps. The quarries, gas fields, military installations, pharma testing." The girl narrowed her eyes, appraising Astrid. "Other places too."

Astrid stood up, her hands picking at her clothes. "Someone will get me out. I didn't do anything!"

The girl continued, affectless, like a teacher delivering a well-worn lecture. "You really don't understand how the world works, do you? Once you're in the system, you pay for the rancid food they give you, you pay for the sack of hay they call a bed. And what do you pay with? You have no money, so all you can trade is your time, your body, or whatever skills you might have. Whatever else someone might want. Some debts never get worked off if you know what I mean.

"In the salt mines, sixteen, eighteen-hour days. Working underground, you won't even know whether it's day or night. And soon enough, you don't care."

Astrid shuddered, hugging herself. Her heart raced. She inhaled deeply and slowly let her breath escape. *This isn't happening. Mother, please!* She swallowed hard, nausea churning her stomach. The greasy stew unsettled. Her vision tunneled, everything dark around the perimeter. The fluorescent lights drained the color from the room, their hum an infernal incantation, the girl in the orange jumpsuit revealed as one of the damned. *I'm going to be sick.*

"The Queens trade in workers—or as they call them, *labor inputs.*" Her mouth shaped the words with scorn. "Part of their obligation under their treaties with the Trutnevas. They siphon off excess as part of the Protsent. My guess is you and a lot of other people are payment by their new ally, that crocodile, Sware.

"You might get lucky and they ransom you back to Richmond. Always money to be made in kidnapping. Are you important? Would someone pay eighty thousand rubles?" The girl studied Astrid. "No, probably not. They would have already determined that before sending you here."

Astrid scrambled across the bed and flung herself over the toilet. The sick-sweet flood emptied out of her. Even after there was nothing left inside, she hung onto the bowl, retching and heaving. *No, no no!*

The girl grimaced and looked away.

Astrid lifted her head and wiped her mouth with a wad of toilet paper, staggered to her bed and collapsed. *Philippa, help. Where are you? I can't do this. I'm so scared.* She stared at her cellmate. The girl ignored Astrid, pacing like a trapped panther. She tugged on the bunk, twisted the toilet, tried prying the food slot off the door, grunting from her efforts. Nothing gave way. Disgusted looking, she plopped on the floor, crossed her legs, rested her hands on her knees and closed her eyes.

Is she meditating? Here?

* * *

Astrid dozed. Her mind spun images so lucid that she believed she was awake while at the same time knowing that she balanced on the edge of unconsciousness, waiting to fall into the abyss of forgetting. Desperate to fall.

Keys in the door. Astrid stirred, propped herself up on one elbow. The girl in the jumpsuit sat on the top bunk.

The guards didn't stop to check on them. They shoved a new prisoner into the cell and slammed the door.

The girl in the orange jumpsuit hopped off and rubbed her hands together. "The Accidental Goddess be praised. Look at you." Astrid tilted her head. The similarity was unquestionable. The two girls shared the same height and build. Same jet-black hair, close in length. The new arrival wore a dirty olive parka over a burgundy herringbone sweater.

The girl in the orange jumpsuit smiled. "Take your coat off. Where are you from? What are you in for?"

The new prisoner assessed the cell, eyes averted. She peeled off the parka. "Philadelphia. Old Town. Got caught stealing from some old lady turned out to be the wyve of one of the Dirae commanders. You?"

Orange jumpsuit ignored the question. "What's your name?"

"January Chen."

"Pretty. Hey, it's your month. They sent me from Harrisburg." She pointed at Astrid. "This one's from Richmond. Thinks some mistake has been made."

January smirked. "Yeah, don't tell them that. I did a year on the rail crew for mouthing off to police."

Eyes bright, the girl in the jumpsuit asked, "How old are you?"

"Twenty," January replied.

"Yeah, me too. I ran away when I was fourteen. Always one step ahead of them until now. Anyone that can buy your way out?"

"I wish. Nobody."

"Too bad. Guess we're in it."

Astrid followed the exchange. *Why is she so friendly with the new girl?*

Jumpsuit girl curled her knuckles into a flat fist, thumb pressed close to her hand. She jabbed—hand just darting out, almost playful—striking January in the ribcage.

"Hey!" January cried. "What do you think you're..." January's hands flew to her chest, gasping. She crumpled on the floor. Astrid rushed to her, lifted her arm. "There's no pulse!"

"Yeah." The girl stripped off her orange coverall. "Her heart stopped. There's nothing you can do."

Astrid lifted the girl's sweater and unbuttoned her shirt. "I know CPR."

The girl shoved her away. "Are you fucking deaf as well as stupid! I *want* her dead. Stop trying to think and do what I tell you. Take her clothes off."

Astrid froze, mind scrambling to understand, heart pounding, then slowly responded. *She might kill me too.* She unlaced January's boots. When the dead girl had been stripped down to her underwear, the girl grabbed her outfit and put it on. She pulled the hood up on the parka. Pointing at the coverall, "Put that on her."

Astrid did as she was instructed. After she finished, the girl kneeled over the body, lifted the head and slammed it against the concrete. Carefully, she wiped up the blood from the floor and flushed the evidence down the toilet.

The girl snarled, "One word and you'll join her. Now call for help. Tell them she collapsed."

Astrid bent over, shouting through the food slot, "Guard, hey, guard, help! Something's wrong with this girl. I think she's dying. You gotta come now!" She didn't need to fake her distress.

At the far end of the hall, the door opened. Three guards approached, one wielding a baton.

Astrid stammered, "She just went down. She'd been okay this afternoon." Her face was flushed and her voice quavering. Out of the corner of her eye she saw the murderer smirk before her face went blank.

"You two stay on that side." The guard with the baton cornered them. Another guard kneeled down over January's body. Her chest was motionless.

The guard hovering over January inspected the body. "Oh, Mother in heaven, this fucking stinks. Nobody's going to believe this. Pointing to the girl, "You, what's your name?"

"January Chen. You brought me in here an hour ago." Her voice even sounded like January's. Then the smirk came back. "Guess we all look alike."

The guard snarled, "Shut up. What happened?"

"It was just like that one said, she was raging about getting out of here. Something about her mother. Said her head hurt. Then she went down."

The guard lifted January's head, studied the wound. "This is where they cracked her head to get control of the situation. It's in the duty report."

One of the guards piped up. "What's the problem, Sergeant?"

The sergeant stood up, scowling. "That's Fang, Zhen Fang. She's dead. This is a major problem. She's the daughter of Xi Fang, the assassin. Political. They had plans for her."

"What are we going to do?"

"We just received new orders. Straight from Glott. We're shipping everyone out. Stick Fang on the train. Put these two in a different car. We'll claim she was alive when she left. Make it their problem. Now get them out of here."

17

– Grayson – January 2079

When it rained, the pumps sometimes ran for days. A wet, throbbing buzz heard everywhere in Hampton Roads. The ground tingled with their vibration. Silverware danced on countertops. Dogs hid.

Valerie Grayson lifted her phone and placed it back on the square of cork—recycled bulletin board—kept for these times. Cushioned surfaces allowed normalcy in the city. Valerie stood up and smoothed out the front of her plain black skirt. The decrypted letter lay on her desk.

From her office facing north, she studied the steam from the shipyard rising and disappearing in the late afternoon air. *So it is with all of us.* The storm left behind gray skies pierced with iridescent pink. The Iowa class, USS Wisconsin listed to starboard just outside her building. A colossal relic from another time. Something that would never be built again. *A kind of alien spacecraft.*

Her second week in office, Valerie was the new Premier of Tidewater. *Nobody expected me to win.* Working late hours learning about revenue streams, carbon measurements and legislative procedures. Briefings on the conflict in the United District.

Valerie twisted the gold wedding band on her finger, her brow knitted. The letter, sent by Kendra Lawson, the Richmond Premier, called for an urgent summit of all the leaders of the Piedmont Republics. Tomorrow, she'd board a train to Charlotte. Tonight, she needed to know everything she could about the Trutnevas.

Valerie stood for office when the last Premier, Elora King, died unexpectedly. A special election. She had never held office before. Growing up in Surry, she mostly knew about pigs and peanuts. Her people were farmers. Love and knowledge of the root and stem. She had been a 5th-6th grade teacher.

On the credenza, her gilt-edged Bible they used for the swearing in. *God showed me this path. I heard Her voice.*

For years, she'd served as deacon in her Pentecostal church, baptizing the children in Crouch Creek. The baby boys sightless, flailing when their heads went under. In the classroom, the girls bringing their brothers, taking turns reading to them. *We women have been chosen. Joseph doubted. Mary was constant.*

Valerie called through the open door. "Alice?"

Alice appeared at the doorway, always striking in one of her tailored vintage suits. "Yes, ma'am?"

"Please ask—strike that, please *instruct*—the Secretary of Civil Security, the Secretary of the Treasury and Secretary of Coastal Defense to join me. We'll be dining here. Please coordinate with the kitchen."

Alice jotted the note. "Anything you prefer?"

Valerie pointed. "I saw some beautiful striped bass down by the harbor. I leave it to the chef's excellent discretion. And a sweet potato mash."

"Dessert?"

Valerie wrinkled her forehead. "How about peanut pie?" *This job's gonna put twenty pounds on me.*

"Yes, ma'am. I'll see what I can do."

"Thank you so much."

Grayson returned to the window. The Queens of the North. Living in opulence behind the Mason Dixon Wall. Keeping their people in, subjugating them. A quarter of the births by artificial insemination—controlled by the Sisters.

She turned on the radio and tuned to the Trutneva station.

Lush, sweeping strings. *Tchaikovsky, Rachmaninov?* Valerie couldn't tell.

A breathless announcer interrupted, "This just in. Reports from our brave soldiers on the front show that the dictator, Pallas Evermore, has amassed troops all across our southern border. Dear friends, our beloved Sisters have offered immeasurable sacrifices seeking only to coexist. The tyrant leader of the United District has torn up every offer! This latest maneuver clearly signals the U.D. demands our blood!"

Their propaganda minister is sure doing a damn good job whipping their people into a frenzy.

The announcer's pitch slowing, "Coming up at the top of the hour, a rebroadcast of the stunning confession of the U.D. saboteur caught by our vigilant security forces in the Reading power plant. Hear from her own mouth the plans for their invasion. We return now to "The Sea" by Alexander Glazunov."

She studied the wedding ring on her smooth brown hand. *I thought I would quietly grow old with Marilyn.* Valerie's two daughters grown, younger one halfway through her required military service at Fort Monroe. *She'll be called up. I will be the one to give the order.*

In the twenty years since they'd met, she and her wyve, Marilyn, had shared two husbands. As was the custom, the men (really, just boys) shared their bed for ten months. They brought gifts to the mothers of the boys to show their respect and appreciation, to honor the sacrifices the mothers made to care for these helpless creatures. The marriages were celebrated three years apart. On both occasions, Valerie conceived a girl. Marilyn bore one daughter also. She and Marilyn cared for the men—loved them—even though they were a mystery. *Life was still a gift, no matter the source.* The days were hard, especially in the early years. The blue-eyed menfolk an extra burden. Only in bed did they seem human, responding to the same touches women did, letting their pleasure be known in sweet growls and moans. Sometimes, at the conclusion, she would feel something pound in her chest, a longing to speak to them, to hear them, to feel their gaze upon her, aware. Mostly she didn't think of this. Days were busy; Marilyn enough of a companion. Yet she wondered. Once men and women loved one another as equals. How strange was that? It was frightening and wonderful to imagine.

"They took advantage of us," Marilyn said. "Made us lesser. We couldn't even vote. You've read about it." Yes. She'd read the other books too, the romances. Only a few left.

She touched her sleeve to her eye. That was history. Now—*their strange songs—fragments of words they'd heard. They each knew my heart. A secret knowledge they could never share as if they'd been given something infinitely rare but at a terrible price. Dying before they lost their youth, remaining beautiful, undimmed.*

Valerie remembered stories about the hard years—the Forgetting—when computers failed, when recorded history disappeared. Global supply chains broke down. Factories shuttered. Riots, militias. Diseases once thought eradicated resurged. Farm folk banded together, remembering their debt to the land. Fishing folk on the coast looked to the sea for survival.

The harsh realities of the world shaped how relationships evolved. The chaos wrought by the mutation rewrote all the narratives. There was no guide to navigate this strange landscape, to offer meaning. There was love—there was always love. She was not the only woman who looked at the new men with a longing, seeing something beautiful and lost, who found the sensation in lying with them held a mystery she could barely grasp. Yet who would not choose a partner with whom one could speak and laugh? Joined with it perhaps a reluctant recognition that other women were the only alternative to being alone. It was not hard to comfort, to find pleasure. Harder for some, perhaps.

Some fell in love with other women as their hearts had always demanded. In one small way, their lives might be less complicated, but nobody judged them particularly favored in this new reality.

Partners often chose to become wyves—a sacrament that they would look after each other in sickness and in health. A helpmate with whom to share the child-rearing responsibilities. Security. In the Republics, marriage provided recognized legal rights.

What would we become? Many women retreated, feeling no desire for each other, afraid of the changing world. There were those who asked only, "What will happen?" as if there were answers. Some offered answers, of course—the priestesses, the fortunetellers, the politicians, the mad. So many answers, wild, beautiful, terrible, ridiculous. *This is all a test. The Garden of Eden is being planted—in Africa. In the Middle East. In Georgia. We will all die at the dawn of the new century. The boys will lead us to an infinite consciousness. We will evolve to reproduce without partners.* And many more stories, always more stories.

Most responded to the silent imperative—live, wait. The drumming in their hearts. The yearning to bring forth life. Their unique strength. Acknowledging without words that they were witness to evolution's hand. The changes didn't signal the end of humanity, but only *what was needed to survive.*

They shall repair the ruined cities, the devastations of many generations.

18

- Grayson/Philippa - January 2079

The train stopped at the Main Street Station. The Richmond Premier, Kendra Lawson, and her retinue joined Grayson in the Tidewater government car. Grayson clasped her hand. Lawson was an elegant slender woman, gray hair in a stylish angled cut. She removed her topcoat and handed it to one of her staff. Beneath it, she was attired in a double-breasted charcoal suit with silver buttons over a sparkling white blouse. A pin with the Richmond seal, an armor-clad woman warrior standing over her fallen opponent circled by *Sic Semper Tyrannis*, shone on her lapel. With Lawson was her senior advisor, General Karyn Poole. Grayson had met both women at her inauguration. Both thoughtful, courageous women. *These women will do what's right.*

The car served as a mobile executive office for the Tidewater Premier. It was fitted out with several sitting areas with comfortable leather chairs where people could face one another, expandable tables, a full bar and a staff of servers.

Grayson guided everyone to a grouping near the rear of

the car. "Little more privacy. May I introduce the Tidewater Secretary of Civil Security, Liis Vesik."

Vesik shook hands with the Richmond delegation. She stood a half a head taller than the group, self-consciously stooped forward slightly. Even with her kinky black hair pulled back, stray locks escaped, brushing her cheek. Her large, black-fringed eyes were watchful.

A server approached. "May I offer you ladies some refreshments?"

Lawson tilted her head up. "A glass of red wine."

"Bourbon, something aged," Poole said.

"Red wine for me too," Vesik answered.

"Just a sweet tea for me, please," Grayson replied.

The server slipped away.

"Now," Grayson began. "What's the news?"

Lawson leaned in. "The U.D. has fallen. Pallas Evermore is dead. Antenora Sware has appointed herself the new Queen. Trutneva troops control many key resources. There is still fighting on the eastern shore and outside the cities. We're trying to make contact. Tidewater will be crucial in our effort to keep supplies flowing. It's vital we keep the eastern front open, keep a portion of their forces occupied."

The drinks arrived. Outside, the former City of Petersburg rolled past, brown grass covering the blackened ruins—the riots in 2032.

Grayson twisted her wedding band. "Of course. We offer our full support. Liis, tell them."

Vesik pushed a stray hair back, smiling. "We're already ahead of you. We have connected with the remains of the garrison in St. Michaels. We have a convoy of ships loaded with food, medical supplies and arms heading there now. A second convoy, also underway, is scheduled to rendezvous up the coast at Dover."

Poole held up her glass. "Well done."

Vesik cleared her throat. "There's more. Our cruisers will patrol the Chesapeake. The Trutnevas can't match our navy. We should have control all the way up to Havre De Grace. We can stop troop movements coming across the Bay Bridge."

Lawson nodded. "Good. Excellent. This is welcome news. Think about it. The Trutnevas have never known real opposition. They've bribed and threatened their way to where they are now. They are strong, no doubt. And clever. We can't make the mistake of underestimating them. Their combined armies are twice the number of the five remaining city-states. But they're going to have to fight *our* war. We can win. We will drive them back behind their wall.

"Richmond is doubling production of biodiesel. We've re-tooled factories to manufacture more armaments and materiel. We've called up all women who are able to serve."

Grayson sighed. "Well, that's two of the five. What of the others?"

Poole sipped her drink, then rested her hands on her knees. Her blunt features looked tired but alert. "They are not on the front lines, so don't expect them to understand the urgency. A treaty is a wonderful thing until it needs to be enforced. I trust they will all see this as an existential threat to what we've built. None of them would ever side with the Trutnevas, so the only choice is to band together. I have faith."

Grayson smiled, her face softening. "I do too."

Lawson cried, "That is our mission in Charlotte. We must be the spark. We must bring the fire."

* * *

Philippa stepped out of the train at Charlotte Station. The clouds hung low, an ice storm looming. She pulled her overcoat close. The mid-January sun, wan and distant, shrouded the scene. *The winter light—always retreating, always indifferent. Only the spring light holds hope or promise. Astrid, I will find you. Don't give up.*

On hearing the news of the collapse of the United District, Philippa offered to resign her commission. She would go north to find Astrid. She would risk capture, risk death. The torment of not knowing was worse. The constant refrain of *I should have done more.* Astrid was not a soldier; she was a dreamer. Philippa had loved that in her, had chosen not to tell her too much of what she saw, what she knew. She didn't know how anyone could not put together the clues, but Astrid, she believed, had understood as much as she could handle. *I should have made many things clearer. I didn't want to scare her into staying with me. I didn't want to talk of the possibility of war.*

General Poole refused her resignation. "You will be far more effective at my side. Alone, it's suicide. They will find you. Remember, Captain...Philippa, Astrid isn't the only hostage. Sware and the Trutnevas will use them to bargain. For now, they will make sure no harm comes to them. I know your every instinct is to run to her, but you have my word that the Premier will do all in her power to bring them all home."

Philippa's eyes welled up. She turned away. Poole stepped around the desk and wrapped her arms around Philippa. Philippa broke down; everything she'd been keeping in washed out of her. She clung to Poole like a lost child.

"I know, I know," Poole repeated. "We'll bring her home."

Government vehicles picked them up at Charlotte Station. The Richmond and Tidewater groups piled in. Philippa sat next to Liis Vesik. The Charlotte capital building, former Hearst Tower, a mere seven-minute drive. Stepping out in front of the sweeping entrance, Philippa overheard the Tidewater Premier, "It's like a cathedral."

Of the Piedmont Republics, Charlotte was the most populous and prosperous. Early on, the city suffered as the vast banking concerns collapsed. Tobacco, marijuana, timber remained core parts of their economy. As the borders between the states faded, troops from Charlotte aligned with Spartanburg to protect the manufacturing base. They shrewdly knew the value of a port city and struck a pact with the Marines at Camp Lejeune to secure Wilmington as part of the new alignment. From the mountains to the sea.

Carolina Industrial Corp manufactured tractor trailers, front loaders, gas turbines. Munoz Engineering ground mountains of tires, extruded and re-pressed the rubber into new, high performance tires. Seventy-five percent of the vehicles in the Piedmont Republics ran on their tires. The Darlington Steel mills produced a million tons a year.

Charlotte schools attracted some of the brightest young talent. During the Forgetting, when many universities failed, Charlotte leaders were quick to retrofit their facilities. Computers were stockpiled, but eventually the components become unavailable. The Asian factories that produced the drives, chips and boards folded. The switches and routers couldn't be replaced. The power grid became unstable, causing the massive data centers to stagger. The Internet dimmed and finally went dark, the gossamer of the digital world clawed away.

But the science was still there. Girls worked on the campus farms during the day and received instruction in the evenings. They served their mandatory military service in the engineering corps, rebuilding bridges and rigging wind turbines. Charlotte and the other republics, as part of their Mutual Treaties, swore to build their futures without damaging the climate further.

The conference room occupied most of the forty-seventh floor. In the elevator, Poole whispered, "Keep in mind, Charlotte maintains extensive trading relationships with the Reginae. That provides them the best information of the situation behind the wall. But it also means that Trutneva money flows all around. The question is whether they can live without it. We need them to apply economic pressure as one more weapon."

The Richmond and Tidewater delegations were the last to arrive. The Premiers and their staffs milled around, turning when the doors opened. Many lifted themselves out of their seats to hug and welcome the newly arrived.

The table sat fifty. A map of the Republics and Reginae territories on the wall near the head. A long credenza offered samovars of tea, pastries, and slices of leek and gruyere omelette.

The Charlotte ministers had not arrived. Poole glanced at her watch. "Ten minutes late to her own party."

Lawson leaned in. "Making an entrance. You know how she is."

The door burst open. Philippa stared across the room. Morgan Ishikawa strode in, radiant in her confidence, her ebony hair in a simple knot. Her cabinet filed in behind her. Philippa's heart dropped when the last woman entered. Eyes wide, she tilted her head in disbelief. She sucked in a deep breath to slow the pounding in her chest.

Kester O'Donnell. Blonde, willowy and brilliant.

Kester O'Donnell who'd fucked her way through half of the cadet class.

Kester O'Donnell, her first taste of heartbreak.

Kester zeroed in on Philippa. "My God, Philippa? You look amazing! How long has it been? Eight years?" She leaned in and kissed her cheek.

Philippa stammered, "Ten, actually."

Kester leaned back. "You haven't changed." Her eyes fixed on the streak of gray, pulled back. No, it was Kester who looked the same, better even. Her foxy face with the pointed chin, hazel eyes—always green against Philippa's regulation blanket— that mouth...No nights on patrol, sleeping on concrete. No rotations. No regrets. For Kester, the rules never applied. Kester smiled, "I'm the Secretary of Economic Affairs here in Charlotte. Morgan is *so* demanding. I have to go. We have to have a drink before you leave. I won't take no." Her polished nails tapped Philippa's wrist.

Philippa nodded. "Sure, that'd be nice."

"Promise?"

"Promise."

Kester dashed to her seat next to the Premier, whispering in her ear. Philippa couldn't take her eyes off her. The delegates took their places. One of them nursed an infant swaddled in yellow. Ishikawa opened, "Ladies, first, thank you for coming. As I look around this room, I am awed just being in your presence. We've shared so much history, so many sacrifices. My only regret is that Pallas Evermore and the brave leaders of the United District are missing. One of our sisters has fallen.

We are called here to liberate them, to free them from the tyranny of the Trutnevas. We must act and act quickly."

Ariel Carter, Premier of Charleston, a formidable woman in royal blue, poured a glass of water. "They will understand that war is costly. They will seek an accommodation."

Lawson bristled. "That's not the issue. They have over-thrown the government of the United District and murdered Pallas Evermore. This cannot stand."

Ishikawa raised her slim, ivory hand. "The Trutnevas are trying to swallow their meal. They know it could choke them if they aren't careful. They will have to absorb their gains and hold the territory."

Lawson battered her fist on the table. "Which is why we must strike and strike hard!"

Ishikawa continued as if Lawson hadn't spoken. She pointed to the map, "Our intelligence reports that Queen Xi Fang is missing. She never returned from the Sisters' birthday celebration. Trutneva forces along with Sachs and Caggiano are attempting to maintain order in Fang's territory. I don't think Fang's officers are waiting to see which of them is captured for treason. They will die first.

"Choi stands the most to gain. She is fully committed and the strongest among the Reginae. She's ventured south before and engaged the UD in several skirmishes to test their resolve. Stafford is weak and terrified the Newmarked will seek revenge. She can only afford to send token reinforcements. That leaves Fairfax and Vasquez."

Poole spoke up, her tone matter-of-fact. "The strength of a treaty is the belief that it will be enforced. The Trutnevas don't believe we will stand together. They succeeded with the United District. They will come at each of us to tear us apart.

They won't stop with the U.D. We've been more concerned with peace; they've been more concerned with victory.

"We must be prepared to provide food and shelter to the thousands who will flee. We must assess who in their command will fold into the new regime and who might form the core of a resistance. We must build new refineries and increase soy production. Most importantly, we must arm ourselves."

The Raleigh leader, Apryl D'allema, interrupted, "We are already stretched."

Valerie Grayson snapped her head around, her voice rising, "How can you say that? Look around. We have nothing but empty houses. We have food to share. We have medical care. *These are our sisters.* Tidewater will do what is asked. I have issued the order calling up all reserves. Our ships are available for transport. As of this morning, we are marshaling our resources for all-out war." Her voice rang with conviction, and D'allema shrank back.

Ariel Carter waved her hand at Grayson. "Two months on the job and you're telling us how to conduct policy, really? War and diplomacy are two sides of the same coin. We must hear what they have to say. If we fight and lose, their terms will be worse."

Grayson replied, "We must fight. I will not see our citizens subjugated to the Protsent."

Carter dismissed her. "A percentage of output, that's all they want. We can pay if it means lives are saved."

Grayson stood up, hands shaking. "And what happens when you can't pay them in goods? They determine the value. They control the currency. What will you do when they decide they want more? When they round up your people and ship them north in payment? Or when they install their own operatives to monitor compliance? *That's what they do.* If they think you're growing too strong, they'll take more and give it to the others. They'll let you keep just enough so you don't kick. Strong enough to do their bidding. They pit the Queens against each other like a dogfight. Caggiano, Sachs, Choi, they all know if they stopped paying, they'd be carved up and served to the others."

Carter shrugged, her pink frosted lips tight. "They will make an overture. We need to be ready to listen."

Lawson interrupted, "Enough. How long before we can mount an offence?"

Ishikawa consulted with Kester. "April would be the earliest."

The generals and secretaries droned on. War, Trutnevas, war. Outside, the looming gray front of ice a reminder of the cold end of things. *So many will be killed and, in the end, the Trutnevas will never be brought down.* Philippa stole glances at Kester, fighting to suppress memories of her first year at VMI. Exhaustion, pain. The drill sergeant, the ratline, breaking her down, stripping her naked of pride, of her illusions, demanding she conform. Reforging her every day. Duty, loyalty, honor. A world devoid of pleasure, of privacy. But then, the rare nights when Kester rapped on her door—three knocks, then two.

One late night in the single bed, Kester's face buried between Philippa's thighs, tongue delicate then consuming, two fingers caressing her insides. Philippa pinching her own nipple, head shaking from side to side, trying not to scream. Falling in an endless wave of ecstasy that brought her to tears. After the storm, Kester nestled in her arms. Philippa kissed her lips, salty and fragrant.

"That was fun. You were so beautiful when you came," Kester murmured.

"I love you, Kester." The words unleashed without warning. Philippa could only watch Kester's face as the words hung in the light through the window.

Kester pulled her head up, her mouth wearing a grin that was like a shove. "Wait, slow down, sweetheart. We're just two girls having fun, making the best of this God-forsaken place."

"Yeah, right, sure. I don't know why I said it." She blinked back tears.

Kester's hand slid down Philippa's torso. She kissed the curve of Philippa's breast. "This will help you forget those crazy ideas. Close your eyes."

Kester dazzled; she lit up the world around her. Philippa, along with many others, orbited Kester's star. A brief and volatile affair. Getting high together before class, Philippa trying not to laugh at the teacher. Kester luring her away from the library (she never needed to study) to explore the mysteries of sex. Philippa cut her hair the same way Kester wore hers. She memorized Kester's schedule so she could run into her. She made plans that Kester never kept.

Finally, Kester stopped knocking.

Then, on a steel-gray day just like the one looming outside, Kester looked her in the eye, emotionless. "Grow up, Calenos. I'm over you. You're boring. Can't you see that? There's just nothing more to say." *Kester, where did I go wrong?* Even ten years later, the words tore Philippa's heart.

* * *

"Red wine. Merlot."

"Martini. Two olives."

"Vodka or gin?"

Kester glared at the bartender. "Understand this; martinis should only be made with gin. The other is watery vermouth. Sterilize something with it. The martini is one of the things men got right."

Kester turned back to Philippa. Her voice low and confiding. "The way I see it, Charlotte is the most important actor in this drama. We have the armies; we have the industrial capacity to prosecute a war of any duration. Wars are expensive. During peace we forget that. Charlotte would have to finance the war. Understand there are a lot of interests here that don't want to disturb the status quo. Nobody wants war. Nobody wants to send young women into combat to be killed. But we have a new alignment now. If they're smart, the other Republics will follow our lead."

"The Trutnevas—"

Kester skewered an olive. "The Trutnevas see the Anschluss in the District as a necessary step in protecting their lands. They are rational in that respect. Don't cry to me about the martyr, Pallas Evermore. Evermore is as much to blame for this mess as anyone. More. She should have stepped down years ago. Know when to quit, right? She could have ensured a transition of power that wouldn't have weakened our alliance. Bloody selfish, really." *Brilliant Kester, always three moves ahead.*

"The Republics survived because the early leaders under-stood everyone needed a stake in the outcome. Everyone needed to understand how their sacrifices would be more valuable if they understood the sacrifices others were making for them. Resilience and all that. They believed and had to convince others to agree that tomorrow would be better than today. If the future value isn't greater, there is no utility in sacrifice. They didn't become paragons of virtue overnight. They knew when to use force and expediency. There was blood on their hands. Working with Morgan, I've seen some of the classified reports.

"War is the most extreme form of diplomacy. The Trutnevas will seek to remove the threat of war with the remaining Republics, at least until their domestic situation is resolved. But they're smart enough to know that our threats are only as credible as our willingness to deliver on them. Maybe we could win, but at what cost? Wishing for yesterday isn't a strategy. We will have to give them something." She closed her eyes briefly as the gin went down her throat. "Maybe cede Baltimore and everything north of old Interstate 70."

Baltimore, Astrid. "What about Sware?"

"What about her? Sware is a tool. They will cut her loose. She doesn't have any real power base of her own. Imperial troops are the reason she rules. As soon as they're gone, she's as good as dead."

Kester sipped her drink greedily, little pink tongue visible. "I say we cut a deal with them. We return one of our own to lead the new, U.D. War is avoided. It's an efficient solution and everybody still makes money. Why are we talking about this?" She slid closer to Philippa, her smile curling up on the right, an old trick. "It's really boring after a long day. It's like being with Morgan. Tell me about *you*."

What was there to tell? Kester's star had only grown brighter. "I've been with the RSC since graduation."

"You're a captain, right?"

"Two years now."

"That's so great. I made colonel here before moving to the cabinet."

Philippa nodded.

"It's really not that great. Always travelling. Washington, Philadelphia, Novi Vasiligrad, Richmond. Now that I know you're there, I've more reason to visit."

"You've met the Sisters?"

"Of course, I've met them. Very impressive, if you ask me. Solenopea claimed the old Philadelphia Museum of Art as her residence. She hosts the most amazing parties. Oh, the Duchamps! I hope you can see them sometime. Traveling with Morgan has brought us very close. We really see things the same way, but she said she doesn't want to see me until this summit has ended."

Philippa started, "Wait, you're in an affair with the Premier? She's married, isn't she?"

Kester looked askance. "Shhh. Officially, I categorically deny the insinuation."

"God, Kester." *Rules never applied.*

Kester feigned offense. "She needs me. I'm the only one who tells her how things are. Everyone else is a sycophant, trying to get something from her."

Kester brushed a stray hair from Philippa's face. "There, better."

They reminisced about VMI; which of their classmates held important commands, who had left the service, whether certain professors were still there. The need now more than ever for leaders.

"Remind me again, what was your service area back then?" Kester asked.

Philippa set her glass down. "I worked on solar installations. Repairs, then some new once a company down in Charleston had started producing the panels. I'd go out with the electricians to mount them and run them to the grid."

"I was in reforesting. Mostly men back then, right?"

"Yeah, mostly. Fewer over the years, like everywhere. I just remember their eyes on me a lot of the time. Few times one of them would ask me out for a beer, but I never went. Why, right?"

Kester leaned in. "So you never..."

A look of embarrassment spread across Philippa's face. She shook her head. "No, never. You? Wait, I think I know the answer."

Kester grinned. "A few. Sometimes it was useful. An older man will do almost anything to be with you if you look half decent. But you make them earn it. Other times it was just for fun. Life is about collecting experiences."

Kester's face lit. "And not looking half decent...do you remember that girl? Big one, strong. She worked there at the college. You know, the one who was always lurking around. Greasy hair, bad skin. She'd always pick up the laundry around the time the basketball team showered. Dumb. Seriously dumber than dirt. What was her nickname? Block, rock?"

"Brick."

Kester laughed, "Brick! Right. Wonder what ever happened to her."

Philippa stiffened. "She had a name...Claire. She just couldn't read. Dyslexia maybe. Also a strange kind of synesthesia..."

"Look at you! What a memory. I never wanted anything to do with her. She creeped me out." Kester laid her hand on

Philippa's. "Why don't you show me your room? When's the last time someone massaged your back?"

Philippa pulled her hand away. "I'm in a relationship." *But am I?*

Kester leaned in. "I don't see her here."

"I don't know what you mean."

A flicker in Kester's eyes. "Yes, you do. Don't play that game. I'm talking about how you used to drive me crazy. How I couldn't wait to kiss you."

Philippa's hand touched her hair, her face flushed. *Yes, me too!* Immediately, she lowered her eyes and tore at her scarred cuticles. "It's not a good time for me. My girlfriend is missing. She was in Baltimore when Sware took control, at least I think she was."

Kester moved closer and wrapped her arms around Philippa's shoulders. "I had no idea. I mean, how could I know? Do you have any information? Where was she going?"

Philippa leaned into Kester's embrace, blinking back tears. She sniffed, "She'd heard rumors of a ship to Europe, but the truth is we'd fought and neither of us could find our way back. It was probably just her way of letting go. But now she's trapped." *Why am I telling her this?*

Kester pulled her close. "The storms far out to sea will swallow any ship. Europe may as well be Mars. To my knowledge there's been no travel for over twenty years. The fucked-up world we've inherited.

"I'm so sorry, Philippa. She's probably alright, but it's a delicate situation. You know that. She's caught up in the net of the larger conflict." Kester stroked her hair. "Listen, we have contacts throughout the Imperial Government. I will make some calls. We'll get a read on the situation and go from there."

Philippa lifted her head. "Thank you, Kester. *Thank you.*"

Kester wiped the corners of Philippa's eyes with her thumbs. "Anything for you."

Later, alone in her room, Philippa sifted through the evening with Kester. She smiled and shook her head, reflecting on their reunion. Somehow, Kester had reimagined their past and found only a lost friendship that needed the smallest breath to rekindle. No pain, no regrets. Maybe that was her real gift.

19

– Philippa – February 15, 2079

Two weeks earlier, the Trutnevas had issued an invitation to all the Premiers; a summit in the former United District ostensibly to discuss trade and cultural exchange. The unspoken message declared: We support Antenora Sware, witness the future.

Philippa rode in a staff car with General Poole, Sergeant Johnson and the driver. Since the last trip to the UD, Johnson had been attached to Poole's security detail.

Johnson remained a flawless enigma. Powerfully supple and in control. So tuned into her surroundings, Philippa almost hesitated to speak to her. As if her 'yes ma'am' or 'no ma'am' might disturb the deep connection.

The warm late February day was sunny, the crocuses poised to bloom, daffodils stretched up out of the ground. Still, Philippa shivered and rubbed her hands. Deep in her bones, she sensed the premature spring was unnatural, another symptom of the fevered planet. Seasons had become mutable, unreliable, subtly undermining faith in the future. Natural cycles on which humans had depended for millennia had fractured, inviting the vengeful return of forgotten Discordia. *Rescue us from the wrath that is coming.*

Kester couldn't have shown more support. Using her position over the vast Charlotte economic machine, she learned that Astrid had been picked up in Baltimore, held in Chester but was now in transit to Washington. Philippa suspected Kester also oversaw part of Charlotte's intelligence service. Kester cautiously offered the hope of Astrid's release. An exchange or transfer had been proposed with the possibility of Astrid returning with Philippa to Richmond. *Hold on, I will find you.*

Kester would participate as part of the Charlotte delegation to the summit. They would be taking the train along with the Richmond, Raleigh and Charleston Premiers. Philippa didn't expect to see much of her. Philippa wouldn't attend any meetings. Security and surveillance.

Looking out the window, she saw piles of trash spewed across the sides of the road. Vinyl siding, pallets, the front bumper of a car that hadn't been seen in fifty years. Miles of plastic waste. High winds gnawed at the remains of the old world, tearing off the shingles, prying the rusted signs free.

Philippa stifled a yawn. She'd endured long days in planning committees and strategy sessions. Richmond now hummed with activity. New recruits were coming to Fort Lee daily in the hundreds. Philippa's orders were to oversee their training, get them ready for combat. The new orders did allow her some time with her horse, Icarys. She sat astride the stallion watching the recruits struggling to carry massive logs, straining to climb the wall. Drill sergeants, inches away from their heads, shouted abuse. Philippa could feel the blisters on their feet, the sprained ankles, the ache in their muscles, the despair that she wasn't good enough. Her first year at VMI was a similar hell.

Will we even have enough guns, enough boots?

Parts of the old barracks hadn't been used for forty years. Teams of workers sistered joists, replaced pipe, ran electrical, and patched holes, finishing sometimes only hours before a new cohort of young women in fatigues arrived.

For now, there's still a possibility for peace.

But what constituted peace in this new alignment was unclear. The Trutnevas appeared stronger now than ever. Their threat to the remaining Republics loomed, a growing shadow. General Poole ordered an inventory of pre-Forgetting technology assets, searching for an advantage, a slingshot for their David. In addition to her exhausting work at Fort Lee, Philippa traveled to Williamsburg to the former College of William and Mary. She reported back to the General on progress.

The College had closed in 2028; however, vital archives remained. Over the last decade, Richmond leadership instituted a research program housed in the remains of the former college. Surrounded by the crumbling theatre of the colonial capital, scientists poured over documents printed before the collapse. The Forgetting was a perforation of history, a place into which very few were willing to look.

Rebuilding the machines was impossible—vital components remained scattered and lost. Microprocessors and the machines that made them couldn't be reconstructed. So much of the technology had come from China, which dissolved into chaos when the mutation struck. In the US, engineers had been redeployed to solve more immediate problems of food production, retrofitting the communications and maintaining the fragile power grid. The state of technology had receded to mid-twentieth-century levels. Massive amounts of more advanced, but unusable technology still existed. Contemporary scientists debated whether attempting to reassemble the past should even be pursued. The raging inventions of men had rent their world, sickened it. Their terrible alchemy seared the land. Women had been charged with knitting it back together into something new. Their research into what was lost sought to find the ideas of science that had never been explored, the glimpses into other futures unknown.

Philippa had mixed feelings. She wished it were not a lost world they ransacked, a world made by men (though Kester had always said it was made as equally by women). How much better to forge a new world, pursue new sciences. There seemed something dangerous in treading a path that had led to this, and yet she feared her own tendency to be superstitious, to believe in goddesses of retribution. Without discipline, without reason, without logic, anyone could believe anything; any history could be declared and used to support any position. She had argued all this with friends over the years, sometimes with surprising passion. Nothing had been resolved—not among her friends, not in her own mind.

Practical matters, however, now took precedence. They must use whatever methods they could, so long as they were effective. The Republics needed a breakthrough to help even the odds against the Sisters—about whom she had no doubts at all. The scientists sought advances in communications, weaponry, deception, production, and she would abide by the consequences of whatever they found.

At the border of the United District, a checkpoint appeared. A crude gatehouse had been built. New barbed wire fencing stretched out to either side of the road. An armed guard held her arm up. The car slowed and halted in front of her. Other vehicles idled on the side of the road.

The driver rolled down the window. Philippa noted the guard's uniform bore none of the former UD insignia.

The guard leaned in. "You are crossing into Tenora. State your names and your business."

Poole barked, "Soldier, this is the United District."

The guard glanced back at the gatehouse. Her flaxen hair was pulled up in a knot below her cap. She paused, then recited a message, "Antenora Sware, regina eternum, has declared that the lands formerly known as the United District shall be known as Tenora."

Poole smacked her fist into her palm. "What a load of crap!"

The driver handed over the invitation and security passes.

The guard studied the documents. "You're from the RSC?"

"Yes," Poole replied.

The guard glanced again at the gatehouse. *She's afraid,* Philippa realized.

The guard whispered, "Stay awake. Tenora is a warped reflection of the United District. Nothing is the same."

Poole cocked her head, her good eye piercing. "What?"

"Long live the District!" She handed the papers back, stepped away and waved them on.

* * *

Past the 14th Street bridge, scrub bushes and vines grew around the concrete barriers separating the north and south lanes. Cherry blossoms drifted by. Clouds of them swirled off to the left around the remains of the Jefferson Memorial.

Philippa sighed; pink was Astrid's favorite color. Her canvases overflowed with it. *Step into the painting, I'm here. You've found me.* The beautiful pink snowstorm called to her, so peaceful and inviting.

A chill wrenched her from her reverie. *Something's not right.* She lifted her eyes and screamed.

"Stop the vehicle!" General Poole shouted to the driver.

Bodies swayed from the street lamps that once displayed the UD crest. Crows had picked the corpses. Even still, the victims were identifiable by their uniforms. These were men and women from the highest ranks of the former UD. They signaled Sware's message to anyone entering Tenora: Defy me at your peril.

Johnson shook her head. "Damn." Poole made the sign of the cross. Philippa's heart pounded, an emptiness filling her. She had seen more than her share of death, but the horrific, *calculated* scene brought forward the sickening realization that their enemy wouldn't be reasoned with. The Trutnevas and their allies were something far more terrifying—an over-whelming and relentless evil.

See how the faithful city has become a prostitute.

* * *

The Trutnevas had planned a parade for the Southern Premiers. Philippa scanned the crowd, glad the temperature held in the forties.

Tomorrow you can sleep. Now, stay focused, you've got a job.

Aluminum stands lined Independence Ave. *There's a joke!* Citizens of Tenora filled the seats and crammed into the space behind the parade barricades. A sepulchral murmur traveled through the spectators. They fanned out across the street. Tenora security forces pervaded the parade route. Teams on horseback patrolled the perimeter, their lifeless eyes scanning between the crowd and the Sisters. Gone were the posters of the starving children. The tent city had been cleared out, not a trace left behind.

Behind her, the Imperial box rose highest. The double-eagle banners adorned the rear wall. Next to it was Antenora Sware's smaller viewing box. No Tenora crest was displayed. Sware sat next to a young attendant with café-au-lait skin occasionally leaning in to whisper something in her ear.

The Trutnevas wore deep blue topcoats trimmed in steel gray curly lamb wool and gold epaulets. Double breasted brass buttons gleamed. Their matching curly gray hats bore golden double-eagle insignia. Their flaming hair was pulled back with platinum hair clips, their strange eyes otherworldly. *I can see what Kester meant. The Sisters are exquisite and powerful. I've never seen anyone like them.* Philippa appraised her own moth-eaten coat and pulled the belt tighter.

In the Richmond box was Premier Lawson, General Poole, Philippa, Johnson and several generals, cabinet members and the security detail. Not far away, the Charlotte delegation watched, Kester seated next to Ishikawa. *Her* coat was new, hugging her shapely form.

To the west, a military march sounded. Heads turned. The Tenora marching band strode towards them as the lead parade unit. Sun glimmered off their instruments.

Tenora soldiers followed, marching in formation. They wore

UD uniforms stripped of insignia. The lead women carried a flag with platinum crown over a bloody dagger. *The Tenora flag.* Sware stood as they approached and returned their salute. Philippa glanced at the Sisters. Both remained seated, their eyes intent on the parade. Identical small smiles played on their thin lips.

Behind the Tenora infantry, light armored vehicles crawled along in formation. UD markings blacked out. Next, UD artillery rolled along.

Companies of Venoma Choi's forces marched behind the Tenora contingent. Their brown and green camouflage distinctive from UD or Trutneva.

Another marching band, then an Imperial horseback company.

Imperial artillery. Massive cannons pulled behind enormous trucks.

We don't have anything nearly as devastating. This is intimidation. And it's working.

Battalions of Imperial soldiers—a sea of ultramarine berets paraded next through the fallen capital. *More are coming every week*, Philippa speculated. *How do we even stand a chance?*

The black fatigues revealed the identity of the next companies: The Dirae Corps. The name resonated with terror. Philippa shuddered and pulled her coat closer. Rumors surrounded their existence. They were the elite shock troops of the Trutnevas. One of them was worth ten regulars. Isolated from an early age, raised in huge training compounds, pushed to physical limits few could endure. Expert with small arms and lethal in hand-to-hand.

For the Dirae, retreat meant death—they fought to the last soldier. In Venoma Choi's bid to become Queen, two companies of Dirae reinforced her army. They had laid waste to the towns—New Oxford, East Berlin, Dillsburg—burning them to their foundations. The smoke was seen in Frederick. Civilians fled into the countryside. Deserters in Choi's army were executed.

They were the shadow of death cast by the unforgiving sun.

Few of the women stood less than 5' 10". They shouldered their black assault rifles. The soldiers marched with a merciless discipline, eyes fixed straight ahead, then, as one, snapping right to salute the Sisters. *Mother help us if we have to face them.*

The loudspeaker blared, "Behold the traitors to the Empire."

A defeated mix of U.D. and Fang soldiers stumbled forward, staggering under the weight of thick wooden cangues. Their hands locked in front of their heads, chains connected the pillories. The lead of the chain was secured to harnesses on several horses. The prisoners had no choice but to walk or be dragged behind if they fell. Their heads were shaved, and their eyes fixed on the ground. Some were fortunate to still have boots, others wrapped their feet in rags. The prisoners were flanked on either side of the road by Imperial soldiers on horseback.

These must be the officers, singled out for this humiliation. 'This will be you' is what they're saying.

Following the unfortunates came a row of flatbed trailers with chain link fence around the edges. Rolling cages. More prisoners were crammed inside, men and women, mostly in orange jumpsuits. Their haggard faces pressed against the wire, fingers laced through the holes.

Lost souls of the damned. Philippa pulled her eyes away. *I won't be a participant in their suffering.* She turned toward the

Imperial box. *I should just kill the Trutnevas right here. Two shots. Put an end to this.*

Her fingers slipped to her holster.

They'd execute everyone, Lawson, Poole, Kester.

She pulled her hand away and tore at her cuticle. Another flatbed passed in front. Philippa squinted.

No!

A small figure in an orange jumpsuit cried out, "Magnificent Sisters! Queens of Justice! I appeal to you!"

Astrid!

"Spare me, please!" Astrid pled.

Philippa shoved several RSC staff aside and climbed over the front of the box. Tenora security waded through the crowd towards her.

"Captain Calenos!" Poole shouted. "Stand down!"

"Astrid! ASTRID!" she screamed.

Movement on the flatbed.

She looked up. I saw her. She knows I'm here. She pushed to the barricade. Behind her, Imperial security circled the Sisters.

Shaking the chain links, the ragged figure called, "Help me! Philippa, please!"

Philippa's heart surged, *Just a short distance. I'm here! Hold on!*

"Captain Calenos! STAND DOWN NOW." The order issued to someone else in another world. Philippa focused solely on the cage.

She lifted her foot onto the barricade. More security forces appeared in her peripheral vision swinging truncheons at the bystanders. One of the horses reared. A murder of crows took flight on the Mall. The crowd swayed, people collapsed. Imperial guards pulled her backwards. She slammed onto the pavement, clawing to regain her footing. Two soldiers pinned her. The other guard wrapped her in a chokehold. Philippa pried at the soldier's arm, gasping.

"Astrid!"

Philippa's vision tunneled, fixed on the flatbed rolling away. She twisted once more—her body so heavy and detached—then fell into blackness.

20

– Brick – February 15, 2079

Brick tugged on the jacket of her House Guard uniform and straightened her tie. *On call again.*

The delegations from the Republics had spent the morning at the parade, enjoyed lunch at the Botanical Gardens and now had returned to their embassies. She'd spent the day with Glott, measuring the loyalty of the U.D. officers. *Sware's purge must have put the fear in them.* From what Brick could tell, though, Sware had killed indiscriminately, eliminating some of the most seasoned commanders. *Settling old scores.* Glott predicted they'd defect if given a chance. If war came, Imperial forces would have to do the job.

I could run this place better than Sware with what I've learned from the Sisters. None of this queen business, surrounded by too many liars. I would know where to apply the pressure to keep the women focused on claiming what belongs to them.

All through the day, the haunting trace of honeysuckle in the hallway, the anteroom to Sware's office. *Let it go!*

Cocktail hour in the rotunda. A string quartet with three

skinny old men in ancient tuxedos, two with over-long silver hair, the other nearly bald, a few wisps drifting over his shiny pate, played light classical music. Brick's eyes left the men – she found men oddly disturbing – and gazed up at the domed ceiling, marveling at the inlays and bas-relief. Marble and bronze statues ringed the perimeter. U.D. ministers in Novi Vasiligrad couture gowns fawned over the Imperial representatives, vying for Best Sycophant. Venoma Choi in black leather pants, heels, and a form-fitting, quilted, aubergine leather jacket. *Only thing missing is a riding crop.* The Sisters wore matching emerald silk bodices with platinum thread stitched into a leaf and tulip design. Blazing hair impeccably coiffed. When she wasn't in uniform, Brick preferred work pants and shirts. She snorted. *Fashion. Women trying to impress other women.*

By comparison, the women from the South may as well have been dressed to change the oil. Boxy dresses rendered them shapeless. Scuffed pumps. Half of them in fraying olive uniforms. Valerie Grayson in her high-collared blouse and jacket, a Victorian headmistress.

A servant announced dinner for the smaller group of mostly the heads of state. The guests strolled into the formal dining room. Roaring fireplaces cast an orange light, merging with the hundreds of candles around the room and on the table. The overhead lights dimmed. Wood paneling covered the room. High on the walls hung ancient oil paintings from the early days of the United States. Battle scenes from Yorktown, winter in Valley Forge, views from the Hudson Valley, herds of countless bison on the prairie. Lafayette, Washington, Madison, Jackson, Ross. *What a world they had. If they hadn't been greedy ...but all humans are greedy. Just look around.*

Near the corner, on an easel, stood a painting in progress: a full-length portrait of Sware wearing a crown. Brick laughed out loud, pleased to be rescued from her thoughts. *Greedy and foolish, yes. Nothing's changed.*

The Sisters took their places at either end. Behind Soleno-pea's chair, resting on a marble column, sat a cube covered with black silk. A single spotlight shown down in it, brighter than the surroundings.

With the precision of a military drill, the servants presented the soup. Carrot with fresh cream, garnished with sprigs of mint. Brick hunched over the bowl and shoveled it in.

Conversations quieted down while the women ate. Many murmured praises for the food.

Just as quickly, the bowls were removed, and the dinner plates delivered. Lamb chops, caramelized Brussel sprouts, whipped potatoes with roasted garlic. The oversized china plates ringed with ultramarine, trimmed in gold with the Trutneva double eagle at the top.

Brick sat to the left of Myrmica. She brushed off attempts at small talk from the foreign guests. *I'm here to listen.* She studied the women, how they looked at each other, *understood each other, spoke a coded language.* Smell of lard pomade, clean skin, Calla lily floral arrangements. From time to time, the iron tang of menstrual blood. *Do they have children? Do they have wyves? Who gets to choose?* She stabbed at the meat.

Myrmica stood, raised her glass, "A toast. To our guests."

On cue, a servant lifted the black cloth. Underneath lay an ornate vitrine. Inside the box, a decapitated woman's head. The mouth overflowed with gold; the hardened rivulets suspended down her chin. The face contorted in an eternal scream, eyes wide with terror. The glossy black hair swayed in the formaldehyde solution, a drowned nightmare. Valerie Grayson held her head and screamed. The table recoiled, some into each other's arms. Drinks spilled; vases knocked over. Liis pressed her hand to her mouth, stumbled out of her chair and dashed to the door. Brick heard her retching in the next room.

Lawson gasped, "That's Xi Fang."

"Steady," Poole whispered. "Don't avert your eyes. This is what we are fighting against."

Brick narrowed her eyes, glanced at the box then studied the women's reactions. *They didn't have to watch.*

Myrmica cleared her throat, beaming. "To our guests. To our mutual understanding."

Morgan Ishikawa stood, holding the edge of the table. Even in the dim light, Brick noticed the ashen pallor of her face. Her words spilled out haltingly and true. "We were prepared to negotiate a truce. We were prepared to offer a settlement. But I see now that any compromise is a slow poison."

Sware reared up from her chair, spittle flying from her lips, "You have *no idea—* "

With a jerk of her arm, Solenopea splashed the water from her glass into Sware's face. "Shut up, crow." Turning back to Ishikawa, eyes sparkling, she smiled, scarlet lips like a wound. "Now we're getting somewhere. The measure of the woman."

Sware retreated, dabbing her forehead with her napkin. Her black eye makeup bled down her powdered cheeks, a sad Pagliacci. Brick shifted in her chair, watching the scene. *If you don't know who the fool in the room is, it's you, Antenora.*

Myrmica swept her arm out. "Look around. The United District is no more. A popular uprising against an inward-looking relic has ushered in the dawn of a new prosperity. This is their will. This is the future they've chosen. Now each of you fine, strong women must choose for yourselves and for your people." Her voice crooning and cruel, hypnotic, repulsive. Brick noted the lies absentmindedly.

The spotlight glared, drawing attention back to the horror inside the box.

Solenopea pressed her hands together, and spoke in a quiet but carrying voice, each word ringing. "You say you want war? What do you know of war? This war you so eagerly seek would be fought here, on District soil. Their officers are your officers. The same bloodlines: Citadel, VMI, The Academy. All once sisters in arms. Do you really want to fight them? Can you look a seventeen-year-old infantry woman in the eye and tell her 'We will win?' You may fool yourselves with your self-righteous rhetoric, but she will see through it. The Fang rebellion has been smashed. We've shown you price of disloyalty. We have seven divisions moving south as we speak."

Myrmica beamed, her eyes moving not quite in sync. "We welcome each of you as equals. Pledge yourselves to the Empire. This country once spanned the Atlantic to the Pacific, sea to sea. Together, we will see that day again!

"Each Premier who agrees will be elevated to the Reginae. You will maintain the boundaries of your city-states. You will enjoy our full support. We have abundant energy. More than we can use in a thousand lifetimes. Our scientists are reopening doors we once thought closed forever. We have made significant recoveries and advances in medicine, in computing, in carbon neutralization.

"We women are responsible not only for civilization, but also the species." Myrmica laughed. "I'm always reminded of chess. Everyone knew the queen was more agile, more powerful. She strode the battlements, took the risks. The king merely limped along, always hiding. Evolution finally caught up with reality. What lies ahead is greatness and prosperity beyond your dreams."

Uneasy smiles crossed the Premiers' faces. Ariel Carter mumbled, "How might this work?"

Lawson jabbed her finger. "What are you saying? You can't be serious."

Carter averted her gaze from the Richmond Premier. "We need to have all the facts is what I'm saying. I, for one, will not rule out an agreement that offers peace for my people."

Lawson exploded, "You can't hide. The treaty binds all of our cities. You remember the treaty, don't you? You remember Pallas Evermore. She should be with us!"

Carter clenched her jaw. "We need to consider their proposal."

Myrmica smirked, a coil of fiery hair coming loose and bouncing on her shoulder. Her poisoned arrow had found the mark. "We propose a gradual process. Today, we start by acknowledging our peaceful intentions towards each other. To open up deeper levels of understanding. We can learn so much from each other, share wisdom and experience. We are the leaders, the natural aristocracy. Do not concern yourselves about the Protsent. We will negotiate a fair agreement when the time is right. My sister and I have nothing but the greatest respect for your many accomplishments."

Brick scraped up the last of the potatoes. Everyone else had pushed their plates away. *Another brilliant performance.* All of speakers believed their own words. Except the Sisters, of course. They traded in lies and half-truths. Myrmica played the virtuous ruler, Solenopea, the tyrant. Sometimes when one of them was speaking, Brick saw the colors circling the other, so close was their connection. And sometimes the color of the lies reversed—not as if they had started believed themselves, but as if reality itself had bent to their wishes. But, luckily, that never lasted. It gave her a headache.

War, Brick mused, *quit all this scratching and let's get to it.* The kick of the rifle, ears ringing. The intoxicating smell of powder and fear—better than any high from a drug. Screaming, heart pounding. Hyper-alive, witness to the presence of the blood-soaked Goddess of the Fallen, Othere. Tribute to the Goddess. She scowled. *As long as the Sisters need me, I'll never see the front again. One of their caged pets.*

Solenopea narrowed her eyes. "We have arrested more than a hundred citizens of your Republics. Spies, who will be tried fairly according to Imperial law." She stared at Morgan. "Some of you here tonight may hold adamantine positions about coexistence. May I remind you, in fixity is death. All that lives changes. We remain flexible and foresee a time when more reasonable, constructive discussions are pursued. Queen Sware has generously deferred prosecution of these enemy agents as a gesture of goodwill. But if there is no way forward, she will have to take measures to protect the security of Tenora." She turned to Sware. "Lovely name, really."

Sware smiled her gruesome smile and nodded. Brick wondered how much her fist would bruise if she punched her toady mouth. *Dear Goddess of the Fallen, these speeches were boring,*

Addressing the leaders again, Solenopea said, "Think about them. Think about the lives you will save by joining us in peace."

The table erupted again. "We demand their release! Where

are you holding them?"

Grayson through clenched teeth, "You have no right!"

A servant removed Brick's plate. She waved off a second offering to fill her wine glass. She crossed her arms and studied the Southern leaders, smirking, *No right, sure. Do yourselves a favor and write them off. The Sisters expect you to show compassion. You'll play right into their game.* The Sisters demonstrated such skill at manipulation, such psychological cunning, Brick almost pitied these adversaries. Time was their strongest ally. Each day that passed under the puppet Sware's rule cemented the status quo, made the new alignment a reality. Every conciliatory feint allowed them room to maneuver. Every wedge they could drive between the Premiers improved their odds.

Brick glanced back at the vitrine. Her arm only recently freed from the cast. The damp brought an ache. *Fang got greedy. The Reginae have closed ranks around the Sisters—for now. The defeat of Fang and the bloodless victory over the UD have taught the Queens a lesson in artful power. But there will be a next time and who will come at the Sisters then?*

Sware stood, the black streaks of her makeup still evident. "Our ministers will review each case and coordinate with your consuls."

Myrmica said, "There, you see—"

Sware interrupted, eyes moist with infatuation. "And I would like to add, long have I dreamed of welcoming Myrmica and Solenopea to the United District. Not the stagnant, corrupt District under the former Premier, but a city reborn. A city awake at last to its strength and unlimited potential as part of the Empire." She raised her glass. "Long live the Trutnevas!" Bright golden-brown sparks.

The Sisters half raised their glasses. The other women remained motionless, waiting for the awkward parody to end.

Lawson stood, the color returned to her face. Poole right behind her. Lawson nodded. "We regret that we must retire early. Our sincere appreciation to our gracious hosts."

They strode out. The other Premiers followed, veiled glances back at the vitrine.

Sware cleared her throat. "Anyone for dessert?"

21

– Philippa – February 16, 2079

In the Old Congressional Cemetery, early morning fog clung to the crumbling cenotaphs and headstones. Philippa and Kester stood in knee-high grass. A leafless sycamore loomed over the graveyard. Faded plastic bags, draped through the branches, fluttered like wraiths.

Technically, Philippa had been relieved of duty after being cleared by the RSC medical officer. She would face a disciplinary review after they returned to Richmond. Dress like a civilian was Kester's only instruction when she told Philippa where to meet her.

Old women in ashen mantles made their way among the graves. *Who do they visit? To whom do they pay their respects?* The roads surrounding the cemetery were quiet. Behind them stood the old chapel. Ahead, the UD correctional facility loomed. The slab walls made of sand and rust-colored concrete jutted out of the ground. *The stronghold of Dis.*

Philippa's heart hammered her chest. *She's so close. Just inside. I haven't failed her.*

Kester took a drag from her cigarette. "Whew, that was some show you put on at the parade."

Philippa winced. "I saw her in that cage. I couldn't stop myself. I know I've made things worse for you and the Premiers."

Kester tucked her sunny hair behind her ear. "Don't torture yourself, love. What's going to happen will have very little to do with your actions yesterday. The state dinner was a horror show. Disgusting. The Trutnevas may have overplayed their hand. Their displays of power and brutality were designed to cower the Premiers into a truce. If anything, it steeled their resolve. But they have scored one victory: Charleston falters. Alliances are cheap when there's little at stake. If they refuse to fight, we will have to face some terrible choices."

"But the treaty..." Philippa's words trailed off.

Grinding the butt under her heel, "Have you always been this naive, Philippa? This is self-interest we're talking about. That feckless bitch, Ariel Carter, thinks she can strike a better deal with the Trutnevas. We have to relieve her of that idea."

Philippa tore at her cuticles, stung. "Thank you...again...for doing this. You never even met Astrid. I can't believe this is happening. You didn't have to."

Kester cocked her head. "I know I didn't have to. I wanted to. Maybe there will be something you can do for me in return sometime."

"Anything, just say it, Kester."

"Someone's coming. Remember, let me do the talking."

An older man in a UD corrections uniform strode across the wet grass. He periodically glanced to either side. *He probably thinks it's a trap.* He approached the two women. Thin whips of gray hair hung beneath his cap. His face was frosted with two-day whiskers.

He cleared his throat. "I was told you would provide documentation."

Kester reached into the inside pocket of her fur-lined overcoat. She produced a document bearing the Imperial seal. Philippa gaped at it.

The officer read the letter. He looked up and scowled. "She must be special. This is, shall we say, highly unusual."

Kester snatched it back. "Swallow it. This comes from above Sware."

"I see. New regime, new rules. I can adapt." The man rubbed his hands. "Maybe something for goodwill, eh? Perhaps a few rubles. There will be questions."

Kester stared him down. "You have your orders. Take us to the prisoner."

The man shrugged. The two women followed him around the perimeter of the prison. He opened the gate with a key and proceeded towards a heavy door. Once inside, the three slipped down a dimly lit hallway. *He's trying to avoid any contact.* At a juncture, they descended a stairway and into a new hallway, this one lined with cells. The walls were painted a deep crimson. The air carried a tang of mold. Water pooled in the low places in the concrete.

Philippa glanced in the cells as they passed. The early hour meant most of the inmates were asleep on worn mattresses scattered across the floor.

The man pointed ahead. "Here it is. Number 29."

Philippa dashed ahead; she could feel Astrid's body in her arms. Her eyes welled up. *At last!*

"Open it!" she cried.

The man fumbled for the key. Philippa peered through the

window.

Her heart froze. *I'll never breathe again.* She beat her fist on the door.

The cell was empty.

22

– Astrid – February 15, 2079

Another train, this time to Washington. For weeks, she and Zhen Fang had been shuttled among different transit prisons. This time they were crowded into a box car with unfortunates from parts of the Empire and the former District. Astrid huddled on the dirty floor in the orange coverall they'd made her change into. A small window allowed a shaft of white light to fall across the prisoners on the other end. Astrid focused on the contrast. *The eye is drawn to what the light reveals.* She concentrated. *I will capture this image. If I get out of here I will one day I will render it. I was here.*

Zhen slept propped against a wall. Her deadly presence enveloped Astrid. *Don't speak. Don't say a word. Remember what happened to the other girl.* Astrid never saw what happened to the body. Everywhere they were transported, January Chen was the name on the manifest.

Her stomach gnawed at her insides. The train had stopped maybe four hours ago. From time to time, she'd stand and stretch, but there was little room to move about.

Why did I ever leave? A baby, that's why. Just because Philippa can't bear children, why shouldn't I? Abandoned before she was one. She never knew her parents. But why couldn't she see that was what I wanted more than anything. It was always there between us, waiting like a coiled snake ready to poison our relationship. The world is terrifying, I get it. There's a million reasons never to bring a new life into this chaos. But she needs to know that a baby, any baby, means hope.

The light through the window dimmed, maybe a cloud crossing the sun. Astrid shuddered. *I probably won't ever see her again.*

A young black girl in a Fang uniform whispered nearby, "I'm from east of Binghamton. We were routed by Caggiano forces backed by Dirae. I tell you, *they were diabolical.* The Dirae commander crucified our squad leader. We stood for twelve hours at gunpoint, watching. I wake up hearing the screams. They rounded up the boys and took them from their mothers."

A red-haired soldier clenched her fist. "We were stationed in Oneonta. Part of the Fifth Division. Sachs came at us from the north. We tried to link up with the Second in Jefferson but were cut off by Imperial troops from the south. Lost a lot of sisters in arms. Good women. Tight on their mission, you know. May the Goddess of the Fallen keep them.

"Guards say Queen Fang is dead. Caggiano, Sachs and the Sisters carved up her land."

The black girl rubbed her forehead. "I heard the same. What do you think they're going to do with us?"

The redhead let out a weary chuckle. "Target practice for the Dirae? No, too easy. Labor camp probably. Railroad chain gang. I heard stories about the creosote factories. It gets in your skin, your lungs. A death sentence carried out over five months. Doesn't matter, we're fucked any which way."

"I'm Douglas." She held out her fist. "Good to know you. Let's stay alive. Look out for each other while we can. Remember the Legion."

The redhead bumped. "Harriman. The Legion...forever."

Clanking outside. The sliding door screeched open. Light flooded the compartment. Astrid rubbed her eyes. Zhen Fang stirred. "What's going on?"

"Up, everyone. Now!" came the orders.

Fang grabbed Astrid's arm. "Stay close," she hissed.

At the threshold of the car, a guard locked a shackle onto each of the prisoner's right ankles, securing them to each other. The metal bit through the jumpsuit. Lines of ten made their way across the platform. Fang walked close behind Astrid. They crossed the main hall of Union Station. Armed sentries oversaw their painful progress.

They shuffled through the main hall. Diffused light streamed through the arched windows. The plaster on the coffered ceiling had broken away in places. The gold leaf stripped. Enormous Trutneva banners hung on the walls. Travelers stared at the procession.

Outside, a row of cages on flatbeds waited. The prisoners were herded onto the trucks. A barrel of water from which the prisoners could drink stood next to each flatbed. Soldiers handed each of the prisoners an apple, a stretch of smoked venison and a slab of bread.

Unlike the boxcars, there was no room to sit. Astrid and Fang stood pressed against the chain links. Astrid tore into her food before Fang could take it.

She wrapped her arms around herself. *Could be a lot worse. This is still February.* She couldn't see the two Fang soldiers she had heard in the boxcar, but there were dozens of other women in Fang uniforms crowded into the cages, dirty, exhausted, and sullen. Captured U.D. soldiers too were among the prisoners. *What will happen to all of us?*

After about an hour, the diesel engines of the trucks fired up. Blasts of burned-grease odor belched out of the exhaust. Astrid steadied herself as the truck lurched forward. They drove northwest on Massachusetts Ave, then west on H St. and finally south on 17th. They passed the ruins of the White House and the former Ellipse, now planted with gardens. The trucks stopped next to the Tidal Basin and idled.

Astrid craned her neck to see ahead, but the chain link of the cage and the crowd of prisoners prevented her. She stared instead at the light glistening on the water of the Basin, each flash a hint of transcendence, all coming so fast. The lovely cherry blossoms swirled and danced to her left like pink ashes.

Other trucks passed theirs. Military music sounded nearby. Finally, their truck plodded forward down Independence. Mounted police rode next to the convoy. Crowds pressed up against the barricades. The fury on their faces assailed the prisoners.

"Die, you scum!"

"Dirty traitors."

"You'll get what you deserve!"

"Long live Queen Sware!"

Astrid recoiled, but there was no room to retreat. A rock crashed against the cage, then a bottle. She squeezed her eyes shut. Blood pounded in her ears.

Guards rushed in to quiet the crowd. Astrid reopened her eyes. The truck lumbered on. Bleachers rose along the side of the road. Here, the crowds merely watched the parade. No shouting or violence. Astrid breathed deeply, trying to slow her heart. The crowd's silence was in some way more terrifying. Their faces betrayed the calm admission that she would be found guilty. An indisputable fact. *I will die here. Truth is nowhere to be found, and whoever shuns evil becomes a prey.*

The Trutneva box towered over the others. Adorned in ultramarine and gold. The twins sat on their thrones, icy and radiant. Hope fought against Astrid's growing sense of despair. *They must still know mercy.*

Astrid clenched the links. "Eternal Sisters! Queens of Justice! I appeal to you!"

Fang squeezed her arm. "Shut the fuck up!"

Other prisoners chimed in. "Yeah, me too!"

"We're all innocent."

Astrid shouted over the din. "Spare me, please!"

A disturbance broke out in the stands. *Someone's coming!*

"Astrid! ASTRID!"

Philippa!

She shook the cage. "Help me! Philippa!"

A swarm of guards dragged Philippa to the ground, choking her. Astrid screamed, eyes wide, finally collapsing to her knees.

The truck rolled on. A new piece of martial music struck up. *Like it never happened. Oh God, Philippa! What have I done?*

Fang pulled her to her feet. "Who was that?"

"That's my...my...wyve, Philippa. She saw me."

Fang clenched her arm. "She's RSC? Does she have influence?"

Astrid winced. "She's a captain."

Fang released her. "Pity. They're disposable. Captains follow orders. They don't make strategy." She tossed her long black hair and stared back at the Trutneva box. "My mother was a brilliant strategist. For my own safety, she did not share any details. That's probably why I'm alive. But knowing her, the plan was flawless. Cursed luck. The Trutnevas should be dead. We should have escaped, but that giant, ugly bitch from the House Guard found out. Somehow. She was there in the basement. She was there when they tortured us one by one. The waiting and watching was almost worse. I witnessed them use a hammer to mutilate the hands of one of our most fierce officers. She had taught me to fight when I was younger."

Her face set, she turned to Astrid. The military march still drifted from behind. "But deep down, where you don't want to look, you're glad. It's sick, but you're glad it's not you. And you hate that you know that about yourself."

Astrid reached out. "I'm...I'm sorry."

Fang glared at her. "Keep your mouth shut next time. We don't need that kind of attention."

Astrid nodded, mutely. *We?*

* * *

The truck pulled up in front of a massive, brutal affront of a building. The grimy beige-rose cement walls crumbled in parts. Even with the missing letters on the sign, the purpose was unmistakable.

Department of Corrections

Central Detention Facility

Astrid swallowed, her throat arid. Her sweat-soaked coveralls clung to her. *Just some water. Maybe once we're inside.* The heat, the standing, and the press of the other prisoners' bodies created a suffocating atmosphere where tempers boiled over. Arriving at the prison unleashed a storm of pent-up fear and anger. Fang soldiers scuffled with UD soldiers. Astrid recoiled from the factions. *Why make this any more miserable?*

A tall UD soldier stroked Zhen's hair. "Maybe I'll see you on the inside, little one. You look like you might need protection."

Zhen clenched her fist but kept silent.

A half dozen Imperial guards arrived. They beat the chain link with their truncheons.

"Shut up all of you. Keep it up and you'll find yourself in the hole."

The prisoners quieted down.

Astrid and Fang remained chained to eight other prisoners. One by one, they dismounted the flatbed and staggered into the detention center.

Two guards flanked the group. They reached a row of cells. A blunt-faced commander stood with a clipboard. She pointed at Astrid and Zhen, "Keep going with these two. Only space left is on C Block."

"A'ight."

One of the guards replaced their ten-person chain with a shorter length for two people, cuffing Astrid's right ankle to Zhen's left. Astrid shuffled alongside Zhen, the manacles forcing them to walk in rhythm.

They limped into the lower depths of the prison. The air was dank and cool, causing Astrid to shiver in her damp coverall. They reached a block of cells.

Suddenly, Zhen shoved her against the wall. Astrid's right leg stayed pinned by the cuff, tripping her. Her head knocked against the concrete block. A flash of crimson clouded her vision momentarily. Sounds came as if through wet wool.

The guards stopped short, confused.

In that faintest moment, Zhen Fang struck.

She spun on the manacled foot and delivered a roundhouse kick to the first guard's head. The woman crumpled on the floor. The second guard swung her baton, free hand fumbling with her holster. Zhen dodged the blow, sliding back.

Astrid slid down, pulled by Fang's maneuvers. Her knee cracked against the floor. She cried out.

The guard locked eyes with Fang.

Fang smiled.

The guard's hand shook. Her sidearm wasn't coming free. She pulled her gaze to the holster.

Zhen pivoted again on her bound foot, this time with a stabbing kick to the solar plexus. The blood drained out of the guard's face. She doubled over, gasping and clawing at the air. She wobbled for a step, then fell to her knees.

Zhen straddled the guard and encircled her head in her hands. Fang jerked and a with a hollow crunch, the guard collapsed, lifeless.

Astrid shrank into the wall, eyes wide, unable to tear her gaze from the slaughter. She pressed her hands to her mouth to stifle her overwhelming instinct to scream.

Fang crouched and sifted through the pockets, soon finding the key. She uncuffed herself and tossed it to Astrid. "Hurry."

Astrid fumbled the key into the lock. "We'll get caught. They'll kill us."

Fang growled, "I will say this once. We just need to get out of the building. Away from the people who can identify us. Once we're out, we're safe. Zhen Fang is dead. January Chen is a nobody. When a system of control is so pervasive, no one looks past the obvious. Someone in a guard uniform is a guard.

No questions asked. I've seen first-hand how they implement these systems. I know how to slip through the cracks. To them, it is unthinkable that escapees would be on the loose. In two hours, we'll be listed as dead. No one in authority is going to admit to the mistake. They would be executed. It's a system built on fear. You just need to know whose fear to manipulate.

"Now move. Put on that uniform."

If I stay they'll hang me for the two dead guards.

Astrid's head throbbed. Her knee stung. The surreal scene of the two dead bodies lying in the fetid corridor kept drawing her gaze. The unnatural positions. The bright color of the blood. The blank faces. It was more like a painting than reality, but the stink and the sounds (gone now, echoing in her mind) were more real than anything had ever been. She followed Fang's instructions like a sleepwalker. She pulled off the trousers, revealing torn pale blue cotton print panties underneath. *Would she have chosen them if she knew she was going to die?*

The uniform was a bit too large. Fang studied Astrid, reached over and straightened her belt. "Going back may be dangerous. Better to press forward, find another way out."

Astrid nodded.

They worked their way to an exit. They passed several guards along the way, but none stopped them.

Outside the afternoon was fading. Clouds obscured the sun and the temperature had fallen twenty degrees. They slipped into the derelict neighborhood. Row houses leaned against each other, verging on collapse. Rats scurried across the street.

"What do we do now?" Astrid stammered. "Do we split up? Maybe I can find Philippa if she's still here."

Fang stared straight ahead. It was a question asked by a fool.

"You're in Trutneva occupied territory. You won't last a day out there."

23

– Astrid – February 16, 2079

Astrid could tell they were traveling vaguely north. They'd woven through the derelict neighborhoods of eastern Washington. One of the guards had stowed a little money—mixture of rubles and libra—in the pocket of her uniform. With it, they purchased food and matches. At a charity thrift store that sold clothing, they bought worn coats and hats. After that, there was nothing left.

Fang stuffed her hands in her pockets—the temperature now below freezing. "Can you handle a gun?" Fang carried the two ancient Glock 9MMs issued to the guards.

Astrid shook her head. "No...I don't know."

Fang scowled. "You had some training, right? Mandatory military service? You can't be totally useless? What do you do?"

"I paint. An artist."

Astrid expected another stinging remark reminding her how ill-suited she was for their situation. *We are escaped prisoners in enemy territory. We have no money, food, or communication. All the world thinks we're dead. I'm dragged along behind a revenge-*

bent psychopath with three corpses chalked up so far. Who the fuck prepares for this?

Fang's face softened. "Who do you like?"

Astrid started. "What?"

"I said, who do you like? What artists? In Norwich, my mother collected many artists for the museum. All periods: Picasso, Rothko, Goya, Jasper Johns, De Kooning, Borremans, Vermeer were some of them. All these priceless works that once sold for millions were all but forgotten. I spent hours there sketching until I was sent to live with the Trutnevas when I was fifteen. Art is a noble pursuit."

Couldn't have seen that coming. Astrid knew some of the names, had seen pictures in the library. She had visited the National Galleries in the District and filled herself with their collections. The fact they still existed was a miracle. She'd heard stories about how the conservators had barricaded the museums during the violent times. There had been an oversized book about Hopper in their Richmond apartment. She would pore over it, sometimes with Philippa's head resting on her shoulder. Philippa liked that one the most, said she recognized the light and the people, their solitude. Philippa knew little about art, but was always so eager to listen. *She never wanted to burden me with the tragic scenes she'd witnessed as a soldier, her understanding that the cruel often won. I was a fool to leave.* Astrid huddled into her coat. "Why were you sent away?"

"Part of the Treaty my mother signed. All of the Reginae are required to send their first-born daughter to the Sisters. The Trutnevas look at it as insurance. Their Queens will comply better if there's a hostage. Don't get me wrong, it's nothing like prison. You have money, servants, you can go to parties, wherever. They treat you with respect. You just can't ever leave the Empire."

Astrid sniffed. "Your mother paid a very dear price."

Fang bristled. "My mother knew what she was doing. She had calculated the odds, knew I would be safe. She understood where the Trutnevas were weak. I learned everything I could about their system and secretly shared it with her. My mother was not like the Sisters. Of course, she submitted to their Protsent—there was no choice. She played their game until she saw her opportunity. She wanted a better tomorrow for all women. She paid for her ambition with her life. Now, our land has been stripped away. Our soldiers have been condemned. I am the only one left *and I will avenge them all.*"

Astrid shuddered.

They stood in front of a row of squat brick houses. Behind them, the former National Arboretum sprawled. The fence that once surrounded it collapsed in sections, the trees reclaiming their land.

Zhen approached the first house. The door opened without effort. Inside, graffiti covered the walls. The staircase sagged. The hardwood floors buckled. In the kitchen, the cabinets half hung, many of the doors missing. In the drawers, old silverware rested. Fang took one of the blunt table knives and used it to pry off some of the trim molding. She handed it to Astrid. "See if you can get a fire started."

Astrid snapped the wood into smaller pieces. The fireplace in the living room housed a congealed mix of soot and ash. She reached up into the chimney and opened the damper. She lit one of the molding shards, pointing it down, giving the fire something to feed on. Placing it in the hollow, she added more pieces. Fang appeared with other scraps. She kicked several of the spindles off the staircase. Before long, the fire grew into itself, casting flickering shadows around the decaying room.

Astrid rolled her guard uniform jacket into a pillow, draping herself with the old woolen overcoat. She pulled her legs in. *I've never been so tired.* Fang did the same, lying just behind her. Sleep overcame her.

Hours later, Astrid's eyes flew open. The fire barely flickered, its warmth stolen. *Her hand is under my coat.* Fang's hand brushed the button of her pants.

Every muscle tensed. Fang stopped. Neither moved. Astrid squeezed her eyes closed again, her heart pounding. *She knows I'm awake. If I resist, she might kill me.* Her thoughts softened. *Still, if it weren't for her, I'd be in jail or worse.*

Astrid could feel Fang's breath on her cheek, pictured her hovering above her with that murderous sneer on her face—the same one she wore when she snapped the guard's neck. After a minute, Fang delicately removed her hand.

She whispered in Astrid's ear, "Suit yourself." Behind her, Astrid could tell Fang had rolled over. Towards dawn, Astrid finally drifted off, assailed by unquiet dreams.

* * *

Not far from the house, a truck repair depot of the former UD stood vacant. Fang and Astrid circled the building, choosing a remote corner to break in. Fang wrapped her hand in her hat and punched the window. Glass tinkled on the concrete inside. She unlocked the door and the two women entered.

The cavernous building held several vehicles in various states of disrepair. Astrid and Fang inspected each, settling on one that appeared to be intact. Astrid found a charging cable and clamped it to the battery terminals. Fang turned the key. After several attempts, the engine turned over.

Astrid poked her head in. "Not much gas."

"It will have to do," Fang growled.

Neither woman spoke of the night before. Fang appeared more on edge, volatile, but Astrid couldn't be certain she wasn't imagining that. For Astrid, the event triggered a series of speculations she hadn't time to construct. *Where are we going? What does she want with me after all? How can I get away? She's right that I wouldn't last a day on my own. For now, she's the lesser evil, but where does it end? Does it end?*

Temperatures hovered slightly above freezing. They drove along Route 1 towards Baltimore. Light sleet *tap-tap-tapped* on the roof. They'd barely made it past Savage when a terrible grinding sound ripped out from the engine. The truck lurched, stopping, then jerking forward. Smoke rose from under the hood. Fang navigated the vehicle to the side of the road.

They popped the hood—a gust of smoke forced them back a step. They huddled over the engine.

"Do you know anything about cars?" Fang asked.

"No," Astrid mumbled. *Useless again.*

"Hnh," Fang grunted, stuffing her hands in her pockets. "Our best option is to press forward and see if we can find another ride."

Astrid nodded. *What else was there to do?*

The sleet stung Astrid's face. She pulled her hat lower. In the distance, travelling from the south, a large truck rumbled towards them.

Astrid drew close. "Should we run?"

Fang pulled her hat lower. "Too late, they've probably seen us. Just keep walking."

The truck slowed. Astrid could make out the markings of the former UD, blacked through and the Tenora seal stenciled on the door to the cab. A soldier leaned out the passenger side. "Hey, where are you going? You need a lift?"

Fang waved her hand. "We're good."

"Is that your truck?" the soldier asked.

Fang continued walking. "Yeah, piece of shit broke down again." She slipped her hands out of her pockets.

The truck rolled to a stop. "We can take you to Elkridge. Get in."

Astrid eyed Fang. Fang's head hung low against the sleet. *We'll look suspicious if we refuse.*

Fang approached the window. "Where are you going?"

"Baltimore, then on to Elkton. We're linking up with the rest of our unit. Get in back." *Baltimore. Where my nightmare began.*

A canopy covered the bed of the truck. Inside, two rows of Tenora soldiers hunched over their rifles facing each other. Casual nods as they slid together to make room. Fang hoisted herself up. Astrid followed.

"Thanks," Astrid offered the group.

"What's the news?" Fang asked.

A young soldier, acne scars on her face, replied, "We just do what we're told. Sware's calling the shots. Can't be any worse than the other one, Evermore. The eastern shore is where we're headed. Renegade troops are dug in there. Defectors. Still loyal to yesterday. We're gonna show them the new reality."

Astrid rubbed her hands together. "Did any of you serve with them?" *Philippa couldn't have done this. Couldn't kill her own soldiers. The RSC was her life.*

"Yeah, I knew some of the traitors, but it doesn't matter now. You gotta fall in line."

Another one chimed in, "I heard this area isn't even secure, so why we're going there instead of locking this sector down? Makes no sense. Fuckin' Sware and her new generals kissing Imperial ass."

"Fuckin' A."

The sleet hissed against the canopy. The soldiers grew animated—maybe having a new audience amped them up. They argued about Sware seizing power and what it meant for them.

"It's gonna be the same shit."

"The Trutnevas are a pair of witches. Sware's just their dick. Sometimes, I think the deserters made the right choice. Shit's not gonna be the same. Gonna get a lot worse."

"Shut up, don't let the captain hear you. They'll throw you in the brig."

"Or worse!"

Their voices trampled on each other, each trying to rise to the top.

The sergeant—tucked in at the front—finally weighed in. "Enough. Now all of you shut your mouths and settle—"

For a fragment of a second, silence—all the air in the world sucked out. In the vacuum, a terrible precipice revealed.

WWWHHHOOOOOOMMMMMMMM

The explosion stopped the massive truck dead. It ratcheted, the bed rising up, above the cab. Shrapnel from the cab ripped through the first rows of soldiers. Astrid flew, weightless, out of the back. Everything slowed. She witnessed the burning cab twist off, the bed finally crashing on its side. *Oh God, Zhen.*

Astrid slammed down onto the shoulder of the road, inches

from a tree that would have decapitated her. She rolled several feet into the grass, sliding on the frozen sleet.

Panting, she pulled herself up. The scene shifted in and out of focus. Flames covered the canopy. She fell back on one knee. On her periphery, shapes bobbed in and out. She staggered up, weaving towards the burning truck. *Let her die. Just let her die.*

"No!" she grunted.

Her ears rang. Sounds didn't sync with her vision, following too late. The heat pushed her back from yards away. Astrid pulled her coat over her head. Acrid smoke swallowed the truck. Astrid lurched towards the rear, fortunately not yet burning. Zhen Fang lay broken on the canopy. She hoisted the legs of one of the soldiers off Fang, wrapped her arms under Fang's armpits and pulled her from the truck. One of Fang's legs bent unnaturally. Shuffling backwards, Astrid dragged her clear of the fire.

Movement from the shoulder. A squad of soldiers, clad in camouflage, revealed themselves. Their faces indistinguishable behind grease paint. They approached slowly, leaning into their raised assault rifles.

One of them yelled, "Hands! Fucking show 'em!"

Astrid dropped to her knees, hands stretched to the iron sky. She clamped her eyes shut. *Mother, please don't shoot!*

The closest of the squad closed on her, never dropping her aim. Astrid's heart thundered, the blood pulsing her vision. Sound still came as if from beneath deep water. Astrid squinted, studying the soldier. Her insignia was United District. Astrid knew from the stripes the woman was a sergeant. She read the breast patch: Borquez.

24

– Moncure – February 2079

Reed Moncure patted his brow with his monogrammed white cotton handkerchief. The sun high, the sky dusted with clouds. Patches of bluets grew through cracks in the sidewalk. Cracks that would only grow as the city inevitably surrendered back to nature. Distant hammering on the anvil inside his skull, getting stronger. Hearing a noise, his head snapped around, eyes wide. *Just a door opening.* The 2001 Vacheron Constantin read 1:45 PM. He would get the supplies and go home. Home was safe. Ellen would help with the long day. He shouldn't have left. His sweat-soaked shirt clung to his chest. He tugged at his collar, sight blurred.

Retired from the army for over a decade, Moncure had spent the years restoring a small estate ten miles out of town that had been abandoned. The county sold it to him for the promise to pay the taxes. One of the outbuildings he converted to a woodshop to recraft the elegant moldings that had been destroyed. The long porch spanning the back of the house looked west across the fields. After he'd rebuilt it, he never missed an opportunity to sit—bourbon in hand—and watch the sun drift lower across the horizon.

The pale winter sun bleached the streetscape. The Mutual Credit Association building stood on the corner, towering granite columns. Engraved in the block on the corner: Farmers and Merchants Bank 1897. *Men built that.* The brightly colored sign in the window read: Sisters! Talk to us about starting a business. Farm loans. Savings yield 2.25 APY. *Oh, how we've been forgotten.*

He'd been gone too long. He wasn't where he was *supposed* to be—the guilty dissonance colored his thoughts. His wife, Ellen, needed the blood pressure medicine. 158 over 80. They needed feed for the horses, jatropha bio for the tractor. Something else? His hands trembled as he patted his pockets for the list. *Never enough time.*

Clang, clang, *clang.* The hammering continued—a white-hot blade being forged. A vein on the side of his head throbbed in time. Passing the shop window, his half-dead face stared back at him. Bulging eye and swollen tongue. Cracked lips. He rubbed his stubbled chin. The Smyth was coming – always at this time of day. The Smyth would crush his bones and swallow him whole.

Seventy-five degrees in February. *Feels like 90. How did I get on Meeting Street?* He grasped his knees and bent over, panting. Standing up, he wiped his brow again. In the doorway of a vacant building, someone had built a shrine to The Shipwrecked Goddess. A little girl's dress covered with bleached sand dollars had been laid across the step. Next to an extinguished candle, a jar of salt stood nearby for worshippers to sprinkle for protection. The Shipwrecked Goddess was one of the many new religions that multiplied during the superstitious frenzy in the years following the onset of the mutation.

The sea wall loomed to the south and east, keeping the city safe. Beloved Charleston pulling in, gathering close. *Jesus, I gotta piss again.* A woman crossed the street ahead of him, one of the blue-eyed miscarriages in tow. The cloudy luminescence like Cherenkov radiation. They were prodigium—the sign of what's to come. *We were once kings, now we are fools. They shouldn't even be called men.*

In the early years, scientists worked to understand their condition. They still had computers to run simulations and databases of proteins and genomes at their fingertips. The economic collapse that began in 2020 eventually took the arrays of servers offline. All the infrastructure built over the previous half-century couldn't be maintained. Computing power become localized. The global networks fractured and quietly disappeared, taking exabytes of recorded knowledge. Books, music, photos, video, all vanished. This was the beginning of The Forgetting.

Developmentally diminished and blind, the boys grew. They acquired language skills but couldn't employ them rationally. Nonsense songs that contained inexplicable, sometimes chilling, bits of insight. Two decades later, nature revealed a new mystery as the blue-eyed adolescents began dying off. Twenty-year lifespans. *Was their only purpose to confound us?*

Where did I leave the truck?

Ellen would be worried if he didn't return soon. He had one duty—get the medicine and go home. Home was safe. '*No place is safe. You know what you need,*' the Smyth roared. '*Escape lies in your prison.*'

Clang, clang, clang. Moncure shook his head. *No, please.*

He walked another block. The pharmacy was not too far ahead. Across the street, a sign for a pub, Cassandra's Gift. The red door freshly painted. *No, the women found a purpose.*

Moncure licked his cracked lips. *Just for a minute.*

Inside, cool dimness welcomed him. Dust swirled in the diffused light through the blinds. Stamped tin roof and wooden floor. Ceiling fans barely turned. The girl behind the bar looked up from the tap she was changing. Exotic features, caramel skin. Hair pinned up in braids. She smiled.

Moncure lurched. "Bathroom?"

She pointed.

Moncure stumbled down the hall, stood over the toilet. *Oh Christ, it burns.* Panting, he zipped his fly. *Andrology. Nobody gives a damn anymore about the diseases of old men. And they blame us, don't they? Saying we held the power, made the decisions. Who did? It was over long before I was born.*

Striding back into the bar, he stared between the bartender and the door. The medicine. Ellen.

Clang, clang, clang. 'Ellen can wait,' the Smyth howled.

Moncure sidled up to the bar, eyes still on the door. He pressed his knuckles to his lips. "Double bourbon, straight. Asheville Creek if you have it."

The bartender sized him up. "Right away."

Moncure sipped. Sweet fire flooded through him, promising the hope of salvation. *Burned clean.* He closed his eyes. The hammering quieted, his breathing slowed. *Spared the Smyth. Safe again.* Opening them again, he noted there were only a couple other people in the bar at this hour. The walls adorned with pre-Forgetting objects. Pennants from sports teams, and old flight board showing departures and destinations. Distant, unreachable places.

"W-what's your name?" Moncure stammered.

The girl looked over her shoulder. "Indira."

"Very pretty...beautiful." Moncure cleared his throat. "I was a general, you know. Broke the Siege of Atlanta. Before it all went to hell."

The girl's eyes widened. "I'll bet you were brilliant."

"Those bastards never saw it coming." Moncure drained the glass. "Saved the city. Young women—your age, kids. Think they put up a statue—just a small one. I...I never saw it. Took shrapnel in my shoulder from a mortar. Laid up in the hospital." He held the glass up. "Another?" Moncure watched her pour. Slender hips, the curve of her breasts under the work shirt. Cigarette smell on her clothes and hair.

She returned, brushing his hand after setting the drink down. "Right, here you go."

Ellen turned cold years ago. Moncure fumbled for his wallet, laid a ten libra note on the bar. "Here, keep it."

She tilted her head, eyes soft and inviting. "Brave and generous too," she purred.

Moncure smiled back. Warm goodwill filled his heart, radiating out, connecting him with what he sensed to be a deep and elusive truth. A truth for him to discover. A buoyant magnanimity that he only wanted to share. *This is how we're supposed to be. Ellen never wants me to be happy.* He raised his glass to the middle-aged women across the room.

Grinning, "Here's to you."

They toasted him back.

Indira leaned over the bar. "Tell me about yourself."

Moncure sighed. Where to start and once he got going, how to end?

"I was born in 2022—the last year for men. Graduated The

Citadel in '43. Earned my commission. Three-quarters of the class were women. First rate soldiers. Give my life for any of them. The Piedmont Republic Alliance was ten years old. Nobody knew if it would hold. We fought in Alabama, two years against that psychopath 'King' Blanchard. Fucking gray and desolate land."

Moncure leaned closer. "In '58 I parted with the Corps and headed west to Louisiana. Me and a few other ex-soldiers had an inspired idea to lead a force and capture some of the gas fields. Made it as far as New Orleans."

Indira tilted her head. "I've never been there. They say the city is underwater."

Moncure took a sip and wiped his mouth with his sleeve. He slid another ten libra note across. "Yea, I saw it. The Cat 6 hurricane chewed up the whole coast. There wasn't anything left. The inhabitants had gone feral, guiding their small boats through the ruins. Practicing dark magic meant to protect them from some terror beyond the stars." *Cloaked in the Voudon raiment that had always been New Orleans. What a place it must have been, a century ago.*

People straggled into the bar. The afternoon sun lighting up the room each time the door opened, each time spiking a pang of guilt. *Ellen is probably worried.* But he couldn't pull himself free. Moncure drank and poured out his heart until Indira placed her hand on his arm. "Hold that thought, love. I need to check on the other guests."

He followed her with his eyes. Shapely legs. *With her, maybe I could get it right.* He looked at his watch: 4:30. He glanced at the door, cold sweat beading on his forehead. *The medicine. Ellen.* His warm feeling had stretched thin, his noble sentiment turned false.

Indira bounced back, smiling. "Now, what were you saying? You were a captain?"

What could she ever want with you? Such a stupid, easy mark. Moncure's eyes glistened. Melancholy settled in—the understanding he was seeing the light from a star that had died millions of years before.

25

– Moncure – February 2079

Secretary of Defense Nguyen flipped through the reports on her lap. The pages were spread out across the back seat of their civilian sedan. "He's a blackout drunk, Karyn. They pulled his commission in 2058. High crimes. It's all right here."

Poole sighed. They'd been driving for hours, stopping only once to fill up with biodiesel. "He is a drunk, but he's a brilliant strategist. One of the few with serious combat experience. Face it, most of our forces are peacekeepers. Moncure's been waging war most of his life. He didn't commit any crimes. I was there. He just didn't fit the mold. He had no place in the future."

Neither Poole nor Nguyen were in uniform. A low profile was needed while they slipped into Charleston.

Nguyen crossed her arms. Her jet-black hair hung in a page cut, accentuating her sharp features. "I don't like it. We've got good women. Leaders. They've been training for years for this. Our troops will never follow someone like him. I don't know why I let you talk me into this, Karyn. We need every hour to prepare our defenses."

Poole shifted in her seat. "I'm right with you, Trinh. I know you are indulging this wild idea and I'm grateful. Either he sobers up or he's out. Moncure *needs* this. And we may need Moncure."

"I'll believe it when I see it."

Nguyen turned, looking out the window. The cleared fields rolled past. Occasionally, the burned or rusted carcass of an automobile spotted the landscape. "And moreover, he's sick."

Poole straightened up. "Sick?"

Nguyen didn't turn. "Heart and prostate. Both enlarged. Alcoholic cardiomyopathy. I pulled his medical records from Carolina Health."

Poole shook her head. "I didn't know."

"I didn't either till just now." She handed Poole the report. "Does this change your mind?"

"It's worse than I thought, but no."

* * *

Moncure's house stood a couple miles outside of the city, a whitewashed brick Georgian revival. Columns spanned the front, supporting the balcony. Behind the house, a glimpse of the pastures and barn.

The two women strode up the flagstone walkway and knocked on the door. A tiny woman answered. Gray hair parted on the side, large brown eyes. She wore a plain skirt and pressed canary yellow blouse buttoned to the top.

Poole cleared her throat. "Afternoon, ma'am. We're here to see Reed. Is he here?"

The tiny woman leaned in. "He's sleeping."

At 2:40 in the afternoon. "We've traveled from Charlotte. Would it be okay if we waited?"

The woman smiled, nodding. "Yes, come in. I'll wake him."

The two generals entered. The tiny woman escorted them to the living room immediately to the left of the door. Inside, paneled, floor-to-ceiling shelves covered three of the walls. The head of a sixteen-point buck stared down from over the fireplace. The rug was old, dark, the color of dried blood, bleached bones and storm clouds. *Probably not what they thought when they bought it. I'm tired of death already, even though it's just begun.*

"Thank you, ma'am." They spoke in unison.

Poole studied a glass cabinet. Inside Moncure's pistols hung: Civil War Colt 1860, Browning 1911, 9MM Luger, Beretta. All perfectly preserved. *Just like new. Maybe he's not tired of it yet. Maybe that's men's secret.*

No. She knew him.

She heard his voice yelling from upstairs, "Who the hell is here? I don't want to see anyone. Only bad news knocks at that door. Nothing but saleswomen, evangelists and beggars. We've gone over this *a hundred times!*"

The tiny woman's voice, pleading. "I don't know. They're waiting in the den."

The man's voice roared, "Waiting! *You let them in?*"

"Please don't be mad, Reed. I..."

Poole stormed to the bottom of the stairs and barked, "Reed Moncure, have you completely lost your senses? Show some respect, soldier."

Reed appeared at the top. Barefoot. Striped shirt draped over a white tee. Unbuttoned olive khakis frayed at the cuffs. His face apoplectic. "Son of a bitch comes into my home...Karyn?

Is that you? Ah, Christ, I had no idea. Give me a minute, I'll be right down."

Poole pursed her lips and returned to the den.

Nguyen sighed. "Certainly knows how to make a girl feel welcome. Honestly, Karyn, the world will be better when they're all gone. We should take that poor wife of his with us."

Poole remained silent. *I wish I were certain of that, Trinh. So far, the results are decidedly unclear.*

A grandfather clock ticked out the moments. The phases of the moon circled the face.

Moncure returned—hair combed, shirt tucked in. The color was down in his face revealing tiny blood vessels lining his cheeks and nose.

"Karyn. My God, what's it been. Twenty-five years?"

He reached up to touch her scar but reflexively pulled his hand back. He averted his eyes to the floor. To Nguyen, "I was there when she received that."

Poole's mouth turned down; her eye glistened. "You pulled that man off me before..."

Moncure interrupted, "Yeah, beat him to death. Stabbed him in the liver with his own knife. Bastard."

Afternoon shadows stretched out on the floor. Pale winter light. Moncure clenched his hands to stop the shaking. *The Smyth will be coming. He will break me on the wheel if I don't obey.*

Poole wrapped her hands around his. "Thank you again."

Moncure shook his head. "Sit, please. May I offer you a drink?"

"No thank you, Reed," Poole said. She waved her hand. "This is Secretary of Defense for Charlotte, Trinh Nguyen."

Moncure nodded. "Honored, ma'am."

Poole continued, "You follow the papers, Reed?"

Moncure's eyes darted between the two women. "Yes, I do. This situation in the north is worse than anything we've seen for years."

Poole leaned forward. "We will be brief. War will be upon us. It's inevitable. The U.D. has fallen. The Trutnevas installed one of their tools to maintain control. They are stronger now than ever. Sware has either turned or purged the U.D.'s officers. Charleston makes excuses. Your city's leadership has failed, leaving the rest of the alliance to face the Sisters.

"We've reinstated your commission. Report to Charlotte Medical for intake. Six weeks, then you'll go to Fort Lee."

Moncure shot glances between the two women. "Six weeks? I'm ready now. I just need a day."

Poole locked eyes with him. "You're going to sober up, Reed. We're not giving you a choice. This is your last chance."

Moncure cocked his head, one eyebrow lifted. "Last chance? Last chance for what?"

"Redemption."

26

Chapter 25 – The Goddess of What was Lost

Illustral, The Goddess of what was Lost. The Goddess emerged from the Forgetting. Like the ancient histories of before the Flood, the Forgetting was a time into which people couldn't look. The digital records of the early twenty-first century had mostly become irretrievable. Traces of humanity only contained in bytes and files permanently destroyed. A devouring void into which all knowledge will one day be consumed. Something lost implies an accidental resolution, a new unwanted reality thrust upon humanity. The aging civilization after the new one was born.

Illustral is said to walk among the people often as an old woman asking questions without answers: "What did your mother tell you in the womb? How do you know what you know?" She cannot remember her name. She is a cautionary tale against the hollow pride of reason. Illustral reminds her believers that both good things and bad are lost in time; therefore, she is also the Goddess of New Beginnings. Believers can be reborn in her. Have faith and forget.

Believers offer sacrifice to relieve the pains of this world. They exchange precious things for the other to "lose" for them. Worshippers pray to the Goddess by selecting a word and repeating it countless times until it has lost its meaning and floats naked as sound. In that moment – if Illustral is willing – the self is lost, and consciousness stretches beyond boundaries.

To honor the Goddess is to care for the senile mother begging in the streets. Shrines to her often include a relic (floppy disks, car stereo, robotic arm) dusted with ash and seed.

27

– Valerie Grayson – Spring '79

War loomed on the horizon. The insidious knowledge of its approach tinged every decision, every choice. Unspoken, like the rasp of the guillotine as the blade is pulled high.

Spring torrents kept the pumps running day and night. Valerie did what she could to keep up with them. She grabbed only a few hours of sleep a night, curled up on the sofa. Her face showed the signs of her efforts: bloodshot eyes, hollow cheeks, streaks of gray hair. *So much to do!* Papers covered Grayson's desk: armament orders, a twenty million libra bond to finance the buildup, intelligence reports, production schedules. Liis Vesik moved a bed in down the hall.

Tenora forces (*the arrogance!*) clashed with resistance fighters from the former United District. The Eastern Shore remained free—for now. Elkton had been the sight of several battles in the last few weeks.

Tidewater frigates fired on and destroyed a section of the old Bay Bridge, shutting down Sware's ability to open a second front. They controlled the entire Chesapeake Bay, delivering supplies daily to St. Michael's. Valerie could celebrate the victories, even allow herself to imagine that the war would pass quickly. But she knew those thoughts were insincere.

The wrath of the Trutnevas had yet to be seen.

Charleston plays its own game with the Sisters. The Treaty is no more. We are witness to the dissolution of everything we've fought for. The prophet Isaiah foretold this. This should be our finest hour, but instead, this day is a day of distress and rebuke and disgrace, as when children come to the moment of birth and there is no strength to deliver them.

Rain lashed the windows.

Tidewater was the smallest of the Piedmont Republics, its standing army a fraction of Charlotte's. The Potomac separated it from Tenora. Sware and the Trutnevas wouldn't attempt a crossing, not when they could easily roll across the border into Richmond. Richmond would bear the full impact when it came.

She picked up the letter from her daughter, Jasmine. Grayson had ordered two divisions of Tidewater regulars to Fredericksburg and all the artillery units. Jasmine's was one of the units. The Rappahannock offered a natural defensive barrier if the attack came from the north.

Dear Mom –

Every bone and muscle hurts. We train eight hours a day. We start with a ruck in the hills or along the river. I'm getting better at keeping up. Lots of alpha girls kicking ass. After the morning march, we work the obstacle course, or climb the ropes. Afternoons are classroom training on equipment (I can't go into details, you know) or arms practice. Sometimes we work on fortifying the defenses. Evenings are supper and another shorter march. Whew!

The waiting is hard. The air is tinged with anticipation and everyone's edgy, but nobody wants it to start. Rumors are that Venoma Choi has crossed through the old District with five divisions and she plans to attack Richmond from the west near Culpeper. Two other Queens have sent their armies too. Charlotte and Raleigh troops are said to be headed there, but I'm not telling you anything you don't already know.

I smile when I think of you with your hands on your hips, asking "What did I get myself into?" I think you're the right woman for the job. Thank you for the care package. My squad loved your peanut cookies.

    I pray to our Mother that I will come home to you.

Love,
    Jasmine

Tears burned in Valerie's eyes. *My baby girl!*

Liis appeared, her hair pulled back, wearing yesterday's clothes. "I've got news from Raleigh. We can expect delivery of the artillery shells by Friday. Our commander will receive them in Fredericksburg."

Valerie, staring out the window, nodded. "Good, very good."

Lightening tore a vein across the sky; thunder crashed. *We are so small. What can we offer?*

Grayson twisted her wedding band. In the harbor, the USS Wisconsin pulled at its moorings. The radar tower had snapped off in some distant time—it dangled across the superstructure.

Rust smeared the hull. The teak of the deck had rotted away in parts. The massive 16-inch Mark 7 turrets stood sentry. Grayson had toured it when it was still an attraction. A weapon of terrible destruction, unmatched by anything in Piedmont or Imperial arsenals. Each of the big guns had a range of twenty-four miles. The shells alone weighed almost a ton.

"Liis, can we do more?"

Liis sighed. "I don't know how, Madam Premier. We've called up every able woman and man. Industrial output is near capacity. Military command is working 24/7. Everybody's running on fumes."

Grayson shook her head. *There must be something more.*

"I want you to reach out to your contacts in Charleston. If their crooked leaders won't join us, maybe there are some strong women—ex-military—who will do the right thing. Mercenaries. We will pay. We will find the money. I want you to select one of your generals to build this new army. And while you're at it, buy all their engineers you can."

Liis frowned. "Ma'am, the cost. We don't have it."

Diffused lightening glowed behind the charcoal storm cloud. A vast, white-hot bolt arced to the to the water.

Grayson sighed. "Consider the cost of failure. Picture everyone you love enslaved by the Trutnevas. We can't afford not to pay."

She pointed at the Wisconsin. "One more thing. What do we need to do to bring her to life?"

Valarie shuddered. The words she heard spoken clearly in her head were like a revelation from the eternal Mother. *We will christen her Solidarity.*

28

– Philippa – February 2079

Astrid lost forever!

Philippa bolted upright in her bed, heart pounding, clutching her chest. She gasped, desperate for air. The clock read 4:11. *She was reaching her hand through the wire!*

Wailing echoed through the room, growing more intense. *Just a siren.* She hugged herself and steadied her breathing.

The shrieking crescendoed, the cry hollow and mournful. *Like the labor pains birthing a stillborn child.*

Finally, the siren cut out. Philippa rolled out of bed and opened the window. Eight stories below, Richmond streets were quiet in the pre-dawn. Days since the summit in the U.D. ground on in a satire of peace—there was no fighting, but the waiting charged the city with unbearable tension.

After returning from the former District, she had been ordered to take a week of medical leave. 'Get your shit together' were Poole's words. She couldn't be at the RSC and she couldn't stand being in their apartment. Everything was a reminder.

Kester had called once since returning. She'd pursued every avenue, but there was no word about Astrid. She'd vanished. Erased. Kester stated flatly, "It doesn't look good."

A pang shot through her abdomen. *Haven't felt one of those for a while.* Philippa clutched her belly, remembering herself thirteen years old, doubled over in the emergency room, holding a towel between her legs to stop the hemorrhaging through her pants. The housemother furious for having to drive her, for wasting a towel. Philippa—pallid and shaking—weakly repeating, "I'm sorry."

The doctors staunched the bleeding and transfused three pints.

"You will never be able to conceive. You shouldn't even try," one of them told her. She'd lived by those words ever since.

Her thoughts drifted to last August, right before she'd pulled her last tour. The summer light, bleaching and hazy, filled the apartment. The windows open, but barely offering relief. Astrid curled up on the couch, crying. Philippa standing by the window, cannabis cigarette in hand, *refusing to cry*. Another fight about a baby, but always the same fight, always circling the dense silence between them. Philippa exhaled, blowing out smoke along with all the unsaid words.

I've got to get out of here.

She threw on her RSC sweats, laced up her trainers and bolted down the stairs. Pounding along the pavement helped her focus. *I need some serious gym time.*

Philippa ran a loop around Church Hill then down alongside the Low Line where the Gaia women lived in the old warehouses without electricity, cultivating their psilocybin mushrooms, seeking other realities according to the cycles of the moon. She'd remembered seeing them sleeping by the river in the summertime, dreadlocked and half-naked, interwoven like cubs. She finished at the RSC fitness facility. Inside, she popped off thirty pull-ups, fifty crunches, and a circuit of free weights.

All ranks filled the gym, lifting, sparring, climbing ropes. In a side room, a yoga class stretched. Alone, across the floor, Sergeant Johnson, her spun-chocolate hair pulled back, executed a series of one-armed pushups, bouncing between hands every tenth. After forty, she changed up to burpees. Her cropped t-shirt revealed her chiseled abdominals. Philippa approached. *I've seen a lot of fit women, but she's in another class.*

Philippa approached. "Hey."

Johnson leaped up and saluted.

Philippa returned the salute. "At ease."

Johnson relaxed slightly.

"What's the word, Sergeant?"

Johnson rolled her shoulders. "I put in for a transfer. It's an honor serving the General and all, but with the war coming, I want to be in the action."

Philippa cocked her head. "How did the General respond?"

Johnson nodded. "She understands and agrees that I'm more valuable in the field."

"The General recognizes skills. She regards you highly as a soldier."

"Thank you, ma'am."

Philippa smiled. "Any soldier serving under you is in good hands. I pity the Trutnevas."

Johnson grinned. "Yes, ma'am."

* * *

Reagan Patel, lead scientist, wearing low heels under her white coat, led Philippa down a maze of hallways to one of the testing labs.

Johnson's transfer had been approved. She now commanded a squad in Philippa's company. Johnson's self-discipline and low-key style of command quickly earned her the respect of her troops. She walked the shit and everyone under her knew they could count on her in any situation. She trained shoulder to shoulder with her unit—an equal. The story of her smiting the raging attacker on the Mall had spread, only enhancing her rep. Philippa invited her to travel to Williamsburg to assess the progress of the weapons meant to improve the odds against the Trutnevas.

Patel, walking fast, turned her head, her coffee-brown hair in waves to her shoulder. Gold studs in her ears echoing her wedding band. "We've got something we think you'll like."

Philippa nodded. "I'm intrigued."

They entered a dimly lit room. A workbench stood against the far wall. Electronic components in various states lay on top along with soldering irons, copper wire, bits of circuitry. Computer monitors added to the faint glow.

The women moved to the center of the room.

Patel stepped away to the workbench. "You are going to hear things. You may feel things. Don't be alarmed." She blinked a few times rapidly, a look of anticipation on her round face.

Philippa stood frozen, Johnson next to her. At first, nothing happened, then she heard light footsteps—very close—but no one else was around.

Johnson flinched, swatted at her head. "Something's in my

hair."

Johnson and Philippa, side by side, heard a voice between them whisper, "You're dead."

Both soldiers spun, Johnson crouching, but again, no one could be seen.

Patel called out triumphantly, "Had enough?"

"Yes," Philippa replied.

"What the shit?" Johnson muttered, a curious smile on her face.

Patel brought the lights up. To Philippa's left the air shimmered. A strange distortion.

Philippa recoiled. A pair of eyes stared out of the blur.

Dr. Patel clapped her hands. "Turn it off, Marie."

The blur resolved into the shape of a woman wearing a skin-tight, black catsuit with what looked like scales covering it.

Dr. Patel grinned. "We call it the Invisible Skin. We made it from tiny cameras salvaged from old smart phones. The screens have been cut down and reshaped to polyhedrons. One suit requires four hundred phones. Copper thread is woven into the Lycra mesh with tiny connectors for the screens and the cameras. The camera captures the image, and the processor displays it on the screens on the other side of the body, creating a mirage. You're still there, in between. There's a small bit of insulation around the edges so they don't make noise if they touch. It's not perfect, but it's near invisible. As you've learned, lower light is better.

"Up close, there's a distortion in the air. Further away, that dissolves. We made a small slit for the eyes."

Philippa shook her head. *Soldiers about to go to war and these geniuses are building toys. Four hundred phones! Must have taken months. We don't have months. We don't have weeks!*

She breathed in and exhaled slowly several times. Dr. Patel's face, so proud moments before, now looked at Philippa with growing concern. "What's wrong?"

Everything! She wanted to yell. "How many of these did you build?"

Dr. Patel shrank. "Only two...so far."

Philippa barked. "How did you think these would be used?"

"We haven't exactly catalogued the uses yet." She attempted a smile. "It is magnificent, though, isn't it?"

"How can you even carry a gun?"

The smile faded. "Yes, well, I see your point. That could pose a problem."

Philippa pressed her face close to the scientist, stomped her boot. "Maybe we can't just say 'Boo' and they'll run back across the Mason Dixon."

Dr. Patel cringed. Johnson interrupted, "Knife."

Philippa turned. "Knife?"

"Yes, ma'am. The sleeves could be lined to make a sheath. Slide it out when you get close to the target. Do your job and slip out. Invisible, like she said."

Dr. Patel nodded eagerly. "Yes, I'd never thought of that. Brilliant."

Johnson approached Marie. She studied the Invisible Skin. "With your permission, ma'am, I'd like the opportunity to try this out."

Philippa stared at the bizarre costume. "Sergeant, against my better judgement, permission granted. You think you can use it?"

"Ma'am, there's one thing you should know about me by now."

"What's that?"

"No one is more lethal."

29

– Philippa – February 2079

Eleven days later, the combined Tenora/Imperial armies streamed across the border. Altogether, there were twelve divisions: light armor, artillery, and infantry. They faced only token resistance as they ground south along old Route 1. The size of the force tempered their speed, but there was no need to rush. The Imperial generals wanted maximum intimidation, maximum terror. They burned everything in their path. *Its smoke will rise forever.*

A panicked ocean of refugees flooded south. For weeks, radio broadcasts had urged evacuation, but there were still holdouts who hadn't believed that war would come.

In the west, Venoma Choi smashed through the RSC border at Opal. Along the way, they engaged with guerilla forces from the former United District hidden in the Catoctin Mountains. After several days of fierce fighting, Choi's superior numbers succeeded in routing them and she moved on.

The command had come down from Lawson: Fredericksburg

must hold. If Fredericksburg fell, Richmond would be next. Choi's maneuver opened a second front, dividing the strength of the remaining Republics. Charlotte, Raleigh and the RSC Second Army converged to meet the Regina's threat.

* * *

Philippa strapped her molle vest over her fatigues, filling several of the pockets with extra magazines. She stood next to the 50-caliber mount on the JLTV, the gun almost as tall as she was.

Lieutenant Scarbrough sat behind the wheel. Her face was set in stubborn lines; she looked very young. "I won't shoot anybody. I can't."

Philippa squinted. "We won't see any action, you have my word. We need to sweep the area. The Trutneva armies will control everything north of the Rappahannock by tomorrow." *And I'll happily shoot any Imperial puta I see.* The image of Astrid in a cage didn't leave her for more than a few minutes. "We have to gather up anyone left out there. We will blow the bridges tonight. We have to get them now. Check your sidearm."

Scarbrough followed the order.

They drove through the mountains of sandbags that fortified their position in the city. Tidewater and RSC troops struggled against time to prepare. Over the years, people who had escaped from the north told stories of life in the Trutneva police state. Everyone had heard them. Arrests in the middle of the night. Condemned to brutal labor camps without trial. Unknown numbers of people sent to their deaths. The boys stripped from their parents and taken to the fertility institutes where they were treated like animals. The Dirae Corp's invincible reputation was also well-known. The Republics could expect no mercy. That's was what they were fighting. Philippa could see the fear in the faces of the young soldiers. Training days were over. *Will it be sufficient?*

They crossed the Cambridge Street bridge and rode along Route 1. Taking a right, they slowed to survey the houses. Collapsed roofs, broken windows, crumbling walls confirmed their vacancy. Faded American flags still hung from poles in front of several. They stopped at houses that appeared livable, running a quick sweep through, checking for people.

Further into the neighborhood, they arrived at a stone house. The ground behind the house had recently been plowed into neat rows. A white sheet hung from a second-story window.

To the north, maybe fifteen miles away, pillars of smoke heralded the coming of the Imperial armies.

Philippa pulled the truck behind the building, grabbed her rifle and circled to the front. She opened the door. "RSC! Is anyone here?"

From upstairs, a voice pleaded, "In here! Please!"

The hardwood floor creaked under their boots as they moved down the hall. In the bedroom, a very pregnant young woman sprawled on the bed, panting. She'd wrapped herself in a quilt, but she was naked from the waist down. Her legs spread and her knees up. Her green eyes were frantic, her face milk-white.

The girl shifted her weight. "It's coming. It's coming now! I don't want it to come."

Scarbrough rushed in. "Shhh. It's going to be okay. We're here to help." She knelt and held the girl's hand, stroked her flushed face. "When did your water break?"

The girl panted. "About an hour ago."

Philippa scowled. "Why are you still here?"

The girl grimaced and nodded towards her leg. "I can't walk. I cut my foot." The skin on the left foot was pulled tight from swelling. The wound was an angry purple color. The dressing had peeled off, revealing a three-inch gash along the sole.

Scarbrough delicately handled the wound, pressing lightly. "It's infected."

The girl shuddered and clenched the sheet. She threw her head back. "Ahhhhhhhhh!" She breathed deeply, then exhaled. The contraction subsided.

"I've never done this before. My aunt said she'd midwife, but I guess she ran with the others. Hope she's not dead. Nobody's come 'round for days. I'm so hungry, but sick feeling at the same time." Her voice was scared and whiny and made Philippa's neck itch. She didn't have time for this. Why didn't people take care of their own? Just as swiftly, duty kicked in, stifling the thought. She would take care of those who couldn't take care of themselves. It would always be on *her*.

Scarbrough handed her canteen to the girl, keeping one hand on her head. "Drink this, all of it."

Philippa sighed, found a protein ration in her rucksack and gave it to the girl. Scarbrough turned to Philippa. "I need to wash up."

Philippa held her arm up. "Let's get her in the truck."

The girl screamed again, the dome of her belly rippling. Philippa stared in horrified fascination.

"Captain, there's no time."

"Dammit, Scarbrough, that's an order. Help me lift her."

"AHHHHHHHHHHHHHH." Another cry ripped out of the girl.

The two soldiers wrapped their arms around the girl and

pulled her up and onto her good foot. The girl hobbled down the stairs, Philippa and Scarbrough supporting her each step. Making it to the living room, the girl clenched her teeth and wailed. She collapsed on the floor. "Oh God, it's coming. Make it stop, please! I'm not ready."

Scarbrough kneeled. "Let me check your dilation."

Philippa glared, the itch traveling to her chest and down her arms. "Lieutenant, we need to move, now!"

Meghan held firm. "One minute, Philippa, please!"

"I'm going to check the road and when I get back, we're leaving." *Who brings a baby into this hell?*

Philippa strode out and unslung her rifle. She pressed the scope to her eye, scanning the horizon. Her heart dropped.

Ahead, an Imperial armored personnel carrier lumbered down the road.

Dirae Corps—part of the vanguard. A quarter mile up the road, the APC stopped. A squad of soldiers jumped out of the back. Tough women, fully armored, carrying HK G36 assault rifles with optics.

She raced back inside. "Scarbrough, we've got contact."

Scarbrough turned, eyes wide. "Now? She's ten centimeters."

"Go out the back. Get her in the truck."

"What about you?"

Gunfire erupted in the front. Glass sprayed the room. Philippa took cover around a corner. Scarbrough threw herself over the girl. Philippa hollered, "GET HER OUT NOW!"

She pulled the charging handle on her rifle, chambering a round. *It's come. Let me brave.* She crawled across the floor of the living room and crouched beside the blown-out window. She peered around the edge. The Dirae soldier had positioned herself across the street behind a brick wall.

Philippa aimed and fired off a few rounds. Nothing.

The Dirae stayed low.

In a minute the entire squad is going to converge on my position. She laid down a burst of covering fire and prepared to dash to the truck. "Changing mag!" she called out to no one.

She backed off two steps, reaching for a new magazine. *BAM!* The front door burst open, the lock and handle shattered. A second Dirae soldier charged in, rifle aimed at Philippa's head.

This is it. Astrid, I wish I could have been more.

CLICK, CLICK. The soldier cocked her head and pulled the gun away from her shoulder.

It's jammed. The thought barely formed when the Dirae charged. The soldier jabbed with the butt of the rifle. Philippa ducked, but it still connected with her helmet. Her ears rang. She staggered. Another blow to the head laid her out on the floor.

Behind her, she could still hear the screams of the girl.

The Dirae pounced, straddling her, wrapping her hand around Philippa's throat. For the first time, Philippa got a look at her. Light brown face, Philippa close enough to see her freckles, the scar on her cheek. The woman sneered, her eyes narrowed. Spittle flew. "Die, you bitch!" the soldier roared.

Philippa clutched the Dirae's arm, struggling to break her grip. *She's too strong!*

With the other hand, the soldier withdrew a slim knife from her boot. The blade matte black.

Philippa heaved, breaking the soldier's hold on her throat. She choked in air and grabbed the knife hand with her right hand. With the other, she swung her helmet across the bridge of the woman's nose.

A popping sound. Blood sprayed in Philippa's eyes.

The soldier didn't react, didn't recoil. "You'll pay," she snarled through blood-stained teeth. The soldier twisted, breaking Philippa's hold on her knife hand. Quick as a snake, she plunged the blade into Philippa's side just below her armor. Philippa screamed. A white-hot sun exploded inside her. The soldier removed the knife, mouth curling in satisfaction. "I'm gonna cut that ugly head off your shoulders."

Pain shot through her. *Just be done with it.* The soldier lifted Philippa's head by the hair. Philippa weakly grappled with her, trying to fight back as her thoughts fled to death, what it was, if it was anything, how much it would hurt. The knife grazed her neck below the ear.

CRACK, CRACK, CRACK, CRACK

The first shot blew the Dirae's jaw off. A strange, questioning look crossed the soldier's face before it too shattered. She collapsed on top of Philippa. *Well, this is death, I guess. Heavy as shit. Not mine, though.*

Scarbrough pulled the body off. "My God, Philippa."

Philippa panted, "Help me up."

The lieutenant hoisted her onto her feet. Philippa wobbled. Pain radiated through her right side, both all-over like a burn and stabbing in discrete bursts. Scarbrough pressed on the wound with a gauze pad, making the captain want to scream. She gritted her teeth and draped her arm around Scarbrough's shoulder. They limped out the back.

"Thank you," Philippa gasped as they reached the JLTV. Philippa let go. "You drive. I'm taking the turret." She snaked up through the hatch and grabbed the grip of the 50-caliber, ignoring the pain or at least telling herself she was. She retracted the slide handle several times, clearing a spent cartridge.

The truck lurched forward, tossing Phillipa in the turret. She hung on to the weapon, feeling blood seep from her side.

Scarbrough wheeled out towards the road. Dirae soldiers opened fire from the right and the left, from nearby and further away. Philippa spun around, unleashing a burst of deadly retribution from the heavy machine gun.

Philippa screamed, her face contorted—a primal, ancient howl against the universe, "AAAAAAARRRRRRRRGGHGHHH." Retribution for the invasion, for the Dirae that nearly killed her, for stealing Astrid. For being born, for being born *now*. She leaned into the 50-caliber, her body braced against the merciless hammering of the powerful weapon. Tracer rounds flared out. She switched among targets. The Dirae returned fire; bullets ricocheted off the turret shield.

Burning cartridges spewed out of the side port. The gentle tinkling of the ejected shells merged with the deep, mechanical *thunk thunk* of the gun, like playing both ends of a piano. The rounds chewed through mortar, trees, through the body armor the Dirae wore. Philippa saw one go down, nearly severed in two. *Jesus Fuck. I did that.* Then, another thought, *She would do the same to you. This is your job.*

The JLTV peeled around a bend in the road. The Dirae fell out of sight. Philippa sucked in air, heart slamming against her breast. The adrenaline edged off. She glanced down. Her fatigues were soaked with blood at the wound.

What happened? The girl's not screaming.

The truck raced onto Route 1 toward the Fredericksburg base camp. Philippa slumped down through the hatch. Her side throbbed, a searing ache. *I'm so tired.* She snatched a fresh gauze pack from the med kit. She pressed it against the wound, wincing. *So heavy.*

Next to her, the girl, legs covered in blood, cradled her infant son. Its impenetrable blue eyes appraised her.

30

– Johnson – April 2079

In the north, smoke fanned across the horizon, mingling with the low-hanging storm clouds. Gray skies in all directions suspending time—impossible to tell morning from afternoon.

Sodapop Johnson strode out of the command building and stared across at the defenses, *Vengeance* strapped to her shoulder. The RSC had only weeks before the invasion to prepare. Lines of ancient cars had been towed and stacked along the river in crude defensive barriers. Trenches spanned the length of the city; sandbags formed exterior walls along the ridgeline. Concrete barricades punctured the landscape. Rows of rusted howitzers waited, clustered in strategic locations behind reinforced fortifications. Minefields spread across the northern border. The condition of the ordinance couldn't be trusted, however. Easily twenty percent of the shells fired during training failed to explode. Power cut out at least once a day. Supply couldn't keep up with the thousands of soldiers bivouacked in the city. Food became scarce, forcing soldiers to hunt deer in the nearby woods.

Here, the fate of the Richmond Republic would be determined. The Trutnevas wanted a knockout punch. If the Sisters captured Fredericksburg, nothing stood between their armies and the capital. The alliance would wither. Raleigh and Charlotte would sign a truce. Tidewater, cut loose, wouldn't stand a chance.

In the chow line, the sentry posts, the headquarters in George Washington Hall, always the same sight—the haunted mask of despair on the faces of the soldiers. *They know the score: capture is worse than death.* RSC and Tidewater soldiers kept with their own, huddled together, eyes drifting to the ground. The reservists—four weeks of training then here—no one wanting to cry, but sometimes too terrified to hold it in. *Kisses and promises at the top, but it's just show. Nobody wants to trust their women's safety to these part-timers and unknowns. We'll have to do our job and theirs too.*

Late afternoon brought the first sightings of the enemy. Convoys of armored personnel carriers rolled down Route 1. Enormous rigs pulled massive artillery pieces mounted on flatbeds. Sodapop studied their deployment. Cranes lifted them off the beds. Four stabilizing legs extended from the barrel mount. Long muzzles arced toward the city. The fifty pieces formed two offsetting rows, stretching a mile across. The soldiers moved without haste. *They know we're watching, that we can't touch them.* Hundreds of olive tents sprouted behind the guns.

She'd shaved her head on returning to the infantry, shed everything that was unnecessary. Keeping the eight soldiers in her squad alive became the priority. She supposed she needed some humanity for that. But no weakness. She ran her hand across the stubble. *We're sport for them—children playing here in our sandbox. And these are bitches that would eat children for dinner if they got too hungry.*

At her squad's tent, four of her soldiers sat cross-legged on the ground playing poker. M-21s lay next to them at close reach. Private Memphis Satterwhite dealt. Red headed. Skin already burned in the April sun. She'd rolled the sleeves of her green t-shirt over her biceps. Cigarette dangled from her lip. She squinted up at Johnson through the smoke. "Sarge, you want in? Wenona's already out fifty libra."

Johnson shook her head. *Let them have their time. The job's gonna get hard real soon.*

Johnson knew not to get too close to her troops. Memphis had served for three years. Wenona Brimmer had also put in time. Only two on the squad were virgins. Those were the two Johnson worried about.

Memphis pulled herself up and pointed. "There's twelve divisions between the U.D. and the Imperials."

"Tenora," Wenona corrected her.

Memphis shrugged. "Fuck Tenora. Stupid name. Sounds like a yeast infection." She shifted to a radio voice, "Suffering from Tenora? Try…"

The women grimaced.

Johnson spoke up. "Guys, we're going to get to the other side of this. We need to stay tight. Keep sharp."

Memphis turned to the sergeant. "There are ten of them for every one of us."

Johnson met her gaze. "Then we'll each have to kill twenty. Keep them from ever coming back."

Over their tent, the Richmond flag flew—a spear-wielding goddess in an armored breastplate surrounded by a laurel wreath. *Sic semper tyrannis.*

Johnson cleared her throat. "Listen up. O.I.C. said Captain Calenos has been wounded. She was on recon north of the city when she ran into Dirae hostiles. Cut her up pretty badly. Captain nearly bled out. So, as of now, we do not have a C.O. Which means?"

Silence descended on the team. Johnson unshouldered *Vengeance*. A wry smile crossed her lips. "Which means we're going to have to ask forgiveness instead of permission."

She twisted a suppressor onto the barrel. Pointing at the deck of cards, "Gimme that." She shuffled through the deck, peeled out a card and tossed the rest back. "No more time for games. We've got work."

Private Jess Cardozo, eighteen, tall and lanky. Division leading three-pointer. "Orders?"

Johnson sighted the rifle. "Tool up, ladies. We're taking the fight to them tonight."

* * *

Hours passed. The timeless afternoon faded into darkness. Across the river, Imperial troops and their conscripts worked under enormous sodium lights erected on poles. The light, diffused through the mist, painted a lurid yellow-orange landscape. Nearly a thousand tents covered the fields. *What are they waiting for?*

Johnson killed time until cover of darkness. She picked three from her squad: Satterwhite, Cardozo and Corporal Theo Kim. Together they slipped down towards the river. Johnson carried a waterproof molle on her back. *Vengeance* strapped crossways. Kim, Satterwhite, and Cardozo attached suppressors to their

M–21s. Grease paint blackened their faces.

At the edge of the river, a row of flatbed boats rested on the shoreline. Johnson wasted no time selecting one. The four soldiers pushed the vessel into the water and grabbed oars. They hugged the pillars of the King's Highway bridge. Dark water lapped at the sides. The women leaned low, careful to muffle the sound of the rowing.

On the other side, they pulled out, not dragging it. They placed the boat in the tall grass along the embankment.

Johnson took a knee. "It's about sixteen clicks from here. We're going to approach from the southeast. I'll handle any sentries when we get close."

The soldiers nodded.

They trekked without talking, passing crumbling buildings. The clouds obscured the moon. The air was damp and cool. The yellow haze of the Trutneva encampment guided them. Reaching the perimeter, Johnson held up her fist. The squad stopped. Silently, she signaled the three to keep watch. She peeled off the molle pack and stripped out of her uniform. She lifted the Invisible Skin out and slipped into it. *All these scales. This is how a snake feels.* Memphis kept passing glances over at her.

Barely audible, "This is untested. Mother be with us."

She switched the power on before zipping up the front. Satterwhite stumbled backwards. Theo gasped.

Johnson pulled a combat knife with a long, serrated blade from her gear. The blade animated on its own, gliding through the night air as she slid it into a sheath sewn into the left forearm of the suit.

"If I'm not back in fifteen minutes, you bug out. Got it?"

Satterwhite hissed. "Sergeant, we're not leaving without

you."

Johnson glared—the only part of her that could be seen. "Fifteen. Not a second longer. And leave my gun."

Theo whispered, "Aye, Sergeant. Fifteen."

Johnson ran lightly across the field. Rubber soles on the bottom of the suit hugged her feet. *This is absolute freedom. I am the wind of wrath. I am the breath of their nightmares.*

Crossing into the camp, she slowed. *The scientists said it was better to keep moving. Holds the illusion better.* The bilious light shone down in circles. Johnson moved along the periphery whenever she could.

She scanned the city of tents. *Size matters.* Tenora tents clustered nearby. *Better to strike at the head.* She worked her way further in. Imperial tents littered the hillside. Johnson targeted the closest oversized tent. A Trutneva banner hung on a cross nearby. She wove her way through the soldiers, keeping distance. Occasionally, one of them would double-take, catching a fractured glimmer or locking eyes with Johnson for half a second. Johnson smiled behind her mask. *I am the shadow of your fear.*

Surrounded by thousands of enemies, Sodapop floated in a calm certainty. *Focus on the mission.* The tent flap was open. The Imperial officer was alone, writing at a makeshift desk. A blond braid hung down her back. Her camouflage jacket lay across the bed, embroidered bars revealing the rank of colonel. Lights hung from the top of the tent powered by the generators.

She twisted around in her chair. "Is someone there?"

* * *

Johnson returned to her squad with two minutes to spare. She shed the Invisible Skin and replaced it with her fatigues. The uproar in the camp eased her escape. The hardest part was avoiding the soldiers storming around in the chaos.

The squad double-timed it back to the boat. A steady rain had started to fall. For now, the Trutneva armies wouldn't look for them. Retribution would come later.

Crossing the Rappahannock, Johnson relived the scene. On the paper on the desk, she had scrawled: *Sic semper tyrannis.* The bloody corpse of the colonel slumped over the table. *Never had a clue. Rest now, soldier.* In the colonel's hand—between two fingers, Johnson slipped the card she had taken from Memphis's deck.

A red queen.

31

– Brick – April 2079

Brick chuckled, knowing that Sware's days were numbered. She had preyed upon a diseased old woman, her one and only trick. She was sly but was no match for the Sisters, Choi, or any of the other Queens. Her weakness was that *she thought she was.* A fatal weakness. Internal Security would come in the night for her. If she survived the war.

Brick's office wasn't one of the grand offices reserved for the generals and ministers, but more than adequate. Wood paneling lined the drab beige walls. Marijka's desk stood next to the entrance. A map of the Eastern Seaboard showing the boundaries of the Republics and the Reginae hung next to it. Brick rubbed the faded cigarette burns on the inside of her forearm, remembering the pungency of burned flesh. *I just forgot the words, Mother. I know what they mean.* Life after the mutation was hard and cruel (maybe it had always been). She'd had to be hard to survive. She took no enjoyment in this fact, rather felt disgust at the nature of reality, that this was all they had. The people who won did it at other people's expense, the Sisters being the most extreme example. People who tried to rise above it were rare. *Honeysuckle. The cadet's hand on my arm, smiling at my accomplishment—a stupid sentence.* Her father had been one of those people, generous when he had so little. She hated herself for thinking him a fool for it. But she'd seen the game played out dozens of times—betrayal was always the best strategy. Look out for yourself. *Be smart, but don't let on.* Love was too much to ask for with her condition.

Everything in the Trutneva's circle was a lie. She'd learned not to ask certain questions. *Everyone thinks you're stupid, so why not act the part.* She'd seen how the Sisters schemed, manipulated, threatened, and used force to maintain and expand. *I'm just as smart and tough.* She knew she wasn't like them, but her gift offered her a certain advantage. *I could conspire against the Sisters. Permitting a lie, like a stiletto, to exist close to their elegant, pale throats. A coup right under their noses.*

Maybe there was something better if they could stop trying to claw each other's eyes out. Be a Queen, but better. Maybe the Republics had it right.

Marijka read her the communiques. Reports from the front so far had been better than expected. Tenora forces backed by five divisions of Imperial troops met little resistance until Fredericksburg. There, they smashed the RSC/Tidewater armies. They pounded their fortifications with their heavy artillery around the clock. The armies of Richmond and Tidewater couldn't match their range. For three days, the guns roared, lobbing explosive and incendiary shells. Even in the downpours, fires burned unchecked through the city.

Their opponents placed charges on the bridges across the Rappahannock and destroyed them before the Imperial troops could arrive. It made no difference. The Engineering Corps built modular platforms for the trucks to use. The RSC shelled them during the night. The following day, the Protsent conscripts would lay new platforms. Nobody cared if they didn't survive.

At the end of the third day, the Dirae led the infantry into the fallen city. *Othere, look with favor upon this offering!*

What remained of the southern armies fled. A rearguard stayed to slow the pursuit of the Trutneva forces. A suicide mission. They were overwhelmed in hours. Imperial flags now flew over the ruins. For now, the pursuit of the enemy armies would wait.

They would train their guns on Richmond next.

32

– Philippa/The Order – April 2079

Late April sun drifted through stained-glass windows, spreading light and color across the room. Philippa blinked her eyes, concentrating to focus.

An older Latina held her wrist. A Cartier wristwatch ticked on her other hand. She wore a light blue hand-sewn cassock of rough weave with a faded beige smock over top. Her long gray hair was clean and showed the streaks of its former deep brown.

The woman smiled, serene and radiant as the light. "You contracted an infection after the surgery. Your fever spiked to a dangerous level. You've been unconscious for six days now. Your pulse is normal. It's good to have you back."

Philippa swallowed and licked her lips. "Where am I?"

"You and some of the other wounded were transported here after the battle."

"Where is 'here?'" she croaked. "Water, please?"

The woman poured a glass. "The monastery of the Sacred Order of the New Christ."

Philippa gulped down the water, ran her hands through her

hair. "Fredericksburg. What happened?"

The nun held her gaze. "Fredericksburg fell. The siege lasted only a few days. The remaining troops retreated east into Tidewater."

Lost. Everything has been lost. "Are the Trutnevas in pursuit?"

"Reports I've heard are the Imperial army is outside Richmond."

Philippa swung her legs over the edge and pushed herself to stand. "I gotta get to my unit." Her face flushed and the room blurred. She collapsed onto one knee. The nun wrapped her arms around her and lifted her back onto the bed.

"You can't go anywhere. Your body hasn't nearly recovered. You've been through a lot. You must rest. The war will still be there."

"Lieutenant Scarbrough. Do you know if she made it out?"

The nun shook her head. "I'm sorry, I don't know her. I don't know if she escaped. She's not here. Thousands remain unaccounted for."

Across the room, another soldier hobbled on crutches, the stump where her foot should have been wrapped in bandages. Two others slept nearby. The wound under her rib throbbed. Philippa propped herself up and pulled back the sheet. Black stiches peeked out under the dressing. Philippa recoiled, her heart hammering. The force of the powerful Dirae crushing her, choking her, returned. *The hatred!* She relived the struggle to keep the knife away. Her hand clutched the gauze. She drank in air, squeezing her eyes tight. The soldier's bloody face reappeared, sneering as she slid the blade in. The scene flooded back in vivid images. *Killing me was more than just duty. She wanted it.*

Philippa's face eased. The nun placed her hand on Philippa's arm as if reading her mind. "Rest, please. Trauma is equal parts psychological and physical."

Philippa knew little of the Sacred Order of the New Christ. Beguines. The Order existed across the Republics. Communal groups of lay women congregated in churches and monasteries. All of the nuns had taken vows—to never marry or bring their own children into the world. Each of their compounds served as orphanages for abandoned children, mostly boys. Many things had changed since the mutation appeared, but unplanned pregnancies weren't among them. Young girls maintained their natural curiosity about sex but weren't ready to be mothers. The nuns asked no questions and passed no judgment, only offering care and compassion. In the Order, the boys were cared for and raised until old enough to marry. Fifteen was the usual age when they left. Life expectancy was only twenty-three.

Philippa settled back in. "Your Christ is not a man, right?"

"We pray for the return of the unity that is the androgynous Christ—both women and men are part of the perfection God intends for all of us. Christ's suffering is all women's suffering. Six hours he hung on the Cross to bring forth a new life. Six hours—the time of an average labor. Christ is the Son and Daughter of God. But on Earth, the Sons of God have been exiled."

That's one way of looking at it. Philippa reached for the water. The nun handed it to her. "More?"

Philippa nodded.

The nun continued, "Maybe they are trapped, their consciousness existing in a kind of extended dream. Perhaps they are witness to the fourth dimension but can't share any of it. For them, there is no time. They are trying their hardest to communicate, but we can't understand."

Philippa carefully rolled over. *Now look what you've started.* She scowled. "They've devolved. That's the only answer that fits. All the scientists, men and women, agreed that a genetic mutation caused their collapse."

The nun pursed her lips. "Science doesn't have all the answers. We've studied what we can of their genetics. We've written down what they say, their songs..."

Philippa interrupted, shaking her head. "Waste of energy. Nothing but nonsense."

"We do what we can for them." She stood up, wringing her hands and frowning. "I'm sorry. I didn't mean to upset you. Please rest. Someone will check next hour."

* * *

Philippa hungered for news. Once able to shower and move around again, she huddled next to the radio. Richmond surrounded. Astrid's paintings, their aerie—lost. The Trutnevas had taken Astrid and any memory of her. They would never yield.

The war is lost. Everyone will submit or be killed. And Astrid! I can't think of her in an Imperial labor camp. It's too much. Every day is a living hell for those unfortunates. Mother, let her be dead rather than a prisoner. The terrible, ceaseless imaginings haunted her from the moment she woke. Her wound throbbed with every step. *There's nothing left of me. I thought I could be strong. The cold north wind will find me, will sweep me off this precipice into the dark, fathomless waters.*

There had been no reports of the Second Army and the

alliance of Raleigh and Charlotte marshaled to fight Choi. They might be the only hope. If they defeated Choi, the remnants of the First could link up with them. She'd learned that the First bivouacked near Miller's Tavern, waiting on fuel.

The monastery nestled south of Tappahannock. Built around 1960, it exemplified a functional architecture without ornament. A large, pointed arch formed the entrance to the main building made of pale, rose-colored brick. A row of abstract stained-glass windows circled the top of the building. Different shingles attested to the repairs made on the roof. In the open courtyard in front stood a circular concrete fountain that no longer flowed. The nuns planted jonquils and poet's narcissus in the basin.

To the side, a play area had been created with swing sets and rocking horses. Several of the younger children played while a nun watched over them. Behind the main house, the decaying stables overlooked plowed fields and copses of pines.

Cannabis tincture was the strongest analgesic available to the nuns. Philippa maintained a steady intake to stay in front of the pain from her wound. It helped with the terrifying thoughts that were never far away. The edges of the world softened. Philippa limped over to the stables. Three old, but cared for, horses shuffled in their stalls. Flies circled the area. At the far end, a boy of maybe fifteen stood in the stall with his head against the neck of one. His eyes were closed. His arms encircled the animal. He hummed quietly.

Suspenders held up his loose khaki pants. His blue work shirt showed a tear near the shoulder that had been stitched. His youthful face bore Asian features. His inky black hair jutted out on all sides—the minor insult of a terrible haircut.

Philippa approached the boy. He snapped his head and

stared at her. His milky blue eyes glowed in the dusty light of the stable. A broad smile lit up his face. Philippa waved then pulled her hand back, "Hi."

The boy laughed. He turned and held his hands out, guiding him along the edge of the stall to the opening.

Philippa studied the young man. Until now, she'd willed them into the background, never seeing them. Never wanting to see them. On base, months would go by without her encountering one. Their nonsensical phrases that parodied human speech. They'd ruined the world and then checked out, leaving women to clean the mess. *The world is collapsing, and he laughs.*

The boy's head lolled, his smile showing his crooked teeth. He stroked his fingers across her cheek, tender. "Read to me."

Philippa shrugged. "I don't have anything to read. Maybe I can find something inside. Do you want to come with me?" Her words trailed off. *He doesn't understand any of this.* She took his hand, strong, but soft compared with her scarred fingers. The boy pulled away, his attention captured by a piece of hay. He squatted down, rustling the piles, tossing them up and shaking his head as they fell. The familiar horse smell wafted through the stable. Philippa inhaled it, remembering Icarys, wondering if he too hadn't been claimed by the Trutnevas.

Philippa imagined the darkness the boy endured behind his dimly glowing eyes. She too had known darkness, the consuming darkness that she tried to hold back with her stoic sense of duty. The boy bobbed back up. "Clear, clear," he shouted. *They will ship you north to one of their fertility institutes.*

The afternoon heat produced a warm closeness to the air. Dust swirled in the light falling on the floor. A slight buzz rang in Philippa's ears. Seeing the young man up close, watching his innocent gestures, Philippa's heart filled with sorrow, a new ache. She swallowed hard, fighting back tears. *He's lost and broken like me. He's thrown in here with the rest of us. Maybe the nun is right. Maybe a part of him is trapped inside.* She whispered to the boy, "You're an orphan too." *Because of your sins you were sold; because of your transgressions your mother was sent away.*

In a pure voice he sang,

"London Bridge is falling down, falling down, falling down
  Catch them all before they drown
  My fair lady"

He laughed and clapped his hands. "Lost."

It's all so terribly wrong. A tear rolled down her cheek.

The boy frowned and stroked her face again. "And you can cry."

If I could only be with Astrid, I could face the end of our world. If I could only see her again, I would never let her go. Her head swam. Thoughts blossomed then fragmented. Behind their chaotic veil, the sense that one pure idea—alchemical in its mystery—struggled to break through. An ancient spell of binding whose incantation had been revealed. She shuddered.

She wouldn't have left if there had been a baby.

She wrapped her hands around the boy's. His eyes lit with a new intensity.

Philippa whispered to herself, "To have her back with me again, I'd never deny her a child."

She inhaled the smell of clay and manure, the sweat from the young man. All primordial elements of creation, of fertility, of the timeless, mystical urge. Her face flushed, the buzzing ring in her ears amplified with her heartbeat. The hazy light throbbed. She touched her side. *My pain has disappeared!* The one pure idea possessed her. *I will plead a deal with the Mother and all the new goddesses: The Goddess of What Was Lost, The Shipwrecked Goddess, The Goddess of the Fallen, The Accidental Goddess. With whomever or whatever awaits us.*

She slid the boy's suspenders over his shoulders. Leaning in, she kissed his cheek, then his lips. He tasted like milky tea and smelled like horses. His lips were so soft, so young. The boy closed his eyes, instinctively pressing his body into hers. Philippa slid her arms around his chest, surprised at the strength in his slender body.

The goddesses will demand a sacrifice.

The doctor in the ER reared up from her imagination: *You will never be able to conceive. You shouldn't even try.*

Philippa cried out loud, "To have her back with me again, I would bear a child."

Hearing the sound of her own words terrified her. *I've crossed a threshold and no longer recognize myself.*

Philippa led the boy into an empty stall. She peeled off her fatigue pants—blood-stained though the nuns had washed them. She kneeled down in the hay, tugging the boy's pants off. He was willing, at least by the evidence of his body. She'd never wondered before how that worked, assuming what she'd been taught—that men were indiscriminate, always ready—was true. Now it occurred to her that it was too easy an answer. "Is this okay?"

He smiled and murmured something.

She lay back and waited, letting him come to her. He followed without hesitation. She guided the boy's penis, wincing slightly as he entered her. It felt curious, more intimate than she'd imagined. The boy's eyes remained closed, his face gentle. He sang so quietly in a lyrical tenor. Listening to the early strains, Philippa understood it as a song for her alone, drawn out of her ache and fear. Gently it began, with an innocence so pure, not touched by the writhing, convulsing world. He whispered in her ear, moving his hips slowly. *This isn't real.* Memories flooded in. He knew her as the abandoned child. She caressed the smooth, powerful coil of his triceps. She thrust her hips in response and let out a small moan. The song changed shape, now filled with a deep melancholy, drawing in the loss and regret. He found her in that solitary cell where time remained suspended at 4:11. That dark place that dawn never found. Found her in the immanence of a terrible future for her alone to witness. *Nobody could know this about me.* She shuddered and felt tears spill over. His deep, rhythmic movements increased tempo. She pinched her nipple. Intense waves radiated from her pelvis. Growing and building, the waves consumed her. She clenched his back, head twisting side to side. He reared up, his silver blue eyes locked on to hers. The song shifted again, piercing the shroud, filling her with something unknown and eternal. An exchange that terrified her, as if learning the hour of her death.

The waves subsided. Philippa gasped, staring at the boy, now curled next to her, gently humming. The spell faded, the veneer worn away, revealing again the gaping maw of the thresher that awaited her. A sharp pang ripped through her abdomen. *You fool! If they are out there, they are deaf to your pleas. Nothing has changed.* The Trutnevas, Astrid. She rubbed her face. *What have I done?* She pushed him away. "Go! Get away from me!" *I can't breathe.*

She pulled on her pants. The boy, naked from the waist down, fumbled on his knees along the row of stalls.

Philippa saddled the healthiest looking horse, a roan mare. She led it out of the stable, swung her leg over, panting through the surging pain. She would reach the First at Miller's Tavern by nightfall. She clenched her jaw, not looking behind, the sweat cold on her back.

33

– Johnson – April 2079

Johnson waded through the tall switchgrass. *Vengeance* slung low in her hands. Rifles ready, her squad followed. The moon waxed over her shoulder.

She'd stashed the Invisible Skin in the JLTV they'd commandeered. The battery in the suit had drained and she needed a hookup to the grid to recharge. Even a single home with panels would suffice—she'd jack into the inverter. Still, charging would take hours, time she and her soldiers didn't have.

The slow-motion nightmare of Fredericksburg remained fresh. By the time the order came to bug out, a quarter of the Southern alliance was dead and twice as many wounded or missing. Who knows how many had dropped their weapons and fled? Chaos reigned. Of her eight, Satterwhite, Cardozo, Kim, and Brimmer remained.

The Trutnevas took their sweet time. They blasted and burned the city 'til there was nothing left. Three days they laid it on. We should have pulled back after we saw their firepower.

The remnants of the RSC First Army and the Tidewater

reserves retreated east. Johnson's unit stayed with the rear-guard. After they evacuated, she and the four left of her squad followed the Imperial Army. *Close, but not too close.* Four days now. When Fredericksburg fell, food and supplies either burned or were left behind. The squad lived off the land, shooting deer, eating purslane and inky caps. They scrounged for fuel—sometimes siphoning it out of abandoned vehicles. They slept wherever they found shelter.

They had nothing left to lose.

Penetrate their perimeter. Remind them they are vulnerable. We will not give up.

The past two nights, she'd used the Skin to slip into the Imperial camp. Daring to go further each time. She'd left the other red queen on the corpse of a major after a dozen other kills. Her last victim—a Tenora captain—only rated the nine of diamonds.

They christened their squad The Red Death.

Without the Skin, they changed tactics. *Not too deep but leave a mark.*

Weeds grew out of the cracked pavement of the parking lot. The squad hugged the rear wall of the abandoned strip mall. Extending to the south, beyond a row of trees, a cul-de-sac of once luxury homes stood. Inside, part of the Imperial Army camped, gathering themselves for the assault on Richmond.

Johnson raised her fist. The squad stopped. She raised the scope to her eye. The 3:00 AM darkness was complete, but down in the street, a handful of lights glowed. Enough for Johnson to define the outlines of the vehicles and the houses. A nearby sentry, positioned at the end of the cul-de-sac, stood guard. The soldier's helmet bobbed over the pile of sandbags. Johnson imagined her peering into the same darkness, the terrifying unknown. Only the comfort of her weapon.

Johnson kneeled, bracing *Vengeance* on her knee, cocking her head to the scope—one of the last night-vision types. She drew in a long breath and held it. Swimming in lurid green, the cross hairs aligned just below the helmet.

PPHHHHHHTTTTTTPPTTTTTT

The suppressor silenced the shot. The soldier crumpled. *May the Mother have mercy on your soul.*

"Target down," she whispered.

The squad waited for a reaction. Nothing but the stirring haint of the recently dead. They approached the edge of the cul-de-sac. Johnson pointed at Brimmer, Satterwhite and Kim, then pointed to the next house on the street. The three nodded and set out, staying behind the houses, out of the street. Johnson watched their movement, then closed in on the nearer house. The French doors leading to the stone patio hung open. *This is too easy.* Johnson's instinct told her not to trust the situation. She shuddered, a chill rippling down her spine. She raised her fist. Cardozo stood frozen.

Something's not right.

She sighted Corporal Kim through the scope. The three soldiers neared the rear of the neighboring home.

Johnson glanced back at the open door. A sliver of moonlight glinted near the ground at the threshold. She kneeled down. A thread of filament ran across the door opening. *Tripwire! Gotta warn them.*

Johnson raised *Vengeance*. *Fire a shot. Abort the mission.* Then she remembered the suppressor. She sighted Kim again, fumbling with the holster of her pistol. The corporal stood inches from the door.

"Cardozo, burn off a round. Now!" she hissed.

Johnson heard the safety click off.

VVVVVOOOOOOOOOMMMMMMMM

The echo of the shot drowned in the explosion. The ground trembled. The rear of the house erupted in flame. Burning shrapnel fell.

Shouts in the distance. Sodium lights rendered a false dawn. *We've brought the whole machine down on our heads.*

"Run!" she cried.

They sprinted through the trees, past the mall. The JLTV, parked under cover, lay a quarter mile ahead. Behind them, engines turned over, shots rang, but nothing close.

Cardozo climbed into the driver's seat, panting. Johnson pulled herself in. *Only me and Cardozo left.* She knew she would feel the weight of Brimmer and Kim's deaths for as long as she lived.

Cardozo hit the ignition button. "Where?"

Johnson stared straight ahead. "Just drive. North. East. One place is as good as the next. We just gotta survive."

34

– Moncure – April 2079

The Smyth waited. The Smyth always waited. The reality of addiction was that Moncure was never completely free. The Smyth no longer rattled the cage or smashed the glass. A subtler game he now played, present in the heat behind every exchange, within the high-voltage tension that permeated the command, behind the events yet to come.

After six weeks, Moncure had put on fifteen pounds—he realized he'd forgotten the taste of food. His eyes shone clearer than in the last thirty years. He walked upright again, but still haunted by the man he once was. The malevolent whispers: *Just one won't hurt. This is not your war.*

As a younger man, Moncure had studied the classics. He reflected back on Orpheus and Eurydice. Orpheus, musician without equal, traveled to the underworld to retrieve his beloved. There in the infernal caverns, he secured the return of his love, his life. The only condition being, he not look back until they reached the upper world. *Unable to stop himself,* Orpheus looked. So close to the exit from Hell, Orpheus couldn't resist. How many times had Moncure quit drinking only to look back and lose everything?

His wife had stayed with him at the hospital. She'd sewn the new rank patch on his uniform. Sobriety unlocked portions of his heart he'd thought long sealed away. He saw in her again the beautiful, young woman he'd married. Alone, he wept with shame at the fact he'd ignored her for years, terrorized her, hadn't been man enough to treat her properly. *But maybe it's not too late!*

What Karyn had said still resonated: Redemption. His last chance at it. A lifetime of violence he'd tried to forget and now more loomed. His commission had been reinstated under the RSC, although at a major's rank. Karyn laid out the rules of engagement: Advise the generals, share with them his perspective, but he would not lead troops when combat came. There was too much at stake. The alliance of Charlotte, Raleigh and Richmond had already frayed without hearing the first shot. Charlotte demanded supreme leadership over all the troops. Nguyen was awarded that prize. Wary of any misstep, she listened to the strategies offered by Poole and the Raleigh generals, but never settled decisively.

The three armies, mostly Charlotte and Raleigh, camped near Charlottesville. Dogwoods bloomed across the hillsides. The bulk of the RSC forces waited in Fredericksburg with Tidewater. They would face the Trutnevas.

Choi, however, was formidable without the Imperials. Her army was supported by Vasquez and Fairfax. Thirteen divisions to their nine. The southern armies would need to punch above their weight to win.

Moncure attended one joint strategy meeting when he arrived in Charlottesville. He didn't speak a word. Karyn sat to his left. Cold eyes around the room darted towards him from time to time. *You are not welcome here.* Still, being back in an encampment with its sounds, smells, the steam from pots for cooking and laundry, the endless needs; this was home, this was where he'd always belonged.

A handful of men still served within the Charlotte and Raleigh armies. Relics, like himself. They gravitated to each other, all of them lost in a world they no longer understood. The Forgetting was more than loss of knowledge, technical understanding, and history. It was also the forgetting of men and their contributions. Most of the aging soldiers had been relegated to administrative duties, watching their time slip away. Fated to watch the final act—the twilight of their kind. Hanging on because they knew once they stopped, their lives would lose any shred of meaning. Wary and silent around the women but wondering aloud what happened when gathered together in twos and threes. They laughed at each other's crude jokes and speculated that maybe tiny pockets in remote places carried on. Had they been judged and found wanting? Were they praying in language God chose to forget? *But your iniquities have separated you from your God.* Would the mutation run its course and males return after the earth had cooled? Moncure sometimes wished his soul would remain on earth, witness to the next chapters. The price of damnation but at least then he would *know*.

They sat in the lobby of an abandoned chain hotel. A nondescript interior of cracked vinyl chairs, peeling tan print wallpaper and generic pastel abstract paintings. Dust lay thick across the floor and counters. Some of the windows had been broken. RSC officers claimed it for their command post. The beds were still serviceable although the elevator didn't run. A map of the area lay spread across the table along with parts of Moncure's Browning 1911. Poole complained privately, "Nguyen has vital intelligence she's not sharing. I'm certain of it."

"But what would she have to gain?"

Poole sipped her tea. "Her? Maybe a comfortable minister's job when this is over, but she can't afford a mistake, can't lose her command. Charlotte plays this game on many levels. She's not going to commit to a strategy. She's trying to keep all her options open, but meanwhile we're left adrift."

Moncure ran a brush down the barrel. "What do you know of the leader, Venoma Choi?"

Poole shifted in her chair. "She's ruled for close to a decade. She is the strongest of the Reginae, the most ruthless. A consuming ambition infused with a sociopathic efficiency. She's coveted the UD for years. Her territory delivers the most under the Protsent, a badge of honor she is quick to remind the other Queens of. She stands the most to gain when they carve up the U.D. That marionette, Sware, won't even see it coming.

"Choi's purged her top officers and officials at least four separate times. Charges of treason. Show trials. If the Trutnevas hadn't needed her to reinforce their gains in the U.D., I suspect they would have knocked her back a couple notches. Show who's really in charge.

"This conflict's been coming to this for years. The Republics have been sleeping in the fitful uncurrence. This is perhaps our best and last chance to halt the threat from the north."

Moncure reassembled the pistol. "How willing is she to gamble? Will she try to win at any cost?"

"Yes, I think so. She has a burning desire for victory. She's vain, having only won battles against scattered militias while she had the Dirae reinforcing her. She thinks she's more skilled at war than she really is. She expects us to roll over."

"Then do that! Roll over. Lure her further in with a series of feints, small battles, but always retreating. Keep her close." He jammed his finger down onto the map. "Lead her west into the mountains. Route 33 in Stanardsville. It's a chokepoint. We can use the terrain to then strike from both sides." His finger slid across the paper. "Send a portion of your forces east before engaging her. Make her think she's chasing the entire army. Once she's taken the bait, use those forces to cut her supply lines once she's followed you in. You'll have her on three sides."

Poole nodded, her good eye flashing around the map.

"Karyn, you have to do it. You have to make the Charlotte leaders listen. I'll tell them."

"Reed, you can't. They won't listen to you. They think you're trying to deceive them somehow. Leave it to me."

Moncure scowled. "What do I have to gain? You all own the future."

Poole nodded, pursing her lips. She didn't say *They aren't used to men. They're superstitious and insecure, wondering why it's all happened. They fear you want to destroy what you can't have.*

An aide rushed in, handed her a message. The General's face paled. Her hand trembled as she placed the communique on the table. "Fredericksburg has fallen."

Moncure leaned forward, resting his hand on hers. "Karyn, It's not over. We've faced tougher odds before."

Her eye glistened. "I know, Reed. Those loyal, courageous women...they're all my daughters."

Moncure gave a gentle squeeze. "It's war, the only constant of humanity. God have mercy on their souls."

35

– Philippa – April 2079

A dead end. After sacking Richmond, the Trutneva forces swung north again, picking up the scent of the retreating RSC/Tidewater forces. From Miller's Tavern, they retreated steadily down the middle peninsula, scrambling to stay one step ahead of the Imperial armies. The York River to the south and the Rappahannock to the north hemmed them in. Only three ragged divisions remained.

Trapped between Scylla and Charybdis. Off the coast, a Leviathan ground towards land. A wall of fury stretching for miles. A harbinger of the Shipwrecked Goddess. The storm would uproot trees and hurl them. It would tear buildings from their foundations. Rains lashed the saturated earth, flooding roads, turning the fields to impassible mud pits. Soldiers slogged ankle-deep in gray-brown sludge, soaked to the core. They'd had to abandon the artillery.

The RSC/Tidewater armies held on to a small area around Gloucester. Waiting to see whether the storm or the Trutnevas would strike first. They marked the hours before their end.

Better to let nature consume me than the Trutnevas.

Philippa couldn't shake the image of the boy, blind and naked, fumbling in the dusty light. *Where is he now? Maybe five years left to live, maybe three?* She knew he would haunt her. Her sleep—compelled by sheer exhaustion—consisted of short periods of unconsciousness huddled in her parka. Inside her boots, her feet sodden, the skin peeled away in places. She'd given the horse over to aid with transporting casualties worse off than she. Her side throbbed, extending through her abdomen. Scarbrough helped her change the dressing, Philippa relieved she'd survived.

Command had broken down. A couple of the colonels who'd made it out of Fredericksburg attempted to form new units. The soldiers fell in line, but everyone knew the score: try to survive. There would be no counterattack against the Trutnevas, no victory snatched from their jaws of death. Ride out the storm then maybe slip across the river. Everyone knew someone who had deserted and doubted their own judgment for not doing the same.

Johnson and Cardozo caught up with the retreating army. She brought the Invisible Skins wrapped in waterproof containers, batteries dead.

Philippa returned Johnson's salute. "Everything you expected?"

Sodapop replied, "Good while it lasted."

A gray shroud hung over everything. Mist rolled along the fields. *Even the spring light has abandoned me.* The three pitched in digging a trench to fortify their position. Black rain pooled almost as soon as they'd tossed the dirt. Philippa scanned the perimeter, watching the line of soldiers work, their mud-streaked faces. *One long grave for all of us. Oh, Astrid.* Her wound flared, a hundred burning knives inside her. She collapsed on a pile of dirt, head in her hands, hair pasted to her cheek. The rain hid her tears.

So, this is it, our last day. All the pretty words and noble sentiments washed away. Talk of peace and victory forgotten. Death with honor here at the end. Still, I am proud to have served with these women. They are my family, my sisters.

From the command tent, a private holding a radio dashed over.

"Captain, Captain you have to hear this!"

Philippa leaned in, the voice, static-clad and unearthly, repeated.

"This is the Tidewater battleship Solidarity. Are we reaching?"

* * *

Solenopea Trutneva ventured from Philadelphia and now personally led the armies. Antenora Sware joined from Washington. She rode next to Solenopea, wearing a fur-trimmed black greatcoat with an officer's cap. Rows of medals adorned her breast. Under her coat, an ivory-handled sidearm hung from her belt.

The labor conscripts were forced to walk behind and push the jeeps and smaller vehicles. The trucks and heavy guns couldn't make it through the mire and would be reclaimed later. They didn't need them anyway to finish off the worthless refuse. The Imperial and Tenora soldiers slogged forward in pursuit of the two armies. The Tidewater/RSC were beaten dogs, cowering in their hole, waiting for their mistress's wrath.

The RSC/Tidewater forces waited a mere two miles ahead. Sware licked her lips. The final battle would be real combat—intimate—not a distant bombardment. *I will lead them to victory. Tenora will stretch south forever. I saw this. I've always seen this. Perhaps I will even show mercy to the defeated. A queen is both strong and forgiving. Solenopea has praised my leadership. She sees me as an equal, not like the other Reginae.*

The Imperial army took positions. Tenora and Imperial troops would attack the flanks. The Dirae would execute a frontal assault. Intimidating in their black uniforms and armor, they attached bayonets to their assault rifles. Rain dripped from their helmets. They didn't mix with the other troops.

Solenopea stood with Sware on a low hillside. An ultramarine beret capped Solenopea's flaming hair. Each peered through binoculars to the east.

A lonely flare shot above the tree line. A second, then a third followed. Blazing white through the gray haze.

Solenopea scoffed. "A distress signal. Fools. No one can save them."

Sware lowered her binoculars. "If they surrender, I will treat them fairly as new citizens of Tenora."

Solenopea didn't avert her gaze from the burning, falling orbs. "We will feed them to the Dirae. Anyone who surrenders will be shipped north. Arrangements have already been made."

Sware bowed slightly. "Of course, yes. That's what they deserve."

To the east, a triad of mechanized thunder sounded. *Doom doom doom.* A second cadence of three followed. A minute later it began again. *Doom doom doom.*

Antenora froze, her blood turned to ice. The unnatural sound terrified her. To Solenopea, she offered, "The storm?"

Solenopea shook her head. "No, something else." *Was there a hint of fear in her voice?*

A shrieking rasp pierced the air. The first shell exploded on the left, among the Tenora soldiers. A fireball erupted from the earth where it landed. Yards away, soldiers reeled from the overpressure. In the blast, hundreds of soldiers were torn apart. Dirt and remains flew. The second shell followed, landing squarely among the Dirae.

Chaos erupted in the ranks. Shells continued to fall all across their position—an infernal whistle followed by burning devastation. Screams of terror and pain rent the air. Vehicles exploded. Fires raged in the torrent; acrid black smoke billowed up. The soldiers scattered, the blind and wounded staggering in the blasted, drowned landscape. The most powerful army ever assembled by the Trutnevas was being devoured by the minute.

Doom doom doom. The deadly triads continued, spreading out. Solenopea ran. Her House Guards ran beside her, doing their best to shield her from the flying shrapnel. Sware fell into the mud, then staggered back to her feet. She wiped the muck off her face. She followed Solenopea, stumbling, hands pressed to her head. *This can't happen. I am a Queen.*

Panic propelled her forward. The hellish rasp grew deafening. Mere yards away, the shell landed. In the seconds before she was decapitated, Sware watched Solenopea incinerated to ash.

36

– Astrid – February 16, 2079

"Who are you!" Borquez shouted.

Hands still stretched, Astrid stammered, "I'm Astrid Gorecki from Richmond. She's January Chen. I just met her this year. We'd been rounded up in the coup, but we escaped. Escaped from prison in Washington. That's why I have the uniform. The truck we stole broke down and the troop transport spotted us walking. It's the truth, I swear."

"I don't believe a fucking word," the sergeant barked.

"No, please!" Tears streamed down her face, leaving icy trails. "My wyve's a captain with the RSC. She's an assistant to General Poole. Please don't shoot us."

With two fingers, the sergeant pointed at Fang, unconscious on the pavement. "What's her condition?"

One of Borquez's soldiers—a medic—kneeled down and checked Fang's pulse, inspected her leg. She pulled out the two Glocks, cleared the chambers and tossed them to one of the others. She cocked her head towards Borquez. "She'll probably live, but we need to get her stabilized. Soon."

Borquez barked, "Get her off the road." Another one of the squad patted Astrid down, checking for weapons. "Why were you going north if you're from Richmond?"

"She said she had friends who could help us."

Borquez's soldiers tied a splint around her leg and fashioned a makeshift carrying sled from the twisted metal of the wreckage. Two soldiers carted the sled to the shoulder of the road. No Tenora troops survived the blast. Astrid and Fang's luck had been to sit at the rear; otherwise, they too would have died.

Borquez huddled with a corporal. Imperial or Tenora troops would surely discover the wreck soon—the black smoke a beacon. Astrid heard the corporal mutter, "We can't pick up strays. They'll slow us down. Cut 'em loose." Borquez nodded.

Astrid pled, "Please! We can't stay here. She needs help. They'll kill us."

The corporal hissed. "You're damn lucky we didn't shoot you."

Borquez clapped her hand on the corporal's shoulder. "Easy, Warker." Turning to Astrid, "You say your wyve is attached to General Poole? What's her name?"

"Calenos, Captain Philippa Calenos."

The sergeant's eyes narrowed. "Describe her."

"Tall, dark hair with a shock of gray. Beautiful earnest face. Kind of sorrowful eyes."

Borquez tilted her head. "No shit. I met her. Months ago. Right before it all went to hell. Before the coup. She was with the General, except I didn't know the lady was a general. They got into a scrape with some protestors. Calenos threw herself in front of the General to protect her. Nothing happened to her. We had their backs."

Astrid sniffed. "That's something she would do."

Borquez sighed. "We'll take you with us. Don't make me regret the decision."

Astrid helped the soldiers carry Fang to their truck, an old pick-up painted green. The truck had sheets of metal bolted along the sides offering protection to the riders. Careful not to disturb her leg, they slid Fang off the carrier and onto the bed. Borquez swung behind the wheel. Astrid climbed into the bed next to Fang. The soldiers piled in.

The riders in the bed bounced as the truck ploughed across the field towards the road. Changing gears, the truck sped west.

Ellicott City, long abandoned after the flooding, served as one of the bases of operations for the rebel UD soldiers. The resistance soldiers moved constantly, never offering the Imperials a chance to strike. Bases were only temporary—they contained nothing that couldn't be gathered in an hour. The former UD forces operated in localized combat groups. Each group worked autonomously, allowing for agile attacks while minimizing knowledge of the other units in case of capture.

Almost all the former command had either been executed or corrupted into supporting Sware. Civilian sympathizers, terrified of the new regime, supported the resistance with food, medicine, and fuel. They armed themselves and formed militias. They passed along information about the Tenora government: movement of troops, opportunities for sabotage or capture of desperately needed materiel. Sware executed her purge of the corps with ruthless speed and efficiency. Loyalists had no time to prepare—soldiers grabbed their gear, loaded their rifles and fled to safety deep in the countryside.

Everyone huddled against the whipping, frigid wind. Astrid caught glimpses of the river they traveled next to. They passed a mill and crossed a bridge. The derelict town sprung up on either side. Smashed cars lined the street where the pavement had washed away. Piles of debris permeated the landscape. Telephone poles dangled by their wires. Stores leaned into each other like enormous dominos. The waters hollowed out the first floors of many of the buildings.

The truck rounded a corner and climbed a hill. It pulled up in front of a blunt, cube-shaped mansion, tan with crumbling square columns. Smoke rose from the chimney. The soldiers piled out. Astrid grabbed an edge of the carrier and shuffled into the old building.

To the left of the foyer, a makeshift clinic had been set up. The embers of dying fire lingered in the hearth. They placed Fang in one of the beds.

Borquez pointed to a chair. "Wait with her. We'll contact the doctor." Addressing one of her soldiers, "See what food you can find for them."

Hearing the words, Astrid realized how famished she was. She hadn't eaten in almost a day. She could hear the soldiers thumping around the house. They'd left her alone with Fang. She glanced down at her. A cut ran across her forehead. Her left eye bruised and swollen. *Why didn't I just let her die?*

Fang's eyes flickered. She whispered, "Do they know who I am?"

Astrid leaned in. "No, I told them you were January Chen."

Fang gripped her arm. "You can't tell them."

Astrid shivered. *I hate you. I want to be as far away from you as I can.* She averted her gaze. "Your secret is safe with me."

* * *

Fang's recovery demanded eight weeks. Leg broken in three places, fractured rib, concussion. Astrid stayed with her, fetching meals, helping her to the toilet, listening to the litany of targets she intended to murder: the Trutnevas, someone named the She Wolf, a giantess from the House Guard. Her eyes were feverish with the sheen of her fantasies, wide open. Astrid found herself memorizing their shape and color, each eyelash, the curve of her brow. It was easier to look than listen, though the words held her, a leash of desire that sparked Astrid's own desires—in her case, peace, safety, Philippa, but strangely connected to the other woman's need for vengeance.

Fang told a story about how the She Wolf forced her and her mother to play a game of Russian Roulette with the explosive candles only to later find out the candles were fakes. The outrage at being tricked simmered on her lips but couldn't disguise the longing. *She misses her mother. This, too, is love.*

To get away from Fang, Astrid trained with the soldiers, going on rucksack marches along the Patapsco, pushing herself to keep up. She hunted with them, foraged with them. Skills she'd learned during her two years of required RSC service came back to her. Although ammo was precious, she practiced shooting with an M-21, gripping it close, the familiar kick with each round. She vowed she wouldn't depend on anyone—whatever came, she would face it. Fang may have saved her life, but they were even. Fang had suffered but Fang murdered innocents to achieve her ends—to her, January Chen's value as a person was only her name. Fang was a loathsome monster. Inertia kept them together. As much as she hated the girl – *did she hate her? Not as Fang hated. Not like that* – she couldn't see any alternative. They were safe for now with the soldiers.

Daily, Astrid fought an unwelcome fascination for the girl—too much the moth to Fang's flaming rage. Her relentless determination to bend the world to her will was intoxicating. The girl had endured torture, witnessed her mother's execution, escaped from two Trutneva prisons, and planned to kill the two most untouchable women in the world. Yet somehow, this terrifying avatar of vengeance had chosen *her*, had exposed her vulnerability to Astrid. This made her deeply self-conscious. *What does she see? Am I weak or merely unfinished?* Reflecting on her life, Astrid realized she retreated into the defined space of the canvas—working with solvable problems of color, perspective, balance, composition—maybe unwilling to grapple with the unknowability of loving someone. Like the inspiration for a new painting, she eagerly fell into love, letting the emotion carry her. She immersed herself in the new relationship, but inevitably started looking for a reason to end the affair, the original perfection in her mind forever lost. Was the baby merely an excuse? Dimly, she recognized that her inchoate heart was part of her appeal to Fang. Whatever else she had the girl wanted, she had doors open; she was not defended. Like a prey animal hypnotized. *I thought I was protecting myself. Just the opposite. And, love. O Philippa, where are you?*

In the fifth week of Fang's recovery, Borquez brought news of the outbreak of the war. Most of the Tenora troops would be drawn south along with the Imperials, taking the heat off them temporarily. The resistance command sought to take advantage of the change and organized larger, more sophisticated attacks. Borquez's unit tripled in number and they launched assaults on major targets. New soldiers everyday rotated through the camp, exhausted, hungry, their gear a random assortment of whatever they could find. They shared cigarettes and swapped stories. More of the former UD soldiers had come over once they'd seen how Sware's officers had eliminated anyone who posed a threat.

'You stay here, you gotta work. Got no room for dead weight,' Borquez had told her. Astrid assisted the influx, helping to prepare food, changing dressings, unloading supplies. She stood sentry from midnight to six. Fang steadily improved, becoming more independent. Astrid threw herself into doing what she could for the soldiers. She wept when one of them didn't return. This camp, these women *were* the war. With a pang of guilt and confusion, Astrid remembered Philippa, realizing she hadn't thought of her in almost a week. *Please, please be safe.*

Fang removed her cast after seven weeks against the doctor's directive. She immediately threw herself into her own physical therapy program, wincing with every step. Within a few days, she was practicing her lethal kicks.

Astrid stood with Zhen behind the building. The spring morning light sparkled on the dewy grass. *I would need a thousand shades of green.* Fang stretched her leg. "While you were gone, I hiked into the old town and found something for you. Here."

She handed Astrid a small sketchbook and pencil. A faint smile crossed her face. "Maybe now you'll show me what you can do."

Astrid fingered the pages. Art had been the farthest thought in her mind. Escape and survival consumed her. *And coming from Zhen of all the people!*

Astrid smiled. "I love it. Thank you."

Fang eyed her. "I've decided we have to keep moving. My

leg isn't one hundred percent but will be soon. The war offers us the best protection. Fewer checkpoints to avoid, less resistance. We can make it there in maybe ten days."

Astrid shook her head. "Wait. They will still be there. You need more time to heal."

Fang scowled, staring into the middle distance. "No, we must leave now. The war won't last. The Imperial forces will crush your armies. The Republics have no idea what they are up against."

Philippa's face flashed before Astrid. "Zhen, this is suicide. How will we even get past the Wall?"

"I'll find a way. Nothing will stop me." She glared at Astrid, an edge in her voice. "Stay here. I don't need you anymore. I never did."

Astrid's heart stuttered. *Why is it hard to let her go?* "Zhen, listen."

"Don't call me that!"

Sargent Borquez strode around the corner. "Why not? That's your name, isn't it? Zhen Fang, daughter of Xi Fang, one of the sadistic queens from the north. Word is your mother's dead and you're on your own. Your homeland controlled by the Sisters, armies gone. Still, it's a riddle how you got here."

Fang shifted her footing—a deadly stance Astrid had seen before, but her leg buckled. Fang braced herself.

Borquez unholstered her 9MM. "Don't even try. If we wanted to eliminate you, we've had hundreds of chances."

Astrid interrupted. "How did you find out?"

"I checked out your stories. Gotta know who's in our tribe. Not everyone working for the new government is loyal. We still have contacts."

"Okay, so now what?" Zhen growled.

"What's your plan?"

"Same as it's always been. I'm going to make every one of those Trutneva bitches pay."

"Doubt you will get within ten miles of Novi Vasiligrad but go with our blessings. What do you need?"

"Guns, food, compass, civilian clothes, explosives."

"How about a way past the Wall?"

"Spit it out. How?"

Borquez cocked her head. "Since you asked so nicely, there's a tunnel under the Wall running through Cardiff. Connects with an abandoned sewer line in the old town of Delta. About fifty miles north. We can get you that far. The rest will be up to you."

"You'll thank me for this."

* * *

The Mason Dixon Wall. Twenty-nine-foot slabs of concrete, each with an eye in the center towards the top where the crane had gripped it. A graveyard of ancient cyclopes. Behind it lay a twelve-foot-deep trench. Rusting steel buttresses flared out from the top on both sides supporting a rampart. Razor wire covered the top. Turret-shaped guard houses with mounted machine guns punctuated the wall every three miles. It had begun in 2029 as a crude line of Jersey barriers and chain link, a line of demarcation stretching from Wilmington to the Susquehanna River. Vasiliy Trutnev telling the world 'This is mine.' The United District had never threatened the warlord, but Evermore had foreseen the ugly shape the young dictatorship would take. A powerful defense was the best deterrent. As citizens of the northern area fled the increasingly harsh rule, the Wall expanded. When Venoma Choi forged her pact with the Trutnevas, the Wall metastasized west past Greencastle. Checkpoints along all the roads controlled traffic in and out of the Empire.

Midnight approached as the truck neared Cardiff. Borquez cut the lights when they were a half mile away. Searchlights wove across the ground in front of the wall. The moon offered little light, enough to make out the shapes of the buildings. They stopped on Chestnut Street. Borquez had drawn a crude map of the town. The tunnel entrance was hidden in the basement of a ruined church.

Astrid and Fang each carried packs with medical supplies, ammunition, a lantern, binoculars, canteens, Imperial rubles, and ten days of food. Two Durham Arms 9MM replaced the old Glocks taken from the guards. They'd also been given a small block of C4 Borquez 'had been saving for a special occasion.'

Astrid and Fang climbed out, Fang still favoring her good leg.

Borquez pointed. "It's at the end of the street. Left side. No outside door. Make your way to the basement. The entrance to the tunnel is in a closet. Good luck."

Fang shouldered her pack. "I don't need luck."

Borquez shook her head. "Yeah, whatever." She held her hand out to Astrid. "The girls wanted you to have this. It's the squad patch. You're one of us. Stay safe. Hope our paths cross again when this is over."

The sergeant's voice softened. "Astrid, there's one more thing you need to know. The RSC made a stand in Fredericksburg. They threw most of their weight behind it. The Imperials burned the city down. Heavy losses. It looks bad. Real bad. I'm sorry."

Astrid's heart seized up. *Oh God, Philippa!*

"Thank you for telling me," she managed to choke out.

Borquez peeled away. Mindful of the searchlights, the two women made their way down the road. Astrid's mind reeled with the information of the RSC defeat. *Maybe I should go back. Look for her.* Only the knowledge that she had no idea how to do this and couldn't do it alone silenced the inner voice. She felt like a sleepwalker. Revenge? Why did she care about revenge? Sure, she wanted the Sisters dead, but what difference would it make for her?

It will make a difference to everyone. You know that.

Several blocks later, they reached the church. The bell tower had collapsed, leaving a pile of bricks. Windows were broken. Only one side of the double doors still hung, glowing pale in the dim light. The nave was shrouded in darkness, broken only occasionally by the passing glare of the searchlight.

Fang grunted. "We'll sleep here and get started in the morning. No sense looking for it tonight."

Astrid murmured. "Right."

They gathered the long pillows from the pews and arranged them in mats. Astrid curled up with her back to Fang. Moments later, Fang edged closer.

"No," Astrid declared to the darkness. *No! Philippa….*

Fang reached her arm around Astrid, pulling her close. "I'm cold."

Astrid stiffened.

Fang's voice cracked. "You're my only friend. The only one I can trust. I've lost everyone."

Almost immediately, the girl's breathing softened, grew regular. Astrid knew she was asleep.

* * *

In the morning, Astrid woke before Fang, sliding out from under her arm. The April morning light brilliant through the remnants of stained glass. She admired her gift—a green circular patch with two crossed lightning bolts embroidered in orange. She gripped it tightly, holding it to her face as tears ran down. The patch symbolized something new in herself as well as a reminder of Philippa's honor, her selflessness.

The Wall. I never thought I would see it. Now, it's just outside. Everything that is wrong with this world lies behind it. It doesn't matter what I do. There's nothing to return to. There's no place for me to go. I may as well see it through to the end with Zhen.

She strode to the window and burst out laughing. Straight ahead stood the Wall. But the bottom eight feet had been colorfully vandalized by an anonymous artist. Someone had painted thick imaginary cracks and a gaping hole beyond which a sunlit tropical paradise waited.

37

– Brick – April 2079

Brick stormed into her office. Marijke snapped to attention.

"Any orders?" Brick growled.

Marijke's eyes darted to the floor. "No, ma'am. The Queen has not called for you."

Brick stood easily a head taller than Marijke. She glared down at the soldier. "Well then, what the hell is going on around here?"

Marijke stammered, "Nothing. Everything's shut down. Other than the memorial service, nobody's saying a word. It's been the same almost every day since…"

"Since Gloucester."

Gloucester. The invincible Trutneva army crushed like ants under a boot. Solenopea, Glott, Sware, all dead. A staggering defeat never seen before by Imperial forces. After the warship's guns pounded the army, the massive storm tore apart the remnants while the Republic armies slipped away like ghosts.

Upon hearing of her sister's death, Myrmica hurled vases

against the walls, slashed paintings, overturned furniture. She shrieked to the point her voice failed her, finally collapsing in the center of the destruction, a spent, sobbing woman in her dragon's haul of broken treasures.

Together, the twins merged into a creature greater than the sum of their individual beings. With Solenopea dead, Myrmica withered.

In the days that followed, Myrmica brooded alone in her chambers. She spoke to Solenopea as if she were still alive. Black shrouds with enormous images of Solenopea's face hung from the roof of the building. Similar black mourning shrouds appeared everywhere around the city. A week of mourning had been declared. The body—never recovered—lay shattered and decaying somewhere in Tidewater filth.

Paranoia clouded Myrmica's once-sure judgement. Rather than regrouping her forces and holding onto her gains, she'd ordered her armies back behind the wall. In her mind, the Reginae now posed the greater threat. *Maybe she's right.*

In the aftermath of the rout, when the Tenora troops started to desert and return to their homeland, the Dirae turned on them.

Othere, Goddess of the Fallen, had seen the weakness of Sware's forces, the treachery of their leader. She found their sacrifices meager and insufficient. Othere rained her favor on the Republics. She'd struck a pact with the Shipwrecked Goddess, who'd sent her demon vanguard, Leviathan.

Brick pointed to the door. "I need to think about some things. Go. Report back in two hours."

Brick leaned back in her chair behind her desk, ran her hands through her greasy hair. File cabinets lined one wall which were wood paneled halfway up. She didn't know what was in them. The double-eagle emblem hung over the doorway. Stale cigarette smell permeated the room. A dull ache emanated from the scar on her head. She closed her eyes.

A new liar had recently gnawed her way into Myrmica's confidence. Odds on she was Imperial Intelligence. The woman came and went without escort. Brick hadn't been introduced, and Myrmica hadn't offered any details. Brick considered this ominous development. Brick offered unique protection for the Sisters. Her presence in almost every meeting guaranteed her safety, gave her privileges she made certain never to abuse. It was a good deal for everyone. *Now is when she needs me the most.* If she was being cut out, that meant she was vulnerable. And she'd made a lot of enemies in her time with the Trutnevas. Plenty of women who would delight in her imprisonment, her execution. Like a migratory bird, the sure voice she'd learned to trust rang in her head.

Time to get the fuck out of here.

38

– Moncure – April 2079

Keep retreating. Keep retreating. Keep showing your tail. Platoons trained for rapid combat kept up a continuous series of small engagements. Still, the Choi armies pressed close, threatening to overrun them. So far, they'd taken the bait laid out by the retreating Republic armies.

Nguyen's inertia threatened to fragment the alliance. Finally, Poole convinced her to lure Choi into the mountains. In secret, the Raleigh general and Poole commanded a portion of Raleigh and RSC troops to peel off. They cut a path east and waited. Their move bordered on treasonous, but Poole saw no other alternative.

The destruction of Fredericksburg and the sack of Richmond weighed on the troops. They alone stood between the Trutnevas and the evisceration of their Republics. Horror stories of life in the Empire spread from soldier to soldier like a plague. Better to catch a bullet than face starvation and deprivation in the labor camps. Fear of capture drove them to dig in and fight harder.

Poole and Moncure walked through the encampment. Poole turned to him. "Don't go. That's not why you're here."

Moncure ran his hand through his buzzcut. "Karyn, I'm going out of my fucking mind sitting in those meetings. Waiting and watching. And don't tell me my opinion is valued. I've seen too much to buy that crap. They're all just humoring you. You see it too. *You* brought me out here. I need to see some action. Need to know that I'm contributing, that I'm not dead weight."

Poole's good eye glared at him. Moncure glanced down. "Reed, you're not dead weight. We both know this could end badly. Even if we defeat Choi, there's still the Trutnevas. Soon enough we will all have some tough choices."

"The future is an unforgiving place."

Poole shook her head. "Don't be an ass, Reed. Everything that the Republics have worked for, everything you and I bled for is hanging in the balance. I hate to admit it to myself, but I'm scared.

"Having you here, after all these years, has been some reassurance. Maybe I'm showing my age...clinging to fragments of the past. I think that we women are still walking around in someone else's civilization, like imposters in borrowed clothes. I remember being a young woman excited about the future. We would have our own architecture, our own governments, our own science. I wondered 'What would they look like?' I was so eager to make a difference. Now I doubt we will ever have enough time to work through our own dreams for a better world. Such chaos we've inherited and the best that we can hope for is to leave something better behind after we're gone."

"It would be a hell of a sight, your world. I'm sorry this is the one you got. You deserve better. But, Karyn, I need this. One mission.”

Poole spun on him. “Listen to yourself. That's just your stupid pride talking.”

A grin slid across Moncure's face. “You're probably...no... certainly right about that. But does that change anything?”

“I could order you.”

Moncure stared at her. His voice softened. “But I know you won't.”

Poole stared back. “Fine, go.”

Moncure embedded himself with one of the platoons engaged in the rearguard action. He hustled with the team, moving gear into the JLTV, panting to keep up. His left arm ached where he'd been wounded years earlier. He rode out with them for one of their attacks, staying close to the platoon leader, Captain Choudry. ‘Stay out of my way' was her only instruction. Choi's forces had been sighted less than a mile away. Quick in quick out. Surveying the area, she ordered her soldiers to take up positions in an abandoned brick warehouse. A faded mural for a feed company covered one of the walls. Kudzu claimed the back of the building. The ordinance team deployed two mortars, calculated distances, and fired in rhythm *thwooomp thwooomp*. The explosions throbbed in the distance.

Moncure gasped, reeling under the weight of the gear. His chest ached where the straps dug in. Women took positions along a row of broken windows. Moncure checked his M-21 and kneeled alongside a strawberry blonde private at the far end of the building.

Thwooomp thwooomp. The mortar crew continued lobbing shells.

Small arms sounded, but no ricochet. *They haven't found our position. Soon enough, though.*

An artillery shell exploded not far in front of the building.

To the right flank, movement along the tree line.

"Contact!" one of the soldiers yelled.

The RSC opened fire on the Choi soldiers. Moncure sighted the barrel but couldn't pull the trigger. The scene blurred in front of him. He squeezed his eyes closed then reopened them, with little improvement.

Your time has passed.

Bullets seared through the open windows and across the wall behind which they fought.

Captain Chowdry cried, "Our job's done. Move out!"

The soldiers darted towards the idling JLTVs. Moncure stood, vertigo causing him to stumble. A shell slammed into the front of the warehouse just feet from Moncure's position. The blast hurled him to the side. Dust hung in the air. His ears rang. The second floor of the building crumbled. Soldiers covered their heads and evacuated. The young private lay twitching not far. Shrapnel had torn her leg apart. Blood spurted below the knee.

Moncure stripped off his pack. *So fucking heavy. Can't breathe.* Outside, Choi soldiers closed in. His vision telescoped in and out, finally focusing on the girl. He crawled over to her. Blood pooled beneath her. Smelling the burnt flesh, Moncure leaned over and vomited. He'd seen dozens of these soldiers—wounded, dying. He peeled off his belt and wrapped a tourniquet around the girl's leg, watching the flow. Moncure's efforts brought the soldier around. She clutched his jacket, screaming.

He wheezed, "You're gonna make it. Hang on."

The color drained out of the world. An inferno raged in

his chest. With all his strength, he hoisted the private over his shoulder and staggered through the debris. His left arm throbbed. As he reached the door, two other soldiers grabbed the wounded private and slid her into the vehicle. Moncure collapsed into the seat.

The JLTV barreled off. Moncure leaned forward, panting. A cold sweat chilled his neck. His wife's face hovered in front of him, radiant as when he first met her. "I'll be home soon," he whispered. Beside him, a medic inserted a needle in the private's arm for the transfusion. Moncure closed his eyes.

Captain Chowdry shook his shoulder. "Hey, you okay?"

Moncure nodded, that deep and elusive truth now so close. "Take care of her. I'll be fine."

39

– Philippa – April 2079

The Tidewater/RSC soldiers charged towards the Ware River. Winds raged and the rain pelted them. Trees swayed, leaning almost horizontal against the powerful storm. The Leviathan would make landfall within the hour.

Immediately after the flares going up to alert *Solidarity* of their location, the massive guns pounded the Trutneva forces. Explosions echoed from the west.

Small boats huddled in the water, waiting. Every minute counted in the race against the storm. Soldiers stripped off their gear and dropped their weapons. Tripping, splashing, stumbling, they ran the two miles to the shore. Some rode the few remaining horses, abandoning them when they reached the departure point. The officers tried to maintain discipline, holding them until the wounded could be loaded, but once that was accomplished, the soldiers clawed and tumbled their way onto the decks. Some fell on their knees in gratitude. Others vomited over the rail as the decks heaved in the waves. The sailors shouted at the soldiers, the soldiers, exhausted and still in disbelief, shouted back, unheard over the raging winds. Shoving broke out and one RSC soldier fell overboard.

Philippa limped between Johnson and Scarbrough. The three of them huddled alongside the stern of one of the boats, the spray splashing cold against their hands and faces. Shivers moved from one to another as if each exhausted body was wired to the next. Johnson had made certain to grab the Invisible Skins along with *Vengeance*, and she hung onto them as if they were her children.

The ships cast off, motoring across the turbulent waters, careening against the waves. Ahead, in the bay, the dark silhouette of Solidarity loomed. Philippa nearly wept; the ship flew the flags of all the Republics. *This is what we've been fighting for!* Clouds of flame erupted from the barrels, casting the ship in stark, otherworldly contrast. Dense smoke mixed with the gray haze. The soldiers cheered each round. The deafening timpani cadence rained hellfire on the Imperial invaders like some terrible herald of the judgement. *Tremble, you women.*

Cargo nets hung from the side. One by one the small craft pulled alongside, perilously riding the waves. Shouts of fear were swallowed in the gun's roar. The soldiers climbed the nets, sailors pulled them over. Stretchers were lowered to collect the wounded. Scarbrough and Johnson secured Philippa along with the Skins, then climbed the net.

Philippa clenched the side of the stretcher with one hand. With the other, she gripped the box with the Skins. The stretcher swayed and bounced off the side of the ship. The jerky hoisting convinced her she was about to fall out at every pull. Her side radiated a hot pain.

Even the colossal ship wavered under the raw power of

the Leviathan. The soldiers were ushered below deck. Hot turkey soup and brown bread with butter waited for them. Crewwomen led Philippa to a bunk in the medical ward. She took in the close quarters and musty smell of the ship. Other soldiers filled the bunks. Scarbrough appeared carrying a tray with two bowls. Philippa pulled herself up.

Scarbrough placed her bowl on a nearby table and passed the tray to Philippa. "Here, eat. I'll take a look at your side after you've finished."

Philippa hunched over the tray. Carrots and celery floated in the broth. Forgoing the spoon, she tilted the bowl to her lips. Nothing had ever tasted so delicious. *I'd thought I'd eaten my last meal ever this morning.*

Scarbrough watched. Her wavy gray-brown hair drifted in front of her eye. She swept it back behind her ear. "They said we're better off anchoring here in the bay until it passes."

Philippa wiped her chin and stared at Scarbrough. "We're safe! Can you believe it?"

"It's a miracle. It truly is." She lifted her hands, looking from side to side. "How could they have pulled this off? Where did it even come from?"

Philippa winced, her hand massaging her wound. "I don't know, but I hope they got every last one of those Trutneva bitches."

Scarbrough leaned in. "Here, let me take a look at that."

She helped Philippa peel off her top and lifted the side of her undershirt. She lifted the dressing and inspected the stiches.

"How is the pain?"

"Comes and goes."

Scarbrough replaced the dressing. "It looks like it's coming along. I'll see what I can scrounge up for the pain. Most everything got left behind. After Fredericksburg, supplies were scarce. Only what we could carry and even that got dropped in the race to the boats."

"I have nightmares about the Dirae soldier that did this. I see her, hear her in my head."

Scarbrough rubbed her hands. "I don't want to ever have another day like that. Brought a new life into the world and crushed another one out."

"They were coming for all of us."

"I can't understand it. What did we even do to them?"

Philippa let the question hang in the air. What mattered was that they'd escaped. They'd slipped the noose. Maybe there was still hope.

Scarbrough offered a weary smile. Philippa realized how the war had taken a toll on her friend. Scarbrough had always been a bit curvy, but now her fatigues hung loose. Her eyes darted, as if anticipating violence. She clutched Philippa's hand. "You and I, we've had some times. I'm going to let you get your rest."

Philippa reclined on the cot. Outside, the guns had ceased firing, but the winds still howled. Carved on the bunk above her was the word 'Yokosuka.' Philippa rolled the sound of the strange word around in her mind. The massive ship rocked, but not violently, lulling her with a not-dared-to-hope-for feeling of security. She closed her eyes, one thought echoing before she drifted off. *Astrid, are you still out there?*

40

– Poole – April 2079

Dear Ellen,

With profound sadness, I'm writing to share with you the news of Reed's passing.

While facing enemy forces, he suffered cardiac arrest. In the minutes leading up to his passing, under fire, Reed carried a young wounded soldier to safety, saving her life. True to his code of honor, he requested she receive medical attention before he did.

I served with Reed many years ago and was privileged to be with him again at the end. His sound counsel benefited our alliance. Although he hated war, his was the spirit of the eternal warrior, fighting for the just cause. He spoke often of his abiding love for you and the promise of starting a new chapter when the war ended.

As we both know, more than the man was lost. I often wonder what he thought about being counted among the last of his kind, a fading ember. That fact makes his passing more poignant.

I have submitted my recommendation that he be awarded the Sterling Saber, the highest award given to a soldier of the Richmond Republic.

From accounts of those who were with him, he was not in pain. I am reminded of the words of Psalm 103, The life of mortals is like grass, they flourish like a flower of the field; the wind blows over it and it is gone, and its place remembers it no more. He is held in the Mother's grace.

With deepest respect and sympathy,

Karyn

Poole signed the letter and sealed it in the envelope. On the table, Moncure's old Browning lay. *You old fool! You had to go and show everybody. Play the stupid hero.* She wiped her eye. Over the years, as men she'd known died, she'd thought about entropy – heat moving away, leaving to colder regions. The mutation felt like evidence of a special kind of it. Men's energy, their creativity, even their destructive demands had vanished, leaving behind a kind of heat-death with the impossibility of return to the previous state.

They were camped west of Stanardsville. So far Moncure's strategy had worked—Choi's forces shadowed them, a day's march behind. Tomorrow they would lead them into the old Shenandoah National Park. The hidden RSC and Raleigh units waited for orders to attack from the east.

Reports still arrived. Little was known of the fate of the Fredericksburg armies. The Second Army lost contact after the defeat. The Trutnevas didn't destroy Richmond as they did Fredericksburg. Perhaps they wanted the symbolic victory of capturing the capital. Another mass exodus of people fled further south. The Imperials garrisoned troops and flew their flag over the city, but their focus soon shifted to finding and eliminating the remaining Republic forces.

In a strange turnaround, however, they had received a report several hours earlier that after only two weeks, the Trutneva garrison had pulled out of Richmond.

One of her aides poked her head in. "General, come quickly!" Poole raised herself up, clenching her teeth and puffing. Her hip stung as she eased her weight on it. A slight limp. She slid the Browning into her holster and chewed a pair of aspirin from the vial she carried with her. By the time she reached the tent flap, her stride was normal although the pain still radiated.

Outside, amaranthine clematis clung to trees. The early morning sun still hung low in the east. Orange-gray mist draped across the Blue Ridge Mountains. General Nguyen and General Dos Passos, the Raleigh commander, stood flanked by soldiers with guns leveled.

A jeep bearing the Choi insignia—orange dragon on a dusty purple field—rolled slowly into the main camp surrounded by Charlotte armored vehicles. Three women rode inside. A soldier in the back seat waved a white flag. The driver stared forward.

Next to her sat Venoma Choi.

The Queen wore camouflage fatigues with a mauve beret. The jeep halted, and Choi swung herself out. "I'll have tea with milk," she snapped.

Nguyen nodded to one of her aides. "Search them."

The soldiers raised their arms. Choi hesitated for a moment, then grudgingly complied.

Nguyen barked, "We should kill you now."

Choi scoffed, "Greetings to you too, Trinh. Don't kid yourself. You see yourselves as too honorable to commit such an act. I've come unarmed, defenseless. How could you live with your consciences? Besides, if I'm not back in three hours, my armies will find you. So it's up to you—how many lives do you want to spare?"

Nguyen pursed her lips. "What do you want?"

"I'm offering a cease-fire provided you guarantee safe passage back to our country. I speak for the Queens Vasquez and Fairfax as well."

A murmur rolled across the soldiers in response to hearing the two magical words: cease fire.

Nguyen jabbed her finger. "Which border? You are occupiers of the United District. Pull back behind your infernal Wall and we may have something to negotiate."

Choi rolled her eyes. "Yes, behind the Wall.

"The situation with the Trutnevas has opened up new possibilities. Your armies engineered a remarkable victory. As you must know, Solenopea and Sware are both dead. As we stand here, Myrmica retreats. We can finish what you started."

One of Sisters is dead? Poole couldn't wrap her thoughts around the idea. *This horror show may be over.*

"It's a trap," Dos Passos cried.

Choi, turning to the Raleigh leader, scoffed. "The gas fields are worth infinitely more than your farmlands. She who controls the energy, rules. There are many old scores that need to be settled with the Trutnevas. We have no reason to trust each other, but perhaps we can agree on a common enemy. If you don't believe me, follow us back to the border.

"Every day, every hour matters. Myrmica may be vulnerable, but she's rich, clever and still commands the Dirae. There won't be a second chance. I'm leaving."

She slid into the jeep. "Follow us if you want. If you're foolish enough to attack, we *will* fight, and your soldiers will die unnecessarily. Their blood will be on your hands. This is the best possible solution for your people. Think of it as a gift."

The jeep spun out. Two of the Charlotte vehicles followed. Poole watched until they rounded a curve. *A gift indeed.*

Poole approached Nguyen and Dos Passos. "Your thoughts?"

Nguyen, "Unbelievable. Just like that, our luck has turned. What do you recommend?"

Poole, "I say we stick to the plan, move deeper into the forest and wait. Send a recon team to follow. We'll advance the day after if she's good to her word. If what she says is true and Sware is dead, we have a chance to reclaim the U.D. if we link up with the resistance."

Dos Passos nodded. "Right."

Nguyen, "Agreed. Get a recon team on Choi and send scouts ahead to get a read on the District, but now I need to radio this into Charlotte."

41

– Astrid – April 2079

Dim light filtered in through the dirty basement windows. Astrid and Zhen ate a quick breakfast of hardboiled eggs and found the entrance to the tunnel. A ladder extended down into the hole. Lighting the lantern and closing the closet door behind them, they descended into the darkness.

Hunched almost in half, they worked their way over the uneven ground. The lantern provided only enough light to see the next four feet ahead. After maybe an hour, the tunnel opened up on a storm sewer, tall enough to stand up in. The sewer extended two directions, but someone had spray painted an orange arrow to guide travelers. *How many people have come through here?*

A rat scurried along beside a thin stream of water flowing down the middle. Zhen and Astrid straddled the stream and forged ahead. Several more arrows led them to manhole shaft with iron rungs bolted into the wall. The women climbed. The rungs led into a small maintenance building. Cobwebs permeated the room. Astrid peeled the strands from her face and hair. The door to the outside waited across the room.

Astrid studied Zhen's face. The girl betrayed little emotion. *Swept along behind this amoral funnel cloud of rage. All the days together leading here—behind the Wall. Any mistake could be deadly. I may have made a terrible decision, but I've got to see it through now, whatever happens.*

Their clothes were simple denim work pants, cotton shirts layered under moth-eaten sweaters and the coats they had purchased after their escape. They carried their supplies in civilian packs and wore their knit hats low. Astrid kept her gun in the pocket.

Peering out the broken window, they saw few signs of life in the town of Delta. The crumbling buildings overlooked weed-choked streets. A three-wheeled shopping cart lay on its side. Small piles of litter accumulated in the corners—detergent bottles, blue tarp material, furniture upholstery, a baby car seat, the handle twisted.

Astrid offered, "Looks deserted."

Fang scowled, "We need to go north to the river crossing, but first, we need to see where we are in relation to the guard towers."

The base of the door ground against the concrete, sounding a hollow rasp. Fang slipped out, returning moments later. "Looks okay. We'll stay close to the road, but under cover. Got it?"

Astrid nodded. This was Venoma Choi's territory, one of the dreadful Queens allied with the Trutnevas. *Philippa said she vied with the Sisters for cruelty. Her raiding parties ranged as far west as Morgantown to capture labor units for the Protsent.*

The countryside could have been anywhere in the Richmond Republic, Astrid thought, deconstructing the scenes into color, balance and composition. Farmhouses speckled the landscape, some with tractors ploughing nearby. Others appeared abandoned. Vehicles traveled up and down the road along with bicycles, carts and other pedestrians. Zhen and Astrid hovered close to the trees lining the road. Fang's leg appeared to be completely healed—she never complained. Nearing Holtwood, they paused on a wooded hillside. Fang studied the horizon with the binoculars. She handed them to Astrid.

"Trouble."

Astrid zeroed in on the Choi checkpoint on the western side of the bridge crossing over the Susquehanna. Two armed soldiers leaned against a truck, smoking. Scanning east, the Trutnevas patrolled their own gatehouse on the opposite side.

"We can't fight our way through that. Have to keep going north." She retrieved the map from her bag and spread it out on the grass. Astrid pointed to their location. Fang's eyes followed the serpentine outline of the river. "There! A railway crossing. That's the best probability. The trains don't stop. The Trutnevas control all the track. She craned her head around. "Not quite noon. We can make it by sundown and cross in darkness."

Astrid nodded. Reaching in her own pack, she produced a tin of peanut butter. Tearing off a chunk of bread, she spread the peanut butter with her finger and handed it to Zhen. Zhen offered a thin smile. "Thanks."

"Sure." Astrid tore off another chuck and smeared some more peanut butter, sucking her finger afterward.

By dusk, they reached the crossing near Mt. Wolf. A set of two tracks with room to walk single file between them. From a nearby field, they surveyed the scene before approaching.

Rows of old suburban homes stood just to the north across the tracks. Scattered lights glowed from the neighborhood. On the bridge, red lanterns strung on cables outlined the contour. An eastbound train blew its mournful horn, slowing into the curve before crossing the river.

"As soon as it gets on the bridge, we move. Stay close."

They dashed across the distance to the tracks. The train lumbered onto the bridge. Astrid smelled creosote. They crouched next to the passing cars. Finally, the last one rolled by. They followed easily, the train's speed barely more than a jog. The fine asphalt crunched under their feet. Thirty feet below them, the river surged against the pilings, a wet hiss mixing with the rhythmic, mechanical clang of the train's wheels. Soon, they reached the opposite shore. The train's horn sounded another weary chord.

Clouds covered the moon, offering only a spare, diffused illumination. Astrid could barely make out Zhen's outline as she trudged forward.

Twisting her head to the side, Zhen remarked, "We're in Trutneva territory. The queendom of the murderous twins. We're one step closer. My mother never trusted them, and they probably never trusted her." Zhen gave a wry laugh. "With good reason.

"There are things I saw in that basement I will never forget. What they did to my mother. You think I am so violent, but I can't even tell you. I want to make them suffer in the same way, but my mother wouldn't want me to descend to that level. It would disgrace her memory. I will avenge her, but after what they did to her, the only mercy they can hope for from me is a quick death."

Astrid felt a twinge of sympathy—and gratitude that Zhen

was not describing the torture—but mostly exhaustion. *This will be over soon, one way or another. If I die, may it also be quick.*

42

– Philippa – April 2079

The howling labor of the storm gave birth to perfect, infinite blue skies without a cloud. Two days had passed. Debris from the storm floated all around, washing up on the banks. Teams reported back from shore that the Imperial army had withdrawn. Carrion birds—the real victors—strode the bloody fields. Sware's remains were identified along with what appeared to be soldiers from Solenopea's personal guard, leading to speculation the Queen had been there. There was no certain evidence that the Sister had been killed, but it was hard to imagine anyone escaping the bombardment. The teams surveyed the battlefield, awed by the destruction wrought by Solidarity. The hulking warship remained stalled in the bay. When the crew tried to sail back to Norfolk, one of the engines burned out, spewing a stream of viscous oil that surrounded the boat. Philippa imagined a dead god of war—summoned, resurrected, sworn to serve—now released from his oath, dark magic spilling out from the broken corpse.

The sun neared its apex, the temperature slightly over eighty degrees. Philippa, Scarbrough, and Johnson stood next to the railing facing east towards the ocean. The teak of the deck had been patched over with plywood in areas. Solar panels had been installed across parts. Rust streamed down the sides of the tower and batteries. A salted breeze blew. The Tidewater flag—a ship on calm waters sailing into the dawn—fluttered nearby. Even the flag of faithless Charleston flew—a silver crescent moon encircled by six silver stars on a navy background.

Philippa's strength improved, markedly. The day before, Scarbrough removed the stiches, after which Philippa walked laps around the deck, reveling in the clear spring days. She breathed easier—the Trutnevas had been pushed back. But it was far from over. She'd spoken with Johnson about the success of the Invisible Skins and was impressed by Johnson's experience. Now was the time to capitalize on the Republics' good fortune. A daring and reckless idea possessed her.

Philippa turned to the others. "One Trutneva down. We need to cut the head off the remaining serpent. Finish it once and for all."

Scarbrough continued to stare at the water. "What makes you think three new ones won't grow out of the corpse?"

"I'll take the odds."

"You'll never get close enough."

"These Skins will give us enough time. We get in, we get out. We can sail from here to Novi Vasiligrad in two days. We can end this once and for all!"

"It's suicide."

"It beats waiting here for their next assault. For all we know, the Second has been defeated. They've captured Richmond. We could be all that's left and how long could that hold?

There's nothing left for me here."

Scarbrough pleaded, "There's everything! *We're still here. You're still alive! That's the whole world.*"

Johnson's eyes followed between the two women. Finally, she interjected, "I'm in. We'll find a way. I've seen what the skins can do."

Scarbrough shook her head. "I expected *you* to talk some sense into her."

Philippa reached out her hand. "Meghan, I own you my life. I..."

"Then don't throw it away!" Scarbrough retorted, her face scarlet.

Philippa held her gaze. Scarbrough pulled away. Without a word, she strode down the deck and into the ship.

Philippa watched her go. In many ways Scarbrough was right. Philippa's idea was incredibly risky—they'd be deep behind enemy line without support. Alone. She turned to Johnson, "I know someone who might be able to help."

* * *

It had taken many attempts, but finally the crew women were able to establish a radio connection with Charlotte. Huddled over the receiver, Philippa laid out the plan she and Johnson had crafted. Kester found countless holes. 'An example of flawed thinking' was her response. She argued that an assassination attempt without inside cooperation was doomed—relying too much on chance. When Philippa described the Invisible Skins, Kester remarked flatly, 'I thought that project was abandoned.' She hinted that a diplomatic solution for peace was in the works. Phillipa tore at her cuticles,

289

listening. Once again, *brilliant Kester, always three moves ahead.*

Only after Philippa held firm did Kester relent. She agreed to do what she could for the mission. Her parting words, 'I hope you reconsider, Philippa.'

43

– Astrid – April 2079

Astrid marveled at the skyline on the horizon. Novi Vasiligrad. Metropolis of Tyrants. The dim, feverish ruins of yesterday's civilization, slowly collapsing in on itself. Rebuilt in the image of the Trutnevas. The heart of the blood money networks over which Vasiliy, and now Myrmica ruled.

They'd made it there in nine days, walking almost six hours a day. They'd traveled through the farmlands and forgotten towns. Across the Susquehanna, the Amish persisted, living their lives as they had for centuries, women now driving the teams of horses and mending the barns, their heads still covered according to God's will. Astrid and Zhen sheltered in one of their stables during a torrent.

Astrid's weary legs carried her forward, swept behind Zhen's driving need for revenge. Zhen's urgency intensified with each step closer to her target. Astrid still couldn't imagine how they could get even remotely close to the Trutnevas without being captured or killed. She shuddered at the thought of being a captive of the Trutnevas again. She resolved that she could perhaps be a voice of reason, protecting them both if Zhen were too blinded by her hate. *But would she listen? And what if she succeeds? How will we escape?*

But all of these were secondary to the fundamental question: *Why am I here?*

Their food supply was nearly exhausted even though they'd rationed it frugally. They still had the Imperial currency. Now that they'd reached the city, new problems rose up. They hadn't accounted for the time it would take to gain entry to the palace. Zhen knew the layout of the building—she'd visited dozens of times when her mother had been an ally as well as during her captivity.

In Newark, they hitched a ride into the city on a produce truck delivering to the southern end of the island. The truck rumbled through the old Holland Tunnel. Inside, the lights flickered in some sections and in others were completely burned out. Greenish-gray mildew smeared the once-white walls. A thin stream of water ran along the side of the tunnel and several times the truck rolled through shallow pools of standing water. Astrid sighed with relief when sunlight appeared at the end.

Piles of garbage spilt onto the road. Decrepit buildings—boards across the lower doors and windows, spray painted with thousands of images—rose up from the broken sidewalks. The truck turned south and entered the canyon of skyscrapers. Astrid marveled at the scale of the city. The center of the Empire thronged with activity—thousands of women going about their daily lives. Regular men doing normal things were mixed in with the young, blue-eyed replacements. On the surface, Astrid couldn't discern many differences between the citizens of Novi Vasiligrad and any major city in the Republics although she noted lines in front of some of the stores winding around the block. Studying more carefully, Astrid observed the furtive glances and unwillingness to meet the eye of anyone approaching on the street. *Everyone waiting to be denounced.*

Closer to Myrmica's residence, she marveled at stores lining the ground floor offering a dazzling variety of goods—jewelry, gourmet foods, couture, flowers, cosmetics, furs, perfume. Fashion items for men, almost unheard of in the Republics. Elegant restaurants punctuated the shops. Several casinos with cheap glittering exteriors beckoned. Decadent opulence, a testament to the corrupt wealth of the Empire. Mounted NV Police patrolled the streets, staring down at the civilians. They wore navy uniforms trimmed in silver, black jackboots and white helmets with visors shielding their eyes.

Astrid and Zhen jumped out at the delivery stop closest to their target. "How often do you make this run?" Zhen asked as they exited.

"Every three days," the driver replied.

Zhen slapped the truck. "Good to know...thanks again."

A block ahead, the imposing stone façade of Myrmica's palace stood. The streets surrounding it had been cordoned off—APCs parked sideways across the road. Armored police stood guard around the perimeter. Zhen pointed, "Look at that." Enormous banners of Solenopea's face hung down the sides. *She must have died. Zhen won't get her revenge on that one.* Zhen's half-whispered repetition of the names of the women who'd killed her mother led Astrid to imagine a terrible bargain with some chthonic deity, the price of which was hidden from Zhen. To Astrid, Zhen's vendetta had revealed a tragic dimension. This impression grew with their approach to Novi Vasiligrad and Zhen's conviction that revenge was within her reach. Astrid struggled with the gnawing certainty that

Zhen's fury had broken her, had stolen her humanity from her, that the girl had gone to a place from which she could never return.

Zhen continued, "We need to understand what's going on. Where there may be a weakness."

They strolled towards the building, acting casually. Taking their time, they, surveyed each side, finally winding up on Maiden Street.

Zhen slipped into a skyscraper across the street from the palace. She pretended to study the office directory, then headed to the stairs.

"The top floors will be empty. Not enough people any more to fill spaces and nobody trusts an elevator that much these days."

Astrid followed Zhen up seventy-two flights. After the thirtieth floor, it was clear nobody had ventured higher in some time—a thick layer of dust settled across the steps. Stepping out into the suite, Astrid looked around at what had once been an office of a Japanese bank. Hiragana and katakana characters covered the papers left behind. Delicate scrolls covered with images of ancient villages hung as tasteful accents to the simple tatami wall coverings. In contrast, the furniture stood out by its ultra-modern design.

"Probably very expensive once upon a time," Zhen murmured. She reached into her pack, pulling out the binoculars. "From here, we can study the scene."

Astrid nodded. They could watch all the activity below. *If Philippa could only see me now.* Astrid stared across the Manhattan skyline and reflected back on their apartment in Richmond. The library with the Napoleonic bee wallpaper and thousands of books. The stationary bike offering a glimpse into the past. Snuggled together on the sofa listening to radio dramas. The soft down on Philippa's cheek.

She found a couch in an office and curled up. Zhen did the same across the hall. She idly paged through a Japanese magazine from 2019. The bright faces of the people, the pictures of the clean, orderly, amazingly advanced civilization, and the indecipherable language prompted Astrid to imagine she was studying an alien artifact. She pulled her jacket close and drifted off. Higher than she'd ever been, above the fevered madness, she dreamed of flying. Wearing a white wedding gown, she traveled to a distant solar system set with two suns. There she gathered moonlight to grind into pigment, enraptured by such pure creation.

* * *

Days of watching. There were two service entrances to the palace on Maiden Street, overhead doors leading to a garage. Most of the building was surrounded by concrete posts except for these entrances. Imperial vehicles came and went throughout the day with no discernable pattern. Zhen kept a log. They took turns slipping down into the city for food, using the money Borquez had given them. Astrid spent time sketching—the views to the rivers, a still life in the office, but mostly Zhen. She attempted to capture the fierce singularity that drove her, that radiated in the glint of her eyes, in her posture that always hinted at a terrible violence waiting.

Zhen peered over her shoulder. "I like what you did with me."

"Take it," Astrid offered.

Zhen pulled away. "Maybe later."

295

But would there be a later? How long would their luck hold? They'd gotten this far, almost in striking distance.

Zhen prepped the C4 with an ignition timer. "I've figured it out. Tomorrow we go in."

Astrid nodded silently.

* * *

A light drizzle fell. Oily puddles produced rainbow film. The produce truck idled outside of the store where they had gotten out three days earlier. The driver huddled over a steaming cup. Zhen stormed up to the cab and waved the gun. "Get out if you want to live."

The driver raised her hands, sliding out. "Take it. Take whatever and go. I never saw either of you." Her eyes never left the gun.

Astrid climbed in the passenger side. Zhen took the wheel, shifting into first. The truck lurched forward. Zhen stared straight ahead, both hands clenching the wheel. She kept the speed down as they circled around the palace. Driving west on Maiden Lane, Zhen downshifted and laid on the gas. The engine revved. Astrid buckled her shoulder belt. Approaching William Street, Zhen began the turn north, but just past the barrier, she pulled the steering wheel left. The truck fishtailed onto the sidewalk. Astrid bounced off the door. Zhen accelerated. Shouts carried from the nearby police. Zhen hunched over and Astrid ducked as shots shattered the windows.

"Stay low!" Zhen cried.

Astrid closed her eyes and steeled herself for impact. The truck bounced across the street and up on to the opposite curb.

The garage door loomed enormous across their field of sight, then the truck rammed into it. Astrid hurled forward against her seat belt. A deafening metallic tearing shriek swallowed the sounds of the gunfire. The door partially gave way, one corner bent backwards. The truck remained wedged in the doorway, the cab poking into the garage bay.

Zhen stabbed the C4 with the timer. "Thirty seconds!"

Astrid and Zhen raced from the truck through the garage. Every yard meant protection from the blast. Astrid counted down in her head.

Twenty-five

A guard was stationed at the door from the garage to the building. Hearing the collision, she sprinted towards the bay door, rifle raised. Zhen fired off three shots. The guard fell on the concrete. Zhen grabbed her rifle.

Fifteen seconds

The door to the building stood maybe forty feet away. The women surged towards the opening.

Ten seconds

Five

WWWWWWHHHHHOOOOOOOOOOMMMMMM

The two women crashed through the door just as the explosive detonated. The garage glowed an infernal orange and the heat stung their faces as they slammed the door behind them. The building quivered. Lights flickered, revealing a gray block hallway. Sirens blared in the distance.

Zhen forged ahead. "This way. I think the interrogation cells are nearby. We'll start there."

Astrid drew her pistol, still dazed. *In ten minutes, the building will be swarming with security. We have no escape route. What have we done?*

44

- Philippa – April 2079

The Tidewater fishing boat stayed just out of sight of the shoreline. The plan was to approach Novi Vasiligrad from the east. Once Kester had agreed to help Philippa, just as she'd been before with locating Astrid, she was all in. Philippa marveled at how deeply the Charlotte intelligence network spread into the Trutneva empire. Kester had disclosed that there was a passage underneath the palace that led into the old subway system. An escape route for Myrmica in case events turned against her.

Philippa stared up at the night sky, searching in the south for Sirius and the Southern Cross. A tiny streak of light traced an arc. *Satellites taking pictures for no one to see.* Later, a mild drizzle fell obscuring the horizon, but not strong enough to send her below deck. Rising sea levels and storm surge eroded the shorelines. The ocean cut a channel through Rockaway Park into Jamaica Bay. The eastern tip of the island around Napeague had been severed, creating a second smaller island crowned by Montauk.

She tore at her cuticles. *Somewhere out there Astrid may still be alive. Is there even any hope of that? It's been months since she was captured. She's probably dead. How could she have survived? She never belonged in this colosseum of suffering we've inherited. Her hopeful search for what is beautiful blinded her to the realities of this world. She sought meaning in art, in creation, in a transcendence far removed from the grief and anguish.*

Astrid, if you are out there, I will find you. It's not too late.

After nightfall, Philippa and Johnson rowed a small two-woman skiff across the bay, landing on the land once known as Fort Tilden. They pulled the boat ashore and hid it in a copse of trees. They sheltered in one of the abandoned buildings.

The next afternoon, they set out. To the left, the community of Roxbury. The collapsing houses overgrown by an aggressive green plant that clung to them. The plant canopied a downed power line. Large sections of the road had given over to weeds and drifted sand. They walked across the desolate bridge into Brooklyn. Although this was the backyard of the Trutnevas, it was unguarded and deserted. The Trutnevas maintained the largest security force, but the reality was that there were far too few to cover all the territory they controlled. Their invasion of the District had spread them even more thinly.

If we succeed in taking out the remaining sister, we stand a better chance of negotiating a settlement. The Queens, the Imperial generals, all of them will fight to fill the void left by the Trutnevas. If Astrid is still alive, we could secure a return of the prisoners.

As was her custom, Johnson kept to herself. Always quietly efficient in her duties but demonstrating a deep understanding of the realities of the world in a word or two. Philippa admired her skills and courage. They'd served together through some desperate times when neither expected to see the other side.

But now at this final challenge—the two of them against the most powerful empire—she couldn't hold back.

"Johnson, how come you never say anything?"

Johnson smirked; her eyes glimmered. "What do you want me to say: 'Yes, ma'am, I love that we're in the shit, eating food they wouldn't feed a dog. I love the fact I gotta carry every mission. I mean *the fucking weight.* I have serious respect for General Poole, but generals stay safe. Generals don't have feet that never dry. I know my job and I'm damn good at it, but I *love* that everyone expects me to keep it together when all I want to do is scream. When this is over, I'm gonna find some sweet thing that knows how to make me laugh. Try to forget the faces of the women and men I've killed."

Philippa laughed. "Damn, glad you got *that* out. You're a good woman, Sodapop. It's an honor to serve with you. I hope you get everything you want."

Kester had provided them with forged identification papers in the event they were stopped. They wore functional work clothes, the kind any service worker or mechanic might wear. Johnson pulled her knit cap down over her ears. In their backpacks, they carried the Invisible Skins tucked under ragged fleece jackets. The long knives they kept tucked in their boots.

They strode through the ruins, casual but with purpose. Burned out buildings consumed many of the streets. Further west, nearer the river, collapsed towers merged into each other—skyscrapers, the likes of which hadn't been built in sixty years. Following the map, they followed the steps down to the subway entrance. The gate was locked, but the rusted hinges pulled free from the wall after the women alternated pulling on it. Carefully, they descended. The sharp edge of mold mixed with the odor of wet concrete. They pulled flashlights from their packs. Rats scurried from the light, squeaking their panic from the intruders in their kingdom. Palpable darkness shrouded them—the tiny lights producing only the smallest incision. Philippa shuddered, imagining the closeness of a tomb. Further in, they strode through a foot of standing water on the tracks. Only having approximations of distance, Philippa concluded they were under the East River from the many fine leaks that bled down the walls of the tunnel.

Miles later—near the passage into the palace—light glowed. The soldiers switched off their flashlights.

Philippa nodded to Johnson. "Let's suit up."

She pulled the Invisible Skin out of her pack, stripping down to her underwear. Skin-tight, unlike anything she'd ever worn. The tiny chips of screen and cameras made movements a little stiffer. Still, the suit had been crafted so well, there was no clicking sound. The hood covered her entire face, leaving a thin slit for her eyes. Inside the mask a vague metallic smell. She slid the blade into the sheath sewn into the sleeve. *This is it. We either take her out or die trying.*

The batteries only guaranteed two hours of camouflage. Kester's intelligence described Myrmica as a recluse since the death of her sister. Therefore, she would be somewhere in the palace. Kester had also provided a diagram of the building. Myrmica lived on the top two floors, which was where she would most likely be. Kester warned them about heavy personal security around the queen.

They switched on the suits. Philippa slowed her breathing, centering herself in front of the mission. Every nerve fired in anticipation. The electric mesh surrounding her acted like a conduit, amplifying her sense of awareness. Philippa grinned behind her mask. *They will never see it coming.*

"This is so fucking cool," she whispered, but she couldn't see Sodapop's response.

Hugging the side of the tunnel, they crept towards the light ahead. Ahead, on a platform, a small group of guards convened around a doorway. Unease crept into Philippa's thoughts. *Why so many?*

Litter and debris covered the ground. Philippa chose her steps carefully—clear spots only to avoid noise. She stepped forward. Under her foot, a slight give—unnatural—like pressing a pedal.

BANG! Liquid exploded up from the ground, spraying her. The paint splattered through the slit in Philippa's mask, blinding her. Overhead flood lights switched on. Philippa staggered. She heard Johnson sprint ahead. "Run!" she hissed.

Sightless, Philippa turned to flee, crashing into the wall then onto her knee. The guards leapt down into the tunnel, guns raised. Philippa swung wildly, but in vain. Strong hands soon subdued her.

It was a trap! The words rang in her head. She struggled against the soldiers holding her down. Through the din, she heard, "I want her alive." Her heart seized. Realization sunk in. Icy horror at the depth of the betrayal caused her to doubt her hearing.

She recognized the voice. Kester.

45

– Brick – April 2079

It's all gone to shit. What am I waiting for?

Brick stubbed out another cigarette and paced across the living room of her apartment, rubbing the back of her head. *Like a caged animal.*

A heavier security presence had descended on the city since Gloucester. New faces everywhere, new liars. Everyone appeared to know about her trick and kept a wary distance. No word from Myrmica; she remained in her paranoid seclusion. The Empire, once an impenetrable, adamantine juggernaut, now fractured, threatening to rend itself apart.

Some of the daughters of the Reginae had escaped—Vasquez, Fairfax and Choi. In the Quiet Room, their guardians evidenced no knowledge of how the three slipped through the surveillance net. The She-Wolf conducted slow, meticulous interrogations with horrifying glimpses of creativity. In the end, they were grateful for the opportunity to confess.

Even Marijke had disappeared. 'Given new orders' was the only response she'd been offered by the squint-eyed new colonel. Trailings that glimmered orange-brown verified her statement. *Her fermented smell like stale beer, sickening. I should have busted her jaw.*

Brick couldn't stay away from the windows—watching the streets below for some clue to their next move. Prowling between the western and southern views. The street traffic revealed little. *I have to be ready if they come at me.* She smacked the side of her head several times until her ear rang. *This fucking curse. I don't want to see everyone's lies. I don't want to wait for them to add up like with Blanca—always better to leave. Better to be alone.*

She had enough money to last for several months. Enough for the bribes that were part of life in the Empire. No longer immune because of her position in the House Guard, she would have to watch her behavior. Still, the decision to escape the Trutneva police state lifted her mood. Chaos was descending on the regime and more chaos was certain to come. She'd make it out before the end.

Tomorrow I'm gone.

West, into the Appalachians—in the rocky hollows and gorges fugitives had hidden for centuries. Evaporate into the rolling mist and ruins of company towns shrouded in coal dust. She'd heard that fires burned deep in the mines, the smoke rising from cracks in the crumbling roads. *I will make an offering to Illustral, the Goddess of What was Lost, who is also the Goddess of New Beginnings. She will watch over me.* There she'd be beyond the reach of the Reginae. She would get there before autumn. Work a ranch or help bring in a harvest in exchange for food and a place to stay for the winter.

Beyond the mountains, she'd heard fragile settlements

existed. Like much of the world, still living off of the corpse of the dead civilization. Warring tribes of old men. She'd heard too that further west, drought and ravenous dust storms rendered the plains states inhabitable. Wildfires consumed the western lands. *Next year's problems.*

A knock on the door. "Commander?"

Brick shook her head, "What?"

"You're needed in the Quiet Room."

Fucking kidding me. Again! Only that morning, she'd witnessed the last session. Interrogations had become routine as if Myrmica was trying to find some imagined betrayal that led to her sister's death. She couldn't lash out at the Republics, so she focused her vengeance inward. Seeking the cancer close to the heart. For weeks now, an investigation—spawned by Myrmica's new ally—had proceeded against groups of Imperial officers, each of them spending hours in the chair, restrained '*for their own safety.*'

"Coming," she grunted.

Brick lumbered down the stairs to the basement. *This could take all night, depending on the situation.* Officers or highly placed civilians demanded several hours. Even when Brick had signaled there was nothing of value, the She-Wolf might continue, casting around for new connections, prolonging it for her own entertainment. *Twisted bitch, that one.* Brick felt her pockets. No cigarettes. *Of course.* Couldn't turn back now; she'd send someone once they got started. *Just one more day.*

Inside the Quiet Room, a woman sat strapped to the chair wearing a tank top and underwear. The hot light already drawing perspiration under her arms. Military-issue. Taller, broad shoulders, wearing the customary leather hood. According to the She-Wolf, the hood produced disorientation in the subject, prevented them from adapting to their new surroundings.

Brick closed her eyes and inhaled, anticipating the pungent, familiar smell of fear emanating from the unfortunate. *There it is.* Sifting through the collage of aromas, one in particular caught her attention. Brick shook her head.

She's pregnant!

She studied the woman's flat stomach. No trace yet showing. Something nagged at her, *something she didn't want to know.* She stepped closer. The woman lifted her head, probing for the source of the sound.

Not her! Please. Honeysuckle. Gentle and patient. Taking a risk to be kind so many years ago at VMI. Helping *her* when no one cared. When she stank of horse shit. When everyone called her, a freak, a monster. *Stupid as a brick.*

Brick's heart hammered. A roaring in her ears drowned out all sound. She swallowed, not daring to breathe. *Early mornings together. She smiled when I read the words. She was alone, like me.*

She tugged the hood off.

I think I love you. Brick's own handwriting scrawled on the note paper. Struggling to make the letters. Too afraid to give it to her.

The cadet. Philippa.

Why did you come here? *How could you not know you were dead the minute you set foot in this pit of liars?*

Philippa blinked in the bright light, trying to focus. "Claire?"

Myrmica strode through the door. The She-Wolf and a new woman followed a step behind. *That must be Myrmica's secret advisor. I've seen her before at the dinner. But somewhere else?*

The cadet turned her head and half whispered, "Kester? Is that you?"

The woman, Kester, glared at Brick. "What is she doing here?" To Myrmica, "See, I told you someone would come. Here she is! Find out what she knows about Choi. She is marching on the city as we speak."

Yes, Kester, the smart one. The cruel one.

Brick studied Myrmica, amazed and disgusted by the once-omnipotent queen. Puffy dark circles ringed her bloodshot eyes. Her clothes were mismatched. Her breath smelled foul, like rot. She stared wildly about. Her formerly radiant hair hung in dull, straggly bunches—she'd pulled patches of it out in her grief. Without makeup or her elegant wardrobe, she appeared like a homeless addict.

"The She-Wolf will get to the bottom of this," Myrmica mumbled.

Kester turned to Philippa. "I never thought you would be so stupid. Oh, Philippa, why didn't you leave well enough alone? Let the grownups work this out. I could have protected you. Charlotte is the rightful heir, and I will not sacrifice that to anyone!"

Philippa pulled at the straps. "Does Premier Ishikawa know you're here?"

Kester leaned in. "Still so naïve about the world, aren't you? Of course not. She'll come around though. This is the only possible solution. Charlotte will control everything south of the Mason Dixon Wall. Queen Myrmica will control the north. An invincible union. Now, where is your partner?"

Philippa's eyes hardened. "Fuck you, Kester."

Kester backhanded her across the face. Stepping back and pointing to the She Wolf, "That's nothing compared to what she has in store for you. Nobody can hold out for long."

Philippa's face burned. She turned. "Claire? Help me!"

The She-Wolf's eyes glittered, having discovered a new torment to exploit. "You know her?"

Claire studied the floor, hoping the question would pass.

The She-Wolf persisted, "You do, don't you? Prove your loyalty to your Queen. Strike her."

Philippa sobbed, "Claire, please! We were friends once." Heartbreaking copper trailings sparkling like the last stars in a dying universe.

Brick swallowed hard. Her chest closed in on itself. *Tomorrow I'm gone. One more night of this horror show.* She clenched her jaw and looked away from Philippa. "Orders." Her fingers formed a fist, anticipating the dull pain when it merged with the woman's face.

"Strike her now!" the She-Wolf commanded.

"Orders," she mumbled again. *Just get through to tomorrow. Do whatever you have to do.*

"Claire!" Philippa pleaded.

Myrmica shrieked, "What are you waiting for, you enormous idiot? You illiterate sow!"

Brick swung, putting her full strength behind the blow.

Myrmica crumpled to the floor.

"Enough!" Brick yelled.

The She-Wolf stepped back. She screamed, "Guargghhhs!"

Brick lunged forward and wrapped her hands around her throat, silencing the She-Wolf's final word, crushing her windpipe.

Kester sprinted to the door.

The She-Wolf staggered in a tight circle, wide-eyed. Her chest spasmed, trying to draw in air. She clawed at her throat, her lips already blue-tinged.

46

– Philippa – April 2079

Claire freed Philippa's arm. "There's no time."

Once loose, Philippa released herself from the remaining straps. "Come with me. I know a way out."

An explosion roared. The building shook. The lights flickered while bits of ceiling fell. A cloud of plaster dust descended on the room. Emergency generators kicked in with a deep rumble. An alarm siren echoed through the building.

Philippa and Claire exchanged glances. She could hear movement in the hall. Through the haze, Philippa could make out two armed women in civilian clothes standing at the threshold.

Philippa cocked her head, "Astrid? How?"

"Philippa!" Astrid cried.

"You!" the other woman snarled, eyes locked on Claire. "You murdered my mother." She raised the assault rifle.

Claire stepped back. Philippa raised her hands. "No...no... NO!!"

CRACK CRACK CRACK. Fang fired off three rounds at point

blank range. Claire fell backwards. Philippa rushed to her. She pressed on the wound. Blood pooled underneath Claire's body, flowing with a fatal urgency. Philippa began CPR. Tears streamed down her face as she counted out the compressions.

"No, Claire, please! Stay with me."

Astrid searched for anything to stop the hemorrhaging.

Claire's head lolled, facing Philippa. She coughed, sputtering blood. "It's over. Go...protect your baby."

Philippa paused, her hands soaked. *Because more are the children of the desolate woman.* She stared, wide-eyed and whispered, "That's not possible."

Across the room Fang spat, "Fuck her. A quick death is better than they gave my mother." She strode over to the corpse of the She-Wolf, prodded it with her foot and grunted. She pulled Myrmica up onto her knees by the hair, a cruel glint in her eyes, "Good, still alive." Myrmica clawed at the woman's arm.

Philippa redoubled her efforts, panting as she leaned into the compressions, all the while knowing it was pointless. Claire had already lost too much blood; her eyes lost focus. A wan smile appeared as her face drained its last bit of color. She reached up and laid her large hand on Philippa's, whispered, "I never forgot you."

Philippa buried her head in Claire's neck. "I'm so sorry, Claire."

Astrid wrapped her arms around Philippa. "She's gone. We have to move."

Philippa turned and embraced Astrid. "I should have done more. She saved my life. I should have..."

Astrid held her. "You tried. Oh, Philippa, you always tried to save us all."

Philippa breathed deeply. Her heart welled up in her throat, every nerve electrified. *I won't fail you again. I won't waste Claire's sacrifice. I'm going to get us out of here. Focus, remember your mission. The enemy will be here any moment. Gotta find Johnson.* To Astrid, "I know a way out."

Astrid handed Philippa her pistol. "Here take this. Let's go."

Fang held Myrmica's face close to hers. "Do you remember my mother, huh?"

Myrmica's dull eyes drifted up, the right side of her face now swollen, closing over her amber eye. "What?"

Fang's tone became mocking. "What happened to you, oh my Queen? Where is your empire? Where are your Dirae? There's nothing left to hide behind. You're pathetic, a beaten cur. Why did we ever respect you? Fear you? I'm going to reunite you with your ugly sister."

Myrmica screamed, a piercing wail that echoed through the room. Fang slammed the rifle butt down on her head. Myrmica's neck snapped back. Her skull split with a wet crunching sound. She clutched her head, continuing to scream. Fang brought the butt down again, then a third time, yelling at the dying queen with each blow, "This isn't over...*I will find you in Hell.*"

Zhen stood over the body, panting, "We won! We did it." She looked wildly around. The siren continued to blare.

Astrid stepped towards Zhen. "Everyone's dead. There's no one left. We have to go." Pointing to Philippa, "She knows a way out."

Zhen cocked her head. "Who's she?"

"This is my wyve, Philippa."

Zhen shook her head, disbelief clouding her face. "Here? With the Trutnevas? *She's one of them.*"

Philippa racked the slide on the pistol. Her heart hammered against her chest. *We're so close. Just find Johnson and clear out.*

Zhen winced. "She's your wyve?"

"Zhen, we have to go now!"

Philippa held up her blood-stained hands, her voice slow. "We're on the same side. Astrid's right. I've got a way out and this place is about to be overrun with Imperials."

Zhen moved towards the door, her back to the threshold, blocking the exit. She aimed the rifle squarely at Philippa. "No, this is not how this ends." She turned to Astrid. "She does not get to take you from me."

Astrid pleaded, "It's not like that...It's never been like that. Don't you see, Zhen, you're free. You've avenged your mother. Come with us."

Zhen shook her head. "No." She motioned with the rifle. "Drop the gun."

Philippa held her breath, slowly kneeling down, the pistol held by the barrel. She placed it on the floor.

To Astrid, "Step away from her."

Astrid held her ground. "You'll have to kill me too."

Zhen blinked, but the rifle never wavered. Tears welled in her eyes like she was a lost child. Her voice was husky. "Astrid, please. Think of what we've been through. We don't need her for anything. We owe each other our lives. I have no one without you."

Astrid held out her hands. Softly, "Zhen, it's over. You did it. Just take my hand. We're going together...yes? Just say yes, *please.*"

Zhen clenched her jaw, fighting down her emotion. "They killed her right here. My mother...Astrid...she was...my world. I wish I could have said goodbye."

Astrid whispered, "Zhen, I'm so sorry."

Philippa edged closer to Astrid. Her bare feet slid across the cool floor. The grisly interrogation room was splattered with blood. Both of their lives balanced on the girl's trigger. Philippa glanced at Astrid, allowing herself a moment of wonder. *I thought I'd lost you, but you're here in this netherworld.*

Zhen's face hardened, as if a mask now covered it, that of a beautiful and murderous demon. She cried, "I should have known you would betray me too." She leaned into the rifle, now moving it between Philippa and Astrid.

Philippa stared at Zhen. Behind her, the dim light from the hall shimmered like heat waves on pavement. A blurry distortion swiftly approached the girl. A flash of sliver drew a red line across the side of Zhen's throat. Blood sprayed from the wound. Zhen collapsed onto her knees; the rifle clattered on the floor. Her hand flew to the wide gash.

Astrid screamed. Philippa seized the rifle. Zhen slumped against the wall, her mouth moving, but the only sound a thick gurgle. Blood slipped through her fingers and soaked her clothes. She flailed out with her free arm; eyes locked on Astrid.

Astrid fell to her knees next to Zhen, took her hand and pressed it to her lips. "No!" Tears streamed down her face. "No, no, no, no." Zhen's eyes clouded. Astrid turned to Philippa. "She didn't know what she was saying. She was lost. Her rage...it consumed her. She couldn't see through it."

A pair of eyes peered out of the distortion. The blood-silver blade suspended in the dusty air. A moment later the blur sharpened into the form of Sodapop Johnson. Johnson scanned the room, nodding to acknowledge the corpse of Myrmica. "Mission accomplished, Captain. Let's go home."

Philippa pulled the charging handle. "What's the situation out there?"

Philippa imagined the smirk behind the mask. "The enemy put up some resistance. Just like I was hoping for."

"It's safe to assume we have a clear shot out of here?"

"For now, yes, but that won't last."

Philippa let out a deep breath. They were so close! Hope burst in her heart like fireworks. She'd found Astrid. The Trutneva Empire had fallen. Dawn shimmered into her 4:11 darkness with the promise she wouldn't be alone. The heaviness she'd carried dissolved, and a new beginning offered itself to her. For once, the terrible thresher that waited for her was silent and she could see past it to a blindingly beautiful horizon. She rested her hand on her belly. *And a baby?*

Philippa choked back a sob. "I'm ready to go home."

Johnson smiled and wrapped her arm around Philippa. Their heads touched. "Good, cause I'm so goddamn tired of savin' your ass."

47

– Epilogue – Summer 2081

Everywhere there were mountains. The panorama of the Blue Ridge.

Philippa dusted off the knees of her jeans. The solar panels were all nearly connected. It had taken her three weeks to complete, working around all the other chores and the demands of a toddler. On the porch, Astrid shucked the first of the sweet corn, the baby next to her.

She and Johnson were hailed as heroes. In a grand ceremony, Premier Lawson awarded them the Sterling Saber. A magazine serialized their adventure. With her severance from the RSC and a loan from the Mutual Credit Association, Philippa and Astrid bought thirty acres in the valley and set about renovating the farmhouse. Astrid took charge of the interior. Philippa tended the sheep and cows. They both spoiled their little girl—Claire. The only name the child could have.

Kester never returned. Philippa speculated she'd probably been killed by Imperials in the hours following Myrmica's death. Her betrayal shook the Charlotte leadership.

Johnson was offered a senior officer post in the new United District. True to her vow, she found a beautiful wyve to help ease her pain. Philippa, Astrid, and Claire traveled to Washington for the wedding. The stone church was filled with flowers. Sodapop, elegant in her dress uniform, never stopped smiling all day.

Astrid spoke little about her journey with Zhen. In some ways, she had become unfamiliar to Philippa. She was stronger, more resilient, than before her ordeal. Philippa admired the change, but tread carefully. Their love for each other never wavered, but once in a while, Philippa would find Astrid paging through her sketchbook, tracing with her fingers the outline of the girl who almost killed them both.

So much had been revealed through motherhood. Her highest duty was to protect and love the child. Claire brought with her a new dimension. Everywhere Philippa looked, she saw the world in warm, brilliant colors. No longer did she imagine the frozen darkness claiming everything she loved.

In the north, the fall of the Trutnevas brought chaos and struggle. Choi waged war with the remnants of the Imperial army, grinding to a stalemate only when New England invaded across the Hudson. The other Reginae shifted alliances when it served them. The Piedmont Republics endured. Still a realist, Philippa knew that the hard-won victory was more fragile than ever. The tentative dawn of a new peace spread throughout the Republics.

But it would always be the same sun and the same sky and night would follow.